*To Dawn
Reach for your Path and enjoy
it once you get there!*

Amanda Booloodian

AMANDA BOOLOODIAN

BOOK ONE

Printed in the United States of America
Copyright © 2016 by Amanda Booloodian
Published by: Walton INK

ISBN-10:0-9973353-1-9
ISBN-13:978-0-9973353-1-6

All rights reserved. No part of this book may be reproduced or used in any manner without the express written permission of the publisher, except as permitted by U.S. copyright law. For permissions, please contact Walton INK.

This is a work of fiction. Names, characters, businesses, places, events and incidents are either the products of the author's imagination or used in a fictitious manner. Any resemblance to actual persons, living or dead, or actual events is purely coincidental.

Walton INK
www.Booloodian.com

Book cover designed by Deranged Doctor Design.

Dedicated to silver.

CHAPTER 1

STALKING A TROLL REQUIRED QUIET finesse. Logan, my mentor and partner, moved silently ahead. For all the noise he made, he could have been walking on carpet. Maybe elves learned that with age. Logan was over one hundred and fifty years old. You can learn a lot in that time. Then you have me. If there was a twig or leaf on the ground, you could bet I would break it.

Logan pushed his sandy blond hair behind his ear. The ear looked misshapen, too thick on top. Then it twitched. Flesh rolled outward and upward. Within seconds, the expanded ear led up to a point, until it was more than twice the original length. The late morning sun showed that the newly exposed pale skin was thin, almost to the point of transparency.

I loved my job. What other humans had the chance to work with elves, much less see them unfurl their ears?

Our quarry was a small cave troll, one of the Lost, an Interdimensional creature that didn't originate in our world. It was Logan's and my job to find him and relocate him. Intel said he would be stocky and around four feet tall.

Being a foot and a half taller than the troll should have made me feel as if I had the advantage. The tranquilizer gun in my hand should have given me some sense of security. However, neither did. My mouth was dry and my insides coiled like a spring.

The Agency for Interdimensional Regulation, AIR, hired me less than a year ago. I had only been in the field for six months. Very few people knew that mythological creatures sometimes enter our world through portals connecting dimensions. We can create portals to familiar worlds, but most are naturally occurring. The Lost slip through to find themselves in our world. Three years out of college and I worked to keep that secret. It was overwhelming and amazing at the same time. For this relocation, I knew that cave trolls were simple-minded, non-verbal, and strong. That was the extent of my knowledge, and I had learned it from a case file.

Logan put a finger to his lips. I stopped moving, anticipating a sound but hearing nothing. He gave the signal to take cover. My steps were noisy but quick. Reaching a tree, I flattened myself against the trunk, keeping a low profile. I scanned the forest floor while watching for more instructions from Logan. Logan crouched behind another tree and considered the terrain.

Mentally walking through where my hands should be placed, I gripped my tranq gun. Finger above the trigger, never on the trigger. Safety off. Pointed at the ground.

A twig broke to the right. I gripped my gun tighter. Turning, I brought it up, ready to shoot. Two squirrels froze for a moment and then zipped away. I pointed my gun back to the ground and let out a steadying breath.

I rolled my eyes and looked at Logan. He was hunched over in a silent laugh. Rubbing my head, I frowned at him. He waved me over.

"Thought you were going to tranq the squirrels." The silent laughter continued and Logan braced himself against the tree.

"That only happened once, and it was a deer." I punched Logan in the arm. I couldn't keep my smile in any longer. Frankly, I was just as surprised that I didn't tranq the squirrels.

My death tight grip on my gun loosened as the mood lightened. "How far away?"

"He's by the creek. The sound of the water makes things difficult to hear. Let's use that talent of yours and see if we can narrow down the search."

My shoulders pulled back and I grinned. How does it happen that a human accountant with no investigative skills is hired to help keep the Lost safe and secret from the world? Obviously, that human must have special skills.

I closed my eyes and took in a deep breath. The smell of warm wood surrounded us. Concentrating on the fringes of my knowledge of our world took a short meditation. In moments, something in my mind stretched tight and popped back into place. I opened my eyes and tried to keep a smug smile from my face.

The world around me had taken on a new look and feel. A shimmer, much like rippling water, pressed itself against everything. Almost everything in the world leaves traces. From the Path, I could read movements, emotions, and interactions of the past and present. Once or twice, I had even caught glimpses of things yet to come.

I am a Reader. The shimmers and colors of the Path tell a story that few can see. There are parts of that story missing.

Looking at Logan, I found the usual blank page. I had never seen an elf leave a Path in our world. Luckily, for my job and me, most other things left fragments that could be followed.

Logan pointed in the general direction of the creek. Pale green shimmers near the ground showed animal trails. I ignored those, as they were too small and too light in color to indicate our target.

The sound of rushing water grew stronger as we moved closer to the creek. The number of animal routes also increased.

Light yellow and blue threaded themselves together with light green. "Got him. The color is darker to the north. We head in that direction."

"Nice work, Cassie."

The ground next to the creek rose up and flattened out. My pace quickened as I followed the animal trail. The Path was recent. I gripped my gun, holding it ready at a moment's notice. Up ahead, the creek rushed out of a small cave.

"The Path leads to the cave." I kept my voice low, but increased my pace.

A yowl came from the left. Looking up, I saw a blur of color and skin, as it crashed into me. My heart skipped a panicked beat as I dropped straight into the rocky shallows of the creek. I scrambled up, blood pumping hard. My concentration broke, the world dulled around me, and the troll was gone.

"Where did he go?" I slid on a rock, but managed to keep upright.

Logan held out a hand and I leveraged myself out of the water. "Spirited little guy. You okay?"

"He ambushed me. Where'd he go?"

"He's feeling cornered so he's lashing out. We'll follow him into the cave." Logan looked me over before heading toward the small entrance. "Watch for crevices and stay in the light. Don't rush at him unless it's necessary. Any questions?"

I shook my head.

Logan rushed forward with fluid movements. I darted after him, my feet squishing water out of my boots with each footstep. I flipped the safety on my rifle and slung it over my shoulder. My gun had smashed into a rock when I fell, but I didn't have time to check on the tranquilizer dart, so I wasn't sure if it was intact. My nerves rattled at the idea of going in virtually unarmed. As we entered the cave, I grabbed a flare out of my cargo pants. Logan had one of his flares lit.

I could throw the flare at the troll, but that wouldn't do much good. There were rocks, but I didn't want to hurt him. Logan would have to take the troll out with his tranquilizer gun.

A threatening cry reverberated out of the darkness. I wheeled around, trying to find the source as the sound bounced around the cave.

Logan took aim and fired.

There was a guttural wail. The troll tried to make a run for it, darting through the water.

"Cassie, out of the way!" Logan yelled.

Adrenaline pulsed through my veins. The troll barreled toward me, his head down, ready to ram me.

SHATTERED SOUL

I dove to the left, once again landing in the water. The troll was nearing the entrance of the cave when he slowed. Logan's tranquilizer took hold. He fell forward with a splash. Then only my rushed breathing and trickling water could be heard for a few heartbeats.

Breaking the silence, Logan dashed through the water-filled cave toward our quarry. I mirrored his actions. The troll landed face down in shallow water. Logan flipped him over. My hands shook as we checked his breathing and pulse. Both steady, relief flooded through me. It seemed like a small job on paper, but being out in the field was still new for me. It sucked not knowing immediately what I should be doing, but my partner was a good mentor.

Logan checked him over for injuries. He pronounced the troll in good health and we moved him onto the damp cave floor.

Logan lit more flares around the cave while I looked over the troll. Many of the Lost had human appearances. Logan and his kids passed for human every day. This guy had two arms and two legs, but his torso was blockier than humans had, with too much skin hanging in folds. His squarish head had a face that looked smashed in.

"Morgan is from the same dimension as this guy, isn't he?" My friend Morgan was also a troll. He was the second Lost I met on the job. "They look completely different."

"Comparing Morgan to this guy is like comparing humans to monkeys. Two different lines of evolution. I'll make him safe for transport."

"I'll check out the cave. Make sure we aren't leaving anything behind." Moving deeper into the cave, I lit another flare and crept forward.

Closing my eyes and concentrating brought me to the Path again. After some probing, I found the strongest Paths the troll had taken. He visited these areas frequently. I started down one dark crevice. A horrid stench brought me up short, no need to go digging into that area. Why he visited was no mystery. The next spot was where he tossed his garbage. Small bones and tufts of fur littered the floor.

Dark repeated layers of color told me that he sat next to the water, or possibly slept next to the water most of the time. Close to the entrance, far from the water, was a small niche in the cave wall. That is where I found his stash.

"I found his treasures." With a blink, I closed the Path. Small crystals sparkled when I held up a small rock from the pile. Each of the rocks held a shiny aspect.

This type of troll couldn't talk, and was more animal than their more evolved counterparts, but they tended to keep small ornamental rocks or crystals. According to others from their world, each piece held an emotional memory for the creature.

Logan came over to examine the contents. "He'll appreciate those in his new home. You grab the rocks, I'll grab the troll."

Pulling a plastic evidence bag out of my pocket, I gathered the rocks.

"Was he placed here, or did he come through a natural portal nearby?" Logan tossed the heavy troll over his shoulder with ease.

"The file said his parents were placed here by the office about ten years ago. The dimensional portal opened up somewhere in central Kansas." I took one last look around the cave, making sure I missed nothing. "They crossed into this dimension and when the rumors started, AIR swooped in."

"We have a tendency to do that," Logan said. We splashed out of the cave into the late summer sun. "We should get a signal now. Call it in."

My cell phone had fared even worse than my gun from the fall into the water. I punched a few buttons, but nothing happened. Maybe this will get me an upgrade, I thought wistfully as I stowed the dead phone. Using Logan's phone, I hit speed dial.

"Hank speaking."

"Hey, Hank, we have our Lost. We'll be heading to the Sanctuary to get him settled into his new cave."

SHATTERED SOUL

"He give you any trouble?" Hank asked.

"No, it went pretty smoothly."

"Really?"

"Sure."

"Then why are you calling from Logan's phone?"

I gritted my teeth. "I, uh, dropped mine... in the water." Which was true. I didn't add that I dropped into the water with it. "Is the doctor enroute?"

On his end, Hank clicked a few buttons. "He's already waiting for you back at the truck."

"All right, got us logged?" I asked.

"You're logged."

"We'll check back in after he's settled." I looked at the time on the cell phone. "In about an hour."

"Talk to you in about an hour." Hank signed off.

Dr. Yelton was waiting for us. His sleek town car looked out of place next to our SWAT style truck.

"Mr. Seale, Miss Heidrich, good to see you two in the field. Any trouble?"

We described what happened, including the troll's collision with me, while we stowed the rocks. Then I helped Logan maneuver the troll into the back of the truck. We cuffed the troll down and the doctor examined the patient, taking temperature, blood pressure, and checking the injection site.

"Everything looks good. Now for you." He turned to me.

"I'm fine," I said automatically. "I only fell into the water."

The doctor frowned. "It's a warm enough day, but get dry as soon as possible. Let me clean up your arm so you can get on your way."

I looked down at my arm. I hadn't noticed the scratch. It would only slow things down if I protested, and I would look like an idiot for doing so. Doctor Yelton cleaned the scrape, slapped on a few bandages, and then was on his way.

Logan had the vehicle started. When I slipped into the seat next to him, I rolled down the window and soaked in the sun's heat. I breathed a sigh of relief and pulled off my wet shoes and socks.

Logan put the truck in gear and headed toward the Sanctuary.

"So this guy's tagged for relocation to the Sanctuary," Logan said. "Lots of fairies there. They been notified?"

"Yeah, I've got the papers here." I pulled a folder out of my messenger bag. Most AIR offices were paperless. We needed an equipment upgrade badly. "Relocation to the Sanctuary west of town. Headquarters warned the fairies two days ago. Travis will keep an eye on our friend here until he gets settled."

"Travis will like having another Lost in the area," Logan said.

"Probably, the park seems a little empty lately." Travis worked for AIR as a park ranger. The Sanctuary is set up to house Lost that need to be relocated. Sometimes it's a temporary stop, and sometimes the Lost get a permanent residence. "There's a werewolf living not too far away from the Sanctuary. Our next assignment is to stop in to check up on him. Should we warn him about the troll?"

"The werewolf will probably be ticked off about the warning. No doubt a werewolf would like to get into a troll tussle." Logan laughed again. Elven laughter had such a musical tone that it was hard not to join him.

"Well, if he wants to tussle, he can join the agency. Or apply, anyway." I paged through the paperwork, making sure I wasn't missing anything.

"That would mean fewer adventures for us. I'd rather he find his own fun."

I could have done with a little less of Logan's idea of fun, but I would never tell him that. This job was a way for me to use my gift without doing palm readings or working the Psychic Network hotlines. Readers are rare and useful in this line of work, but I'm sure I wouldn't want to face down a Lost, or any person, armed only with my gifts. If used for too long, my power sapped the energy out of me.

SHATTERED SOUL

Logan started singing under his breath, something about tumbling tumbleweeds. Elves grab onto things and stick with them for ages. He had been stuck on Westerns for over a month.

His solo didn't last long. "Our troll is up early." Logan's hearing was well beyond my range, even with his ears mostly tucked away.

"I'll take your word for it." I rummaged around in my bag for my med kit.

After we exited the interstate, our drive didn't take long. We reached the Sanctuary's drive and wound around a copse of large trees before ending in an empty parking area near a cabin. Logan pulled to a stop in front of the building. Travis came out and greeted us by the truck. His long brown hair was not so neatly pulled back.

"Cassie, you look as lovely as ever. Logan, it's a pleasure to see you again. You've brought a new friend to join us?"

"Didn't put up much of a fight," Logan said as he walked up to Travis and shook his hand. "But we'll have to put him out before taking him back to your cave. ATVs ready for us, or are we taking the horses?"

"I didn't know how the horses would react, so the ATVs are ready to take our new friend to his home."

"Are we all clear?" I asked. Sometimes, regular people entered the area despite the warning signs at the entrance.

Travis spread his arms wide. "It's just us."

Med kit in hand, I walked to the back of the truck. Our troll slumped in the corner of the truck looking dismal. Pushing myself into the Path, I took a read on the atmosphere. I could see agitation and fear rolling off him in waves. Taking a deep breath, I closed my eyes and felt around inside myself for a feeling of safety and trust. I let that warm feeling fill me up and roll out of me, spreading it out onto the surrounding Path. My energy eased away the other emotions.

After dropping the Path, I crept into the truck with my syringe, approaching the troll quietly. My hand trembled. I had given the shots before, but not often enough to be confident as I approached. It only took a moment. I stuck him with the needle. It took about thirty seconds for him to fall asleep again. Logan carried the troll out to the ATV.

Travis led the way through the Sanctuary. The ATVs roared through a forest for a while. We rounded close to a lake glittering in the sunlight and headed for some bluffs. It was hot enough that I was dry by the time Travis pulled to a halt at the bottom of a white rock cliff. We cut off our ATVs.

"The cave is through the woods. We have to go by foot from here," Travis said. "Too much undergrowth."

Logan lifted the troll. His curious elven strength made the task easy. "Sounds like a prime place."

He was right; we couldn't have asked for a better location. The hike through the woods was about a half mile with the cliff base remaining always to our right as we walked. Large gray boulders, weathered with age, lay among the trees. The cave had only a small opening. It was dry, but the air was cooler at the entrance. Travis assured us that it went back far, but dead ended. A few tunnels led off the main cave, but none of them was more than fifteen yards long.

I couldn't tell what fifteen yards looked like unless I was standing on a football field. Even then, I might not be certain, but if the cave tunnels all dead ended, then that was good enough for me.

Logan went into the cave to settle the troll with his stack of treasured rocks.

Travis and I stood in awkward silence for a moment. Curious, I took the opportunity to read his Path. Cool greens and warm oranges drew in around him. He felt good-natured and a little excited. There was a slash of dark gray buried in the middle. He was hiding something in the core of his being, but most people were.

"Have you met our new werewolf?" Travis asked.

"We're stopping by to see him after we're done here."

SHATTERED SOUL

"He's come out here to run a few times." Travis leaned against a tree. He smiled, but looked uncomfortable. Around him, the orange colors started to roll together, making their presence stronger. "Do you run?"

"I like the idea of running, but I suck at the execution."

Travis laughed. "If you ever feel like hitting the trail, this is a good place for it."

Logan emerged from the cave. "He'll be waking up soon. We should—"

An echoing crack cut through the conversation.

A chill rolled through me. "Gunfire? Here?"

CHAPTER 2

NOISE REBOUNDED FROM THE BLUFF. I tried to figure out which direction the shot came from while pushing back the rising panic.

"That couldn't have been in the Sanctuary." I tried to sound resolute, but couldn't quite pull it off.

Logan was on the balls of his feet, and his ears at their points, alert for any hint of noise.

"Call it in." Logan tossed me his phone and took off toward the ATVs. "Travis, what's the shortest way to the fairy homestead?"

I called while running to catch up with Travis and Logan. The chill dug deeper into my system.

"Hank here."

"Shot fired in or near the Sanctuary," I panted, trying to keep up with the others. "Troll is secure. We're heading to the fairy homestead."

"Do you know the location of the shot?" Hank's usually calm demeanor turned demanding.

"Logan, which way was the shot?" I asked as I jumped onto an ATV.

"Couldn't pinpoint with only one shot. Tell him western central toward the fairies."

The ATVs roared to life as I relayed the information.

Over the noise, I could hear Hank. "We'll try to grab a satellite and pull up the area. Stay safe. Call on the fives."

Mashing down the throttle, I stayed within sight of Logan and Travis. It felt like pixies were running wild in my stomach as

SHATTERED SOUL

I started second-guessing our approach. A silent approach would be better, but what if someone was hurt?

Wind pulled through my hair as we charged through the landscape. The other ATVs came to a halt in front of me. Logan jumped off and started heading into the woods. I cut the engine and followed. My heart battered my chest.

Travis started to follow, but stopped short when Logan looked back and shook his head. "Stay with the ATVs."

"Do you have a weapon?" I asked as I hurried by, pulling out the cell phone again.

"I'm covered." Travis fell back as I pressed speed dial.

Hank didn't wait for an introduction. "We've got a team moving in your direction. Tell Travis to meet part of the team by the front entrance."

I paused and yelled back to Travis. Immediately, he headed out.

"The other team members will be entering the area through an old logging trail on the west side of the property. We have no satellites in position for the next twenty minutes."

"We're heading toward the homestead. Going silent." I left the connection to Hank open, trusting that he would mute his end, and shoved it into my pocket.

Logan slowed and listened. The woods were denser as we reached the fairy forest. Tall trees cast shadows, making the air cooler. A soft buzzing noise, which one might mistake for bees, could be heard in the branches and behind the tree leaves. This meant the fairies were keeping a close watch on us. I tried to calm my breath and slow my racing heart--not an easy task. The still sounds and gentle whir of fairy wings helped.

Closer to the heart of the fairies' realm, Logan pulled up and turned to me. "Keep that brain of yours open."

I closed my eyes and took a deep breath, opening the part of my mind that reads the Path. I mentally kicked myself for not having the Path open.

Logan left no trace, but occasionally, I caught a fleeting

glimpse of movement over the fabric of the Path. Fairies barely left their mark on the Path, but it was enough to let me know they were here.

Logan stopped short as several fairies flew out in front of us. They buzzed around, blocking our way. They rushed at us through the air, turning moments before smacking us in the face. From my view, angry orange sparks burst and dissipated as they flew. Their little bodies and colorful butterfly wings created a beautiful display, but from their chirping and hisses, it was obvious that we should move no further.

"We seek an audience with the Speaker," Logan said. One of the fairies disappeared in a blur. Essy, the Speaker, appeared moments later.

"Logan and Cassie, I recognize you as AIR servants," she said, her tone formal, but she too was emitting angry orange sparks. "We have a complaint against the walkers of this world."

"We will oversee any complaints," Logan replied.

"A human has entered our territory and assaulted our tribe."

An immense billow of red fury sprang from Logan into the Path. I took a few nervous steps away. The red turned dark and swelled, and then it stopped. Logan had bottled his emotion up once more. His rage marred the landscape. The eruption of red was frozen. The rippling waves of the Path did nothing to push it away. I bit my lip and eyed the blight.

"Is he here?" From the sound of Logan's voice, you would never know his fury lurked beneath.

"It is gone," Essy chirped angrily in between words. "One of our own is dead."

I sucked in a sharp breath. "Was he shot?"

Essy quivered from head to toe. "The metal missed. He was struck by flesh."

Logan turned to me. "Let's go track the person who did this."

Essy took off from her perch. "It attempted to ensnare Uriah while he was in the wildflower field." Essy led us to a blanket of flowers that covered a small meadow.

SHATTERED SOUL

As we approached, I could see the Path the person had created and I motioned to Logan to stop.

"It appears to be human, or someone who's at least lived in this dimension its whole life." A chill curled in my stomach. "Not one of the Lost. I can see that in his Path." It was the feeling of his Path more than a physical manifestation.

I took the lead and explored the man's movements. "He grew aggravated at the wildflower area, but he wasn't emotional when he came through here." After following the man's imprint for a while, I stopped short.

"This doesn't look good, Logan," I said. "Someone else met up with him. They were here at the same time. It's," I fumbled over the words, "he's human, but his imprint is twisted."

I shivered and followed a second trail of ugly colors. Grays, browns, and greens took on dark hues. They tangled together in ways that I had never seen. Lines of bleached orange were dispersed. The usual rippling stream in the Path was muted and stagnant. "His colors don't flow." I pressed forward. "They bend and twist around." I gripped my stomach. "It's not normal." Nothing else existed except the twisting rivers of color and me as I became absorbed in my work.

The two Paths met and led to a dead end on an old rutted road in the woods. I blinked at the blending of their Paths. They left the area on a motor vehicle of some sort, and the trail ended. The man's Path left me unsettled.

Logan put his hand on my shoulder. The world blurred and Paths disappeared. I blinked a few times and swayed. Logan gripped my shoulder, keeping me steady, while I looked around for Essy. "Where did she go?"

"She left a while ago. Others delivered messages to her. We traveled too far for a fairy not expecting an expedition. They relayed all information to her. I also told her we would send a guard to watch the area."

I sighed and swayed more. If not for Logan, I would have followed the invisible world until collapsing into exhaustion or beyond. There were stories of readers who followed a Path into death. They may not have noticed death's approach while absorbed in the shimmering river pressed onto the world. My limbs shook and I blinked my eyes rapidly.

Lines of worry marred Logan's face before relaxing once again into his casual grin. Remembering how he created a Path while outwardly remaining calm made me wonder what emotions he hid. I sighed and rolled my head on my shoulders.

"There's a team meeting us back at the ATVs," Logan said.

Having no idea what to expect, I followed slowly behind, crunching through the debris on the ground.

We heard Travis when we approached. "I know it's frustrating, but we have to wait. Logan, so glad you're back. The fairies made it clear that they want no one near their home."

"Can't say that I blame them." Logan eyed the group. A few seemed to shrink, leery of Logan. "We don't need to go to their homestead."

One of the men started to protest, but Logan cut him off. "The attack took place in a meadow not far away. There was a single shot that we heard. The fairies have confirmed that the man who fired the shot also killed the fairy, Uriah. We haven't recovered the shell casing."

"If you find it, don't touch it." Clancy, a squat man with a demanding tone, took a step away from the group. "You know I can't work with it if it's been touched." Like me, Clancy had his own gift.

The men nodded. A few rolled their eyes. I recognized some of the faces from the office, but I hadn't worked directly with any of them.

"Let's head out," Logan said. "I interviewed the fairies while Cassie worked. They gave us the description of one man, about my height, white, brown hair. Travis, you're with me to see if we can get any more details. They'll mind us less than others and we need to talk with them before their memories fade any further. Cassie will mark their movements through the meadow. Everyone else, start the grid search with the metal detectors."

SHATTERED SOUL

We all went to work.

Travis and Logan joined us again as I was finishing marking the trail with flags.

"Do they know why he fired the gun?" I asked.

"He tried to grab one of the fairies. They started dusting him and tormenting him. It seems he lost his cool and shot," Logan said.

"But he missed the fairies," I said. "Essy said Uriah was struck by flesh, not metal."

Logan started moving again toward the meadow. "Yeah, he missed with the bullet but clipped Uriah with his hand while he floundered around."

"Did we get anything else from them?"

"Just that Uriah died out here."

Logan handed me an insulated bottle. I took it and almost choked on the bitter black coffee.

"Clancy brought this from the office," Logan said. "He figured you would need it by now."

Making a face, I drank more down.

"Take Travis through the trail you marked earlier. I'll catch up," Logan said.

We moved out of the meadow, each of us holding a bundle of flags. I pushed one into the ground here and there along the way. I checked the Path off and on, but our trail from the first time was pretty noticeable at this point. I pulled out Logan's cell and found it dead.

"Do you have a phone on you? I need to call Gran and let her know I'll be late."

Travis looked up at me and smiled.

"She'll probably worry." I kept my tone light. Gran had moved in with me a few months ago. We were still trying to figure out how to live together.

"Margaret? She already called me." Travis grinned wider. "Not even sure how she got my number, but she called. She wanted me to let you know that there was no reason to call her."

23

I breathed out a sigh of relief.

"Your Gran is something else. How did she know?"

"She's a psychic. The real thing."

"I meet the most interesting people on this job," Travis said.

Logan caught up with us and we met another team at the old logging trail. Logan sent them to work and we hitched a ride from one of the agents back to the Sanctuary parking lot. The sun was starting to dip in the sky and a dull, tired ache had spread through my limbs.

Once we were in our own vehicle, I stretched out before rummaging through my purse for acetaminophen to dull the ache. Logan called his kids first, ever the family man. Most elves that visited our world stayed here for a short time. Logan went to and from this world for fifty years, but set up permanent residence twelve years ago when his wife died. I was pretty sure he didn't want to face his own world without his wife. He brought his kids with him. Like all the Lost that arrived in our world on purpose, they had their names assigned to them when they settled into this world.

"Next up, we need to interview the wolf."

"The werewolf? I thought another team would take that."

"The world keeps movin' as we work our case. Besides, he lives close to the Sanctuary. We need to see if he was in the area."

I should have known that. I needed a lot more investigative training.

"Who's the wolf we're seeing?" Logan asked. "Let's get the details."

"Rider Wolfe," I said, pulling out the file. "Who decided that was a good name?"

"Better get our chuckles out of the way early. It could be a rough translation of his real name to English."

"I've never met a werewolf," I admitted.

"Werewolves can be touchy. I've met a fair few in my time here."

SHATTERED SOUL

"What are they like?" I asked, punching the address into the GPS.

"Private people, don't like strangers much, but once they consider you a friend, you would be hard pressed to find a more loyal one. They're friends for life. They also like their space."

"Hmmm." Not quite the B horror movie werewolf I had pictured.

"Bit grouchy," added Logan. "I'll let you do the introductions. I'll back you up when you need it."

My first werewolf, I thought, as we pulled up and got out of the truck. I smoothed down my sleeves as we approached the small house. The clapboard siding was painted yellow, peeling in spots. Shutters were painted green. There was a garden, brown and overgrown, at the side of the house.

I rang the doorbell and a sound like wind chimes came from the house. It took some resolve not to gulp and take a step back when a man opened the inner door. He was easily over six feet tall with stark black hair, which set off his tanned skin. His eyes were strong and aware. He seemed to be sizing me up as I stared. His entire frame was muscle, but it wasn't bulky. Instead, he had the muscles of a runner.

That made sense. I bet he ran all the time. On four legs.

"Um," I stammered, trying to break the tense silence, "are you Mr. Wolfe?"

His eyes focused on me and he nodded.

"My name is Cassie Heidrich, and this is Logan Seale. I think you were expecting us?"

Again, he nodded.

"We, uh, ran into some trouble earlier, so we're coming by a bit late. Sorry about that." I clamped my lips shut to keep from jabbering on. Looking to Logan, I waited for him to say something. He rocked back and forth on his feet, humming softly to himself.

"Um," I said again, silently berating Logan for not stepping up to help the conversation. "We wanted to stop by and see how you were doing, Mr. Wolfe. Maybe talk a bit?" I didn't mean the last part to come out as a question, but it did nonetheless.

"Call me Rider," the man said at last. He opened the screen door and stepped out. I took a mental note of the hostility in his voice.

"Rider. I do like that name," Logan said.

Rider nodded. "Logan Seale?" Rider asked. He didn't catch Logan's infectious smile. "Not what I would expect for an elf. I was expecting tree names or something." Logan nodded, smiling broadly. Rider's gaze landed once again on me. "I've never met an elf before, or one of you. What are you?"

I was stumped. I had never been asked what I was before and wasn't sure how to approach it. "Ah, I'm human."

"Sorry, I have only met a few people on this side. You smell different from the others."

"Oh, you're smelling the Reader on her."

I gaped at Logan. He never told others what I could do.

Logan noticed my dumbfounded expression. "Ah, well, anyway," Logan stammered before catching himself. He turned once again to Rider. "We wanted to see how things were going. Make sure you've found the grocery store, maybe met some locals and that sort of thing."

"How often will you be checking in?" asked Rider. He watched me.

Was he smelling me? How creepy is that?

"Oh, probably every other week or so to start. Once you get settled in, we'll come less frequently if you'd like."

Rider nodded. "Do you need to know names of people I have met?"

"Nothing like that," I said quickly. Rider was guarded, and I wanted to put him more at ease. "We want to make sure you're fitting in and have someone you can ask questions. That sort of thing."

"Travis has mentioned you two before," Rider said. He looked at me as if I were a puzzle to solve.

SHATTERED SOUL

"Excellent!" I grasped onto the subject. "Travis is trustworthy and should be able to answer your questions."

"Sure, Travis shelters a few fairies and helped us set a troll up in one of the caves. Have you met any of the fairies?" Logan asked.

"I met Essy while out on a run," Rider admitted.

"Get too close to her homestead?" asked Logan. "I swear that little woman nearly took my ears off when I went out looking for her one day. She dusted me so much I thought I'd itch for a week."

Rider seemed to loosen up a bit at hearing this. Fairies live among the plants and trees in the woods. To ward people away, they sometimes drop dust from ground-up poisonous plants. In Essy's case, it's usually a mix of poison oak and poison ivy, something that most people would be allergic to. She was trying to find something that would bring a reaction from me, so she could add it to her mix. Not that I had aggravated her, I had only met her a few times, but fairies kept their weapons close at hand, just in case.

"Something like that." Rider's voice lost some of its edge and the atmosphere around our little group became a bit lighter.

Logan scratched his temple and looked at me pointedly. "The fairies have had a bit of trouble recently."

I took the hint and opened the Path.

Rider was a leery jumble of raw emotion. Pain, joy, anger, and happiness were under the surface. His Path rippled. Shades of green and brown vibrated from instinctual animal to the more complex hues and turns of human. It was beautiful to watch.

And I was watching. Staring really, and Rider was staring right back, with his head cocked as if trying to examine my actions. I pushed the Path away and cleared my throat. I felt my face blush in the light of the sun.

Logan said. "Were you around the Sanctuary today at any time?"

Rider didn't take his eyes off me. "No." He didn't offer any additional information.

"It might be best to give the fairies a wide berth for a while. Have you seen anyone out there recently, besides them and Travis?"

"No," Rider said.

I cleared my throat again. "Have you seen anyone around your house recently? Someone that didn't belong here?"

Rider looked confused. "I have seen you."

"Anyone besides us?" Was my face getting redder?

"No."

"Everything else going well?" Logan asked.

"I have met a few people. I have found the grocery store. I do not have any questions right now. Anything else?"

An abrupt way to end our visit, but it was effective. We said goodbye and let him know to call us if there was anything he needed. Rider only nodded.

As soon as we were back in the truck, I asked Logan, "Do I smell weird?"

Logan laughed and nodded toward Rider. For the first time, I could see a grin on the werewolf's face. Logan laughed again and started the truck. Without looking into a mirror, I knew my face was fully crimson.

"He could hear me?" I asked.

CHAPTER 3

"OH YEAH," LOGAN RESPONDED. "Werewolves have very good hearing. Better than most any creature that I know of. You smell fine," Logan explained as he turned the truck around and started back down the driveway. "You smell a little different than most people. Actually, to a werewolf, you probably smell a great deal different. Each gift leaves a mark on the person. Did you get anything off him?"

"His Path didn't cross the ones we walked last night. His Path is— well, it's unique. I would have noticed if he had been in the area of the wildflower field."

"At least we've ruled him out. We can head to the office."

I contemplated the different scents we had. What other kinds of markers do beings from the other side discern in us?

All the way back to the office, Logan bobbed his head to music only he could hear. Every now and again, he would belt out something about being in a saddle. I listened while focusing on the coffee we stopped for. It had taken years to tame the West. I hoped this fad didn't last as long. Still, it was better than show tunes. Logan's last partner shot him over show tunes.

Our offices were located at the Farm, a massive area of land fenced to look like a horse ranch. I vibrated with all the sugar and coffee coursing through my veins as we went through security. The only time I reflected on the fact that AIR was a government institution was when I received my paycheck from the US Treasury Department and when going through security. Logan entered the code to get past the first gate. Further in was a second gate and a much larger fence. Surveillance cameras monitored the fences twenty-four hours a day. Logan swiped our ID cards and moved on through.

The job came with a government clearance, but that seemed to be a requirement for getting into the Farm. As far as I knew, we didn't actually answer to any government agencies. We had never been audited, for instance, and there were never any inspections. As a former accountant, I had genuinely been curious about the audits so I looked it up. I couldn't find a single record of one.

We parked our car in front of the main office, a four story white stone building with many windows. Around back, you could reach the first basement level through loading docks, but sub-basements could be found under that. In the darkness, the glass doors to the building were well lit both inside and out. After pressing the fingerprint scanner and going through the deserted reception area, we went straight down the hall to command central. We had to swipe ID cards and perform a retinal scan before accessing the main room. Our boss, Barry Milner, and his shadow, Assistant Director, Kyrian Thorne, watched large monitors on the far side of the room. Most of the staff at the Midwest branch of AIR was human. Several agents had special abilities, but neither Barry nor Kyrian did, unless being suited for government work was a gift.

From what I had heard from others, Barry, at one point, had been a remarkable field agent. Once he started moving up the chain of command, he moved quickly. Kyrian seemed good natured and nice to everyone, but it was fake. She didn't want to step on any toes on her way up. It seemed to work for her, because she now shadowed Barry, even though she had only been with the organization for a few years. She had never done fieldwork, but that was probably for the best. She didn't seem like the type to get her hands dirty.

"Good timing," Barry said as we approached. "We have a full team still at the Sanctuary. Have you interviewed the fairies?"

Logan took the lead. "We have all the details they remember. I'll get it written up tonight."

SHATTERED SOUL

Barry handed a stack of papers to Logan. Logan promptly handed the papers off to me. Logan was allergic to paperwork. He preferred talking to people.

"Put a copy on my desk. I want to know what they know," Barry said.

"There might be a related case." Kyrian pulled out another file. Barry lifted an eyebrow. "A gnome went missing in Tennessee."

I moved to take the file, but Barry reached it first.

"We'll do more exploring to see if the case is related," Barry said. "In the meantime, you two get to work on the case in front of you. Don't get distracted."

Kyrian looked at me, a pleasant expression plastered on her face. "Cassie, during the interviews, uh, did you spot anything out of place?"

Sighing, I started to say something fairly unfriendly about Kyrian's complete lack of understanding, but Logan interrupted and started to lead me away. "We'll make sure it's in the report," he said over his shoulder.

"She's clueless," I muttered to Logan as we went to our desks.

"True, but I doubt she'd appreciate hearing about it from you."

We had an office we could use, but we mostly worked on the main floor. Logan wanted to be around other people, not stuffed in a corner. I started reading the information in the files. Before clearing the second page, I rubbed my forehead, trying to relieve the building pressure. Everything ever written down about Essy's tribe was in front of me. Tons of information needed to be waded through.

Our job was usually simple. Set people up in their new homes, relocate, and make sure the Lost maintained their secrecy. We settled squabbles, helped them find suitable jobs, and made sure everyone found their way in their new world.

This was murder. This was way over my head.

31

Logan interrupted my reading with a fresh cup of coffee. "You should be scanning instead of reading."

"If I scan, I might miss something."

Logan sat on the edge of my desk. "Have you seen any new information?"

"Nothing." I sighed, seeing Logan's point.

"At this time in the investigation, it's better to talk to people than read about it. If we wait around to read about it, we're behind."

"Where do we start?"

"All the information is getting funneled through Hank. I started with him while you read."

Hank is our handler and he reigns over the computer in the central hub of offices. He works with three teams of field agents.

"The field team found the bullet and Clancy has brought it in. He's the only one that might have something new at this point," Logan said. "We'll follow up with him next."

Clancy's face was tense with concentration when we entered the office. His face was sweating. We waited.

Clancy let out a breath. "Your staring isn't helping."

I immediately looked elsewhere.

Logan smiled. Some of Clancy's tension fell away.

I'm not immune to Logan's contagious smile, but I ached with tiredness that wouldn't allow the corners of my mouth to turn up.

"How's it going?" I asked.

Clancy adjusted his tie and stared at the bullet casing. "It's been handled too many times. Like someone passed it around to a bunch of people so we can't get a fix on any one of them."

Logan raised an eyebrow. "On purpose?"

Clancy shook his head. "No, no, that's just the outcome of what they did."

"Maybe you should get some rest, and try again in the morning," I suggested.

"Maybe," Clancy said. "I'll send a field report to your printer now. That'll give you all I know."

32

SHATTERED SOUL

"Then, I guess we'll mosey along," Logan said, and tipped an imaginary hat.

Our printer was back in our actual office, so I headed in that direction while Logan went back to the central office. Was I doing everything that I could? I sat at my desk, which had more dust than I expected, and the printer sprang to life. I thought through each step I had taken so far in the case, while pages spit themselves out. I was pretty sure we killed three trees a day by having the confidentiality disclaimers and protocols printed repeatedly. Our system and protocols seriously needed updating.

Someone knocked on the office door.

"Come in," I said while tossing the confidentiality clause pages to the side.

"Cassie?" asked the man who entered.

"Hi," I said. "Are you working on Essy's case?"

The man had dark hair, which looked like it had been cut short a few months ago and in bad need of a trim. He closed the door behind him and smiled at me.

"Not exactly, I'm Vincent, from the Pacific North-West office." He held his hand out for me to shake it.

I clasped his hand and almost immediately began to feel a tug, not physically, but a pull on the energy surrounding me. I started to yank my hand back, but Vincent clamped down in a vice-like grip.

"Hey!" I started. Vincent no longer smiled. He didn't look mean, but wore a look of stony indifference.

"Fiend, you will no longer be parading around in this world. There is no use struggling."

I began struggling like hell. His grip prevented me from wrenching my hand away, so instead, I kicked out, catching him in the knee. I felt my energy being drained away, forming a whirlpool with Vincent at the center. I used my free hand to reach for his face in an attempt to inflict maximum damage. He batted my hand away with ease. I tried again to pull away.

"What are you doing?" I yelled. Instead of pushing away,

33

I launched myself at Vincent. He was caught off guard and I smashed him up against the wall. With my free hand, I tried to punch him. I made contact, but not hard enough to break his grip. I felt weak all over. I tried to knee him in the groin, but he sidestepped me. I kicked out again, but there was no force behind my kick. Panic set in and I struggled, trying everything to get away from him.

"Fiends are not allowed in the world. You will do no murder here."

CHAPTER 4

"What the hell are you talk—" I fell to my knees before I could finish the sentence. I tried desperately to alter the flow of the power rushing away from me. Trying to open the path, I thought I could counteract Vincent, but it didn't open and I felt myself being emptied away. Thoughts flitted through my head. Who was going to take care of Gran? Logan needed me. I was not finished yet!

The man started lowering me to the ground. The struggles were futile, but I tried to pull back. I was spinning in a vortex with him at the center, all of me, not just my strength. I fell away. My eyesight began to dim. After failing to raise my arms in one last attempt of defense, I looked straight into Vincent's eyes.

He looked back and his indifference snapped. His eyes widened in surprise, and then his face filled with anguish as I stared up at him. His mouth opened in a yell, but I couldn't hear. Who would have guessed that I would meet my murderer today? Closing my eyes, I fell into darkness.

Someone talked, but I wasn't cognizant enough to make it out. My own breath was the only noise I could make sense of. Dragging my eyes open was a challenge. They were only open for a few moments before a blinding light forced me to close them again.

Once the light disappeared, an incessant chatter of words filtered in. My eyes opened with less effort the next time. I was propped up in a bed with Dr. Yelton standing over me. He was calm, but working quickly.

Once I was able to focus on his words, I realized he was bombarding me with questions.

"Can you tell me your name?" He paused. "Do you know where you are? Can you hear me?"

I tried to answer the last question but the words came out wrong.

"Can you understand me?" he asked.

I think I nodded. I started to feel different parts of my body in detached ways. Again, his little flashlight glared into my face. I tried to push myself back, but my arms might just as well not been attached to my brain. They moved, but not in the directions that I wanted. Panic welled up. My breathing increased as I tried to get my limbs to work.

Dr. Yelton tested my reflexes, while a blood pressure cuff tried to murder my arm. "Stay calm. We're told that the effects are temporary. Do you know what happened?" he asked.

I processed the question and thought hard. I remembered going to the printer.

Vincent, my office— the handshake! Everything fell back into place. I looked around the room, worried about what I might find. The doctor and I were alone.

"He's in custody."

Gibberish popped out of my mouth when I tried to speak. The doctor winced.

A nurse came into the room. "Test results are ready, Doctor."

Dr. Yelton continued to talk as he pulled information up on the computer. "I need you to tell me your name."

I took a few deep breaths, concentrating once again on the sound the air made while inhaling and exhaling.

"Cassie," I said. Finally, things were starting to flow again. I focused on my fingers, getting each one to bend and flex. Bit by bit, I began regaining control of my body.

"Tell me what happened," he said.

SHATTERED SOUL

I told him my story while he nodded at the computer screen. My sentences were choppy at first, but strong by the end. It was a short story.

"You've had a run in with a Walker," the doctor said. "Scans look good. There doesn't appear to be any internal damage. Let's check your reflexes again."

He poked and prodded and my body started to respond.

"The Walker, Vincent Pironis, said the effects would be short-lived."

"Where is he? How did he get in here?" I asked.

"They took him into custody. He'll probably be in the first floor cells."

"He's waiting in the interrogation room." Logan strode into the room. "What's the prognosis, Doc?"

Dr. Yelton gave a questioning look. Even at AIR, the patient doctor relationship meant something. Maybe not as much as it should, but the doctor wouldn't say anything in front of my partner without my permission. I nodded my approval.

"She's recovering. As Mr. Pironis indicated, all damage was temporary."

"How did he get in here?" I asked Logan.

"Barry's reviewing with security now. Damned Walker, he could have gotten in from anywhere. It's what they do best."

"What is a Walker?"

"They're accursed. Portals connect two dimensions by cutting through the between areas, but Walkers can slip in and out of about anywhere because they can slip between dimensions." He paused. "Are you okay?" He momentarily lost the cowboy twang which let me know he was genuinely worried.

"I'm doing better," I said.

Logan gave me a long look and nodded.

"It never actually hurt," I said. "I was tired, but even that was almost gone now. What exactly happened?"

"I'm going to find out," Logan said. "We've let him sit for a while."

"I'm going with you." I leaned forward on the bed. My body responded, but slower than I expected.

"We need to go over a few things first," Dr. Yelton said.

I shook my head and each word became more forceful than the previous. "This guy came in here and almost killed me. I'm going down to see him."

"You were unconscious not that long ago. That's never a good sign."

"Neither is someone trying to kill you," I said. "I need to know what happened."

Dr. Yelton stared at me a few moments while clicking his pen. "We don't know what side effects might occur. And we only have Mr. Pironis's word to take for what actually happened." He clicked his pen a few more times and looked at the chart. "Your lab results are all normal. Even so, I'm putting you on restricted duty for three days."

My mouth automatically opened to argue.

"Three days, Miss Heidrich. We have no idea what the full effects will be."

I kept my mouth shut in case he tried to make me stay longer. He told me to keep an eye out for anything abnormal.

Logan impatiently shifted from foot to foot. He started walking the moment my feet hit the ground. I would never say it aloud, but I was thankful that it was a slow walk.

"You're not going inside the room with him," Logan said. "You're going to watch only."

"But, what if—" I started.

Logan shook his head. "No, you're watching only. Barry will be going into the interrogation room with me."

"The Director interrogating?"

"He's one of the best, but he wants me to take lead on this. No reading the Path either. You look like you're about to fall over as it is, so let's not add to it. We've got this guy. He'll talk."

My stomach twisted with anxiety as we made our way downstairs. I went into the viewing room, and Logan and Barry went into the room where Vincent waited.

SHATTERED SOUL

Vincent sat at the table. His hands were cuffed and his face could have been a stone carving. He stared straight ahead, not even looking around when others came into the room.

"I trust that she is okay?" Vincent asked. Even his voice held no emotion.

"What makes you think that?" Logan asked.

"You are calm," Vincent said.

"You exceeded my calm threshold the moment I heard you were here," Logan said. "How did you get in here?"

"Through the front gates," Vincent said.

Barry shifted in his chair, but allowed Logan to continue.

"Now, how did you get in those gates?" Logan asked.

"I put in my ID card and had my retinas scanned. Same as any other agent," Vincent said.

"You're trying to say you're an agent?" Logan asked.

"From the North-Western branch," Vincent said.

"Why come here? Why attack another agent?" Logan asked.

The first sign of life flitted across Vincent's face as he minutely flinched.

"I was told that the Mid-West branch of AIR had been infiltrated by a fiend," Vincent said.

"Who told you we had a demon here?" Barry asked.

"The orders came from my supervisor at the North-Western office," Vincent said.

"You were told by AIR that a fiend was here in the office? Why were we not informed?" Barry asked.

"If one fiend had entered, why not two?" Vincent asked.

"So you were here to check things out?" Logan prompted.

"I was sent here to dispose of a fiend." Vincent's voice was steady and void of feeling. "Cassandra was in my file, named as said fiend, so I started to dispose of her. First, I took her energy, and then started with her essence." He paused and looked away. "It was then that I realized that she was not a fiend."

Cold tendrils wrapped around me. He pulled my essence? I had no idea what that meant, but it didn't sound good.

39

"The process of starting to pull essence and stopping again? I've never heard of it happening before. It shouldn't be possible. I couldn't tell you how relieved I was that I was able to stop, and return her essence." He looked back at Logan.

"What does pulling her essence mean exactly?" Logan asked.

"Once I pulled all of her energy, I tapped into what makes her, her. Her essence. It's referred to in different ways, psyche, soul, essence. It's all the same."

"You pulled her soul out?" Logan asked. Fury swept across his face.

"No, I pulled part of her soul out." Vincent looked at the mirror. He looked at me. "I put it back. It's all there."

"That's it then. You pulled part of her soul out and then pushed it back in?"

"As she's probably experienced, there might be some side effects. It could take a while for things to resettle." Vincent faced the mirror, looking very uncomfortable. "Her soul is all there, but it is not whole. It's broken."

Broken? I wasn't sure how to take this news.

Logan slammed his fist on the table. Vincent went back to staring straight ahead. All signs of discomfort left and his face was an unreadable blank mask once more.

"She's broken now. Tell us how to fix her!" Logan yelled.

I had felt abnormal when I woke up, but now? There was something different. I could feel something was off. I wasn't in pain and there wasn't a mark on me, but something wasn't quite right.

The smallest hint of a frown appeared then retreated from Vincent's face. "This has never happened before. I will talk to other Walkers, but I'm not sure how to fix this."

"You're not talking to anyone." Logan leaned back in his seat. "You attacked an AIR agent. We're tossing you into a hole somewhere."

Logan's words didn't faze Vincent. "I was sent here to dispose of a fiend, not a woman. My instructions were explicit. I was doing my job."

SHATTERED SOUL

"Why did you stick around after the job?" Logan asked. "I bet you could side-step your way out of this world right now."

"I could at any time, but I will not leave until I've made this right," Vincent said.

Logan started to speak, but the Director broke in. "We're going to talk to your superiors to work on confirmation. At this time, you are to remain confined."

Logan looked angry, but left the interrogation room. Barry followed behind. As soon as they left the room, Vincent's face turned toward the glass. He didn't say anything; he only watched what must have been his own reflection.

I jumped when the door to the room opened, and Logan and Barry walked in.

"I didn't know the company employed Walkers," Logan said.

Barry raised an eyebrow at Logan. "I'll find out what the other office knows about this incident and we'll proceed from there. We'll have him transferred to a cell shortly."

"A cell's not going to hold him," Logan said.

"If he's an agent, he'll stick to his cell," Barry said.

When Barry left the room, I turned to watch Vincent again.

"You're looking better, but not one hundred percent," Logan said. "Back to normal?"

Telling Logan should have been easy, but when I went to say I felt a bit off, it came out as, "I think so."

The word broken kept coming to mind over and over again.

"Why would anyone want to kill you? Have you ticked anyone off? I'm with you most the time, and I haven't noticed anything out of the ordinary."

"Could it be I was mistaken for someone else?" I meant it as a throw away comment.

"Mistaken for someone else? You're the only red headed female in the office. You're one of only a handful of women." Logan thought for a bit, and then latched onto my train of thought. "Could be that whoever sent out the warning got the

41

wrong person. That could be it. It's possible that we have a fiend running round. Someone noticed or sensed the fiend and went outside our office to get it taken care of." Logan seemed pretty happy to link those thoughts together.

"Shouldn't one of us have noticed a fiend?" I asked.

"Maybe, but we're not in the office that much."

"That's true," I said, trying to hide a yawn. "Listen, Logan, about Vincent." I stopped, not knowing how to continue.

"Walkers are an odd type. They walk between worlds, and don't need a portal to go through, or to drag others through. No one trusts them. They can do whatever they want and slip away. I don't like that he's some sort of a hit man, even if he is supposed to be on our team. He's dangerous."

An uneasy feeling crept over me at the thought of sending Vincent away. "Do you think there will be any side effects to what he did? Something that he could fix?"

"I hope there's nothing. If he broke something, maybe we should keep him around until it's fixed."

"If he's right and we have a fiend in the office, will we lead the investigation?"

"One of his agents was nearly killed. Barry will head this one. We've got our hands full now. Let's go check in with Hank again. It's been hours. Maybe something new has come across the desk."

"You go ahead," I said. "I'm going to wait here."

I could see Logan's frown from the corner of my eye.

"I'll stay until he's transferred to a cell," I said.

Logan nodded. "Don't go in the room with him."

I agreed. Logan left and I went back to watching Vincent.

What am I doing? I thought. There was something about Vincent. Something that wasn't there when I first met him, but I couldn't put my finger on it.

Without thinking, I reached for the Path. My breath caught as a flood of color and light swamped my senses. I gripped the back of a chair. Blinded by the Path, I didn't dare move.

42

What the hell?

I thought I was back to full strength, but my legs started wobbling after a few moments. I struggled against the river of information. Using what little strength I had, I pushed it back. The light faded and the dim world returned. I fell into the chair and slumped forward, breathing heavily. I wanted to believe that some outside force caused this. Maybe a portal was open. My powers often worked oddly around open portals.

This was different though. This was new.

I fumbled for the microphone to the interrogation room.

"How long will the side effects last?" I stared into the room.

Vincent paled. His mask of indifference fell away.

"Are you okay?" Vincent asked.

"Answer the question." Panic filled my voice. What if I could no longer read the Path?

Vincent must have heard the panic. "Do you need a doctor?" He came to the mirrored window as if he could peer in. He leaned against the glass with his hands cuffed behind him. "I thought things would have settled by now."

"Mostly they have. But…" I didn't want to go any further. I couldn't tell a homicidal stranger that my power was impaired.

Somehow, though, he didn't seem like a stranger to me.

"Have we met before?" I asked.

Vincent sighed and leaned away from the mirror.

"No, we've never met." He paused. "You should know, however, that I know you."

"That sounds creepy." He was a stranger, a stranger who tried to kill me. When I looked at him though, there wasn't any fear.

"I took in your essence, Cassie, so I know a great deal about you now."

"That sounds creepier."

"That was not my intention. I'm sorry for what happened."

"I don't understand. How do I fix this?"

Vincent shook his head and returned to his chair. His

emotions were stripping themselves from his face once more.

"I will do whatever I can to make this right," Vincent said, "but I don't have the answers you're looking for."

CHAPTER 5

FROM THE MOMENT I LEFT the office, my mood went downhill. It felt like I left something behind, but I couldn't think of what it was. Maybe because I didn't have a phone? The disquiet rose and Logan started to look worried. I let him know that I was tired and in real need of sleep. That wasn't a lie. I felt like I could sleep for days.

Fragmented dreams where I searched for something left me feeling worse in the morning. I was itchy in my own skin. Something was missing.

When I dragged myself downstairs, Gran was in the kitchen. After her second husband died, I had been worried about her rattling around her house all alone. I convinced her it was worth a try living together. It took some adjustments, but after living together for five months, we were starting to get comfortable with our routines and with each other.

"Mornin', Sugar," Gran said.

"Morning, Gran." I took in the state of the kitchen. Gran liked to cook, but with the amount of food strewn across the counters, it looked as if she was preparing for a feast. "What's with all the food?"

"You're going to have a guest for dinner tonight."

I made a face and joined her at the counter. "It's not Mom, is it?"

"Not sure who it is, but I don't think it's your mother."

"So an uninvited guest?" I asked.

"You'll invite them by the end of the day. I thought I'd whip you two up a meal, but I'm not sure what's suitable."

Seeing the mixture of materials, it was easy to tell she wasn't sure what to cook.

"Maybe by the end of the day I'll have things narrowed down," Gran said.

I wasn't sure how I felt about a visitor right now. We had a dead fairy and someone had tried to kill me. My hands were already full. All that was nothing compared to the feeling that a large hole was being drilled through my chest.

Gran's hulking gray cat swaggered into the room as I flipped on the coffee pot. He took one look at me and hissed. A guttural growl built up as his long hair started to stand on end.

"You know, Cassie, you silly thing," Gran said.

The cat looked at Gran and then back to me. In one quick motion, he turned himself around, lifted his tail straight up, and then marched out of the room.

"I thought we were getting along," I said to the retreating back of the cat.

"Somethin's off today. You feelin' all right?"

"I feel fine." To myself I added, unsettled and hollow, but I can move past this.

"Okay, dear," Gran said. She was peering at me.

I didn't want to talk about yesterday. In fact, I wanted to forget the entire incident with Vincent.

"I'm going to grab my bag," I left Gran's protruding gaze.

Mostly, Gran's exactly how I wanted to be when I got older: a crazy old psychic lady who kept a cat in the house, a fairy in the garden, and spent her days baking sweets for the elves down the street. Sounded like the perfect way to spend my golden years.

Having the same person as a roommate, especially when you wanted to hide something, wasn't the ideal situation.

I took my time grabbing my bag and getting the rest of the way ready for work. It took time to convince myself that I wasn't forgetting anything and that there wasn't anything wrong with me. When I found myself looking through all my bedroom drawers, and not knowing what I was looking for, I knew I'd

SHATTERED SOUL

need more than a few minutes to persuade myself that all was normal.

When I made it back to the kitchen, sun glinted through the window in the back door. Grabbing a travel tumbler, I filled it with coffee, milk, and sugar. Logan knocked on the back door and entered. He had helped Gran and I find our house. Several agency members lived in the neighborhood.

"Morning," Logan said. "Feeling all right?"

"Sure," I said taking a quick gulp of coffee.

"She'll feel less shaky once she gets to the office," Gran said.

"Nothing out of the-" Logan started.

"It's summer, but Halloween is around the corner," Gran said, giving me a quick hug. If she psychically knew what had happened yesterday, she didn't say anything. She knew I didn't want to talk about it though.

"Yeah," I said, grabbing the subject, "my favorite holiday."

"Morgan and I are gettin' together this Saturday," Gran said, "to start on our costumes. He said he has some ideas."

Morgan Renner was one of the Lost. Even though he came to this world on purpose, as a refugee, the term Lost was still applicable. He was a troll that AIR set up with a little house in the country. He visited one day and met Gran. She wasn't even surprised when a troll knocked on our door. She served cookies with tea and settled in to get to know Morgan, just as she would anyone else. They had been friends ever since.

Like me, Morgan's favorite holiday was Halloween. For him, it was the ability to walk around downtown surrounded by people, and being able to blend in seamlessly. For me, it was more about dressing up.

"He say what any of those ideas are?" asked Logan.

"Now, you know it's a surprise," Gran said shaking a finger at Logan. "How about you? What are you dressin' up as?"

"I'm thinking Doc Holiday this year."

"That'll be great." I knew that this would fuel his cowboy fascination.

47

"Gerald has already decided to be a Roman Centurion," Logan said.

Logan's youngest son was twelve years older than I was. As an elf though, he was mentally much younger. He studied art at a local college. I'm betting he studied Roman art. He was probably as wrapped up in that as Logan was with the Old West.

"What about you, Cassie?" Logan asked.

"I'm not sure yet." In secret, I wanted to be Super Girl, wearing a short skirt, tight shirt, and knee high red boots. I'd freeze my ass off, but it would be worth it. To pull that off, I would probably need to lay off the sugar and ditch about ten pounds. It was hard to think about that when I felt so discontent.

Logan stood. "What do you have on the agenda for today, Margaret?"

"Oh, Dee Dee and I are gonna get our hair done and scope out the seniors walking the mall," Gran said. Dee Dee had been friends with Gran through both husbands. "Dee Dee has an eye on one of the hotties who's a regular."

Snatching a forgotten pear, I looked over at Logan. He and I both grinned at the thought of Gran scoping out guys at the mall.

"We're going to get a flat tire on the way out of the mall," she added.

We both took this in stride. "Do you want us to swing by?" I asked.

"Don't even think it." Gran patted her gray curls. "Dee Dee's little hottie will be around to call triple A for us."

"Give us a call if you change your mind," Logan said.

"Anything for us?" I asked, inspecting my pear.

"Be nice to Cassie's guest."

That was a little puzzling, but once again, we took it in stride.

Out of habit, I reached for my phone, only to find it missing. I forgot it had suffered a watery death. With a wave, we left the house.

The truck cab was stuffy when I slid into the passenger seat, but rolling the windows down proved to be a cure.

SHATTERED SOUL

Heading toward the office made me feel better. Throwing myself into work would help me avoid thoughts of Vincent. It might also help to fill the hollow feeling that seemed to be ready to swallow me from the inside.

I thought over the case. Who would hurt a fairy? Who would even know about them? Dozens of questions threatened to swarm. Most were ones I probably should have asked ages ago, but being thrown in to a job like this wasn't easy. Frequently, I learned as I went along.

I cleared my throat. "Who knows about the Lost besides AIR?"

"There are a few other organizations that know. MyTH, in St. Louis is a non-profit organization that watches out for civil rights of the Lost. Most governments have organizations like ours. The Lost have been in the world longer than most countries have been around. Some say there are non-government organizations that are older, but if there are, they keep quiet. Besides that, you've got Native American societies."

"That's it? I would think more people would have noticed."

"Most folk think they'll be labeled as crackpots if they say what they've seen. Or they deny that they saw it in the first place."

I shifted uncomfortably in my seat. Late in college, I had a boyfriend, Zander. We were close and had even discussed marriage. I had thought I could bring him in on my secret. Let him know that the world was larger than he knew. He refused to see the truth. He loved me, but thought I was crazy. It went so far that he tried to have me committed. Mom and Gran had to step in.

I pushed Zander from my mind. Logan sang an old Western song under his breath again. For a few minutes, I listened to my partner sing old trail songs about cowboys long dead.

"We've done relocations and integrations of the Lost, but I haven't seen a murder. Is this type of case normal for AIR agents?" I asked.

"It's not your usual case, but they pop up from time to time."

"I'm not exactly ready for this."

"You've had training."

It was true that before starting in the field, I went through six months of intensive training. Since then, I had been training when not in the field. Learning about the Lost and working with them was one thing, but forensics and investigation was another beast all together.

"Training yes," I said. "Experience, no. Any tips?"

Logan thought it over for a moment. "Use your skill and follow my lead. We've been told that Darla's being brought in."

"Darla Clance?" I couldn't hide my awe.

"Yep, the human lie detector herself."

"Hasn't she been retired for years?"

"She has. Barry brought her in to root out the fiend," Logan said.

"Wow, she's a legend! Have you worked with her before?"

"She was in the office when I started years ago. That woman is something else. Made interviewing suspects a lot easier."

"Tell me about her."

"She can size a person up and tell you if they're lying within a second. Doesn't matter if you're Lost or human, she knows. She'll make short work of the investigation. I never thought I'd see her back in the office again. Hope she has a go at the Walker while she's here."

I practically bounced in my seat by the time we pulled into the office. The restless feeling loosened its grip as we walked in, replaced by anticipation. Darla is one of those rare humans, like Clancy and me who have a gift. Stories of her reached my ears the first week in the office. She could close more cases than any three agents could together.

Everyone talked in hushed tones when we entered control central. There were a few people queued up outside one of the conference rooms. I watched as an agent left and another employee entered. The people in line looked anxious, and those

50

SHATTERED SOUL

who left looked relieved. No one stayed in the conference room for more than a minute.

"I've got your times set up," Hank said as we approached his desk. "You've got about an hour before you go in. Don't be late."

"Anything come in about the case?" I asked.

"No fiend has been discovered so far," Hank replied as he shifted folders on his desk. "Agent Pironis's office confirmed his assignment."

"I meant the fairies case," I said.

"Oh." Hank sat back in his chair. "Agent Pironis has everyone in the office scared of their own shadow."

I raised an eyebrow at Logan.

"So no new information," Logan pressed.

"Nothing new. This mess should be over with today. It would be good to have you two on hand to take a guard shift. After you've been cleared, of course," Hank said.

"Are agents guarding Darla?" I asked.

"If she marks someone as a demon, I doubt she'd make it out of the room without guards. She's a formidable old lady, but I don't think she'd stand a chance," Hank said.

I blushed. Of course, she would have a guard. What the hell was I thinking?

"Is she interviewing Vincent?" I asked.

Hank sighed and frowned at me. "He's slated in at the end of the day. Since his office confirmed the orders, we're checking all the employees first."

Pulling together paperwork took some time. With a relocation, things seemed much easier. Integrations were a little more difficult, but most of the Lost that needed to be mingled in with normal society had already learned plenty about our world. Paperwork for a murder seemed more complicated. It also felt heavier. It might be the same amount of paper, but it seemed to weigh more all the same.

Logan let me learn by doing. This meant that I had to go and ask Hank questions five times instead of once. I was not sure if the joke was on Hank or me. Hank wasn't in the mood for the interruptions. I had never seen the man as terse as he was acting today. It didn't help that I hadn't learned anything new, and that nagging feeling I had lost or misplaced something seemed to take up permanent residence between my shoulder blades.

We queued up well before our time to meet with Darla. People came and went like clockwork. I felt a tight roll of anxiety before walking in the door. I kept wondering what she would ask and say.

When I walked into the room, I was met with a night shift team guarding Darla. The woman was taller than I was with gray hair and dark skin. She was muscular in a way I never expected of an older lady. She was probably about the same age as Gran.

"Are you a demon?" She asked.

"No," I said.

She nodded and that was it. All that tension over one question. I started for the door.

"Wait," she said.

I stopped.

"Are you the girl that was attacked yesterday?" she asked.

"Yes."

Do I have to keep to yes/no answers? I thought.

"That must be why you feel so off. Good on you, girl. You took on a Walker and lived to tell the tale."

"I wouldn't say I took him on—" I started.

"You survived! That's enough for me. Good on you."

I grinned and she waved in Logan. After he was cleared, we went over some paperwork and checked in with Clancy, who couldn't add anything to our investigation yet. In the afternoon, Logan and I stood guard for Darla.

We set in for a few hours of mind numbing guard duty. Everyone was asked the same question. Everyone gave the same answer. Some employees cast dirty looks in my direction. I figured they must blame me for having to go through this ordeal.

SHATTERED SOUL

Toward the end of the day, Hank was helping track down the last few agents that needed to see Darla. Darla was less than patient.

"I ain't got all the time in the world for this. Let's go see that Walker."

She strode out of the room and down the hall with purpose. She knew exactly where she was going. Someone was a few steps ahead of us and Vincent was already waiting in the interrogation room. I hesitated at the door. My stomach doing flip-flops pushed out the feeling of something missing that I had carried around all morning. Darla shooed me into the room in front of her. Logan stuck with us as well.

It was the first time Vincent and I had been face to face since the incident.

Vincent's eyes widened subtly when he saw me; the rest of his face was as blank as ever. He looked tired, though. He needed a shave and his wrists were red. He'd probably been cuffed and re-cuffed several times in the past day. He saw me looking at his wrists and lowered his hands below the table.

I should hate him, but I didn't. Something about him pulled at me, but I couldn't peg down the feeling. It was confusing the hell out of me.

"Do you know who I am?" Darla asked as she sat down. I took the vacant chair beside her.

"I do not," Vincent replied.

"My name is Darla. They pulled me out of retirement for you. I've got a special set of skills to set this mess straight."

Vincent nodded.

"Tell me why you're here," Darla said.

Vincent relayed his story from the day before.

Darla nodded, satisfied with the story. "Okay, girl," she said to me, "ask him your questions."

I blinked in surprise. I had never questioned someone before.

I decided to go with the obvious. "Do you want me dead?"

Vincent put his cuffed hands back on the table and leaned forward slightly.

"I do not want you dead." He looked straight at me, his eyes never wavering.

I didn't need Darla here. I believed him.

"Are you okay?" Vincent asked.

"We're doing the questioning," Logan said.

"It's okay," I said. "It leads me to my next question. You said my soul wasn't whole anymore. What exactly does that mean for me?"

Creases formed ever so slightly around Vincent's eyes. "I'm not certain yet. We have embarked into new territory. Please understand that I will do everything in my power to correct this mistake."

"Mistake?" Logan said. "You read a name in a file and my partner ends up almost dead. That's more than a mistake, it's criminal."

"I know you don't really believe that," Darla said. "Have you put yourself in the boy's shoes?"

"No," Logan said.

"Liar," Darla said.

"I understand Logan's concerns," Vincent said. "If Cassie had died—"

"But I didn't." I stood up. "I don't have any more questions."

"I have one," Logan said. "Does someone want my partner dead?"

"It's a possibility that we must consider," Vincent said. "As long as I am here, it will not happen."

Darla shook her head. "You've got to tell the truth."

Vincent frowned almost unperceptively. "As long as I'm here, I'll do what I can to stop anything from happening."

Darla nodded, but the frown never left Vincent's face.

Logan took a long look at Vincent. Finally, he nodded and left the room.

"I've gotta go look over a few more agents," Darla said.

"I'm sure you'll be out of those cuffs soon," I said to Vincent.

Once again, he put his hands under the table.

SHATTERED SOUL

"I'm right behind you, Darla," I said.

Hank waited outside the conference room again with two agents. Darla made quick work of them. By the end of the day, everyone had been cleared for duty.

After delivering the news to Barry, we said our goodbyes to Darla.

"Never thought I'd meet a Walker," she said on her way out. "Never thought I'd meet someone who had survived a Walker. But still, this day was boring as shit."

I grinned. "It could have been worse. Someone could have said yes."

Barry cleared his throat and thanked Darla for her service. Once she was gone, he turned to Logan and me.

"Vincent has been cleared." Barry narrowed his eyes at me. "Cassie, you have the right to bring up formal charges against him."

I shook my head.

"He has requested a temporary transfer to this office. If you two have any reservations, I need to hear them now."

My stomach tightened. Did I have any reservations about him? It had been an accident. Even without Darla, I was sure about that.

I shrugged.

Logan took more time to answer. "I guess I'm fine with it."

"Good to hear. He's working with your team," Barry said.

"Having him in the building is one thing, but—" Logan started.

"He's a skilled investigator and he wants to keep an eye on the, ah, situation he has caused," Barry said.

Logan crossed his arms. "I'm an investigator, and we have plenty of others around."

There was a knock at the door.

"And now you have another on your team." Barry raised his voice. "Come in."

55

CHAPTER 6

HANK POPPED HIS HEAD INTO the office. "He's here."

"Send him in," Barry said.

Vincent came into the room, for once without cuffs.

Barry got straight down to business. "You'll be working with Logan and Cassie. Let me be clear on this. Logan is the lead at all times. You will defer to him in everything."

"Agreed." Vincent's voice was impassive.

"Don't sound so damned excited about it," Logan said.

Barry ignored Logan. "We'll see about arranging accommodations for you in the short term. Normally, I'd ask an agent to house you for a few weeks, but for now, we'll set up a short term housing fix."

Vincent nodded without saying anything.

"Logan, Cassie, get him caught up on the case." Barry turned his attention to a file on his desk. "Hank will have information on accommodations."

Logan looked resigned when he walked out of the office. I followed behind Logan and the office door clicked shut behind Vincent.

"Go talk to Hank," Logan said. "We'll meet you in the control room."

Vincent nodded and we watched him retreat down the hallway.

Logan moved away from Barry's door before talking. "If you don't want to work with him, we can get him removed from the team."

My eyes were still on the hallway that Vincent had been in moments before. "Will he be able to help?"

Logan shrugged. "Not if we don't trust him."

"Do you trust him?" I asked.

"He's like a blank slate. You can never tell what he's thinking."

I frowned and looked at Logan. "What do you mean?"

"It's like he has the world's best poker face, but he wears it all the time. By looking at him, you'd never be able to tell if he felt anything."

This didn't mix with what I'd seen of Vincent. It was hard to tell what he might be feeling, but the slight movements he made seemed to speak volumes about what he was feeling.

"You don't get a feel for anything he's thinking or feeling?" I asked.

"The man's a clean slate."

I cast my eyes back down the hall again. Usually it was Logan that caught way more than I did. Maybe I was seeing something that wasn't really there.

It wasn't a comforting thought.

"Maybe he's that way because he doesn't know us," I suggested.

"You're okay with this arrangement?" Logan asked and started down the hall.

Keeping step, I said, "If he can help, I think we should let him join."

"No one knows too much about Walkers," Logan said. "Maybe we'll get the chance to find out more."

Hank was across the control room reviewing the massive bank of computers with large display screens. Vincent stood nearby, also watching the screens.

Something in me loosened as we approached. It was almost as if I had been holding my breath and had only now found that I could inhale again.

"I've got an update for you," Hank said. He pulled something up on the wall monitor. "We aren't sure if this is related to your case, but it's too damned coincidental. We have four Lost that haven't been seen in the past week."

"Four missing?" I didn't mean it as a question, but it popped out that way.

"Two gnomes, a fairy, and a pixie," Hank said. "Not confirmed missing, they haven't been seen. It's not that rare with the Lost, especially these particular races. We didn't think it was related at first, but then we had a call from the Ozarks this afternoon."

"What's going on down there?" Logan asked.

"The centaur tribe thinks someone is missing, but they aren't sure yet. Centaurs tend to wander, so sometimes it's hard to tell. Humans were spotted in their territory yesterday. The centaurs grew uneasy and had it called in."

"Could be a connection," Logan said. "Who's down there? What do they say?"

"Someone from the Ozark hub is with them, but they aren't saying much," Hank said. "They're having some language issues. We're sending you down to join up with them and find out more."

"When do we leave?" I asked.

"You aren't leaving," Hank snapped. "You're on restricted duty, so you'll be staying close to home. Logan is meeting up with agents at the AIR hub. Here's the case file."

Logan raised an eyebrow at Hank.

"Everything okay today?" Logan asked him.

"I—" Hank had started to sneer in my direction but stopped. He cleared his throat. "Not sure what's gotten into me."

Hank handed the file off to Logan. Logan started to hand it to me, but stopped.

"Looks like we need to head home so I can pack," Logan said.

"I have Cassie's new phone." Hank moved a stack of papers and uncovered a smart phone. "Take care of this one."

Logan turned to go, but stopped short. "Your arrangements made?" He asked Vincent.

SHATTERED SOUL

Vincent nodded, but didn't say anything.

Hank filled in the blanks. "Nothing is available in the area, but we've rented him a room. As for the vehicle," Hank looked apologetic, "we don't have one ready for him yet. He'll have to use the truck for now."

"Cassie and I have our own cars. It'll work," Logan said. "You'll have to drop us off first though."

Vincent nodded.

"And stay for dinner," I added.

"You want him with you and Margaret?" Logan asked.

"You don't have to do that," Vincent said.

"Gran's expecting him."

Logan shook his head but then smiled at Vincent. "Margaret's expecting you. Know ahead of time, I'll kill you if you make a move against either of them."

My partner looked entirely too happy about that prospect.

With that threat still on the air, the ride home was completely silent. Three could easily ride together in the truck, but having a virtually unknown third person was awkward. I passed the time by examining my new phone.

Gran was getting ready to go when we arrived home. "It's bingo night! Dee Dee and I are going."

"I thought you were staying for dinner," I said.

"No, dear, he's your guest." Gran spotted Vincent and led us into the kitchen where she had a tray of cookies and some iced tea waiting.

"Margaret, I have a few concerns about Agent Pironis. What do you get off him?" Logan asked.

"Hard to read," Gran replied without hesitation. She shrugged. "He's dangerous, but not dangerous to us. That's all I can tell. With time, I'll get more."

A small crease in Vincent's forehead made him looked uncomfortable. "I assure you that I am no danger to you or your family."

"Of course not." Gran smiled sweetly. "I just said that."

"I guess I needed to hear that before I left," Logan said. "I'm heading out of town, but I'll send Jonathan over to check on things."

As soon as Gran headed out, Logan got down to business.

"Margaret has given this guy a clean bill, but the fact of the matter is, he was sent to kill you," Logan said. "Now, I trust your grandmother, but he could have been sent here to insinuate himself into our lives."

"What reason would I have to infiltrate Cassie's life?" Vincent asked.

"Maybe you need to get some information," Logan said.

"First off," Vincent started, his emotions flitting across his face, "she should be dead now." He looked pained for a moment, but pushed on. "I wasn't exaggerating yesterday when I said it was unheard of to stop when someone's essence has started pulling away from them. I was sent here to dispose of a fiend, a demon. That was all."

I felt Logan and Vincent's bottled up emotions starting to uncork and pour themselves around the room.

"Why couldn't you tell she wasn't a fiend right off?" Logan asked. There was no trace of his smile now.

"You don't look at a person and know," Vincent countered. Lines of anger were playing across his face.

"Paperwork?" Logan said. "Someone writes something down on a piece of paper and the Walker just follows along."

"I've already admitted it was a mistake. I requested this transfer in order to rectify that mistake." Vincent's words were low and intense. Anger started seething out of him.

That was the last push. The world broke around me and the Path opened. There was no attempt on my part to read the Path. It was just there. My breath became raspy as my senses were assaulted. The usual shimmering ripple of the Path had turned into a deluge that poured over me. I squeezed my eyes shut tight, but the Path was still there. I might as well have had my eyes wide open. Looking at Logan, I gasped and nearly fell out of my chair. Logan and Vincent were talking, but the words were not penetrating my reading of the Path.

Eyes glued to Logan, I saw him like never before. What was once cloaked from me was no longer hidden. Golden hues wound their way around a gleaming core. Seeing the bright sun that was Logan's Path took my breath away. It was beautiful and frightening at the same time. How had this hidden from me for so long?

As he leaned in toward me, I pulled back. Covered by that brightness, I felt something buried deep in Logan, something that I never wanted to see break out. As I looked at the crushing waves of information, Vincent's Path came into view. I felt like I was drowning. Layers of suppressed emotions hung around him. Other darker spots clung to him. They seemed a part of him, but at the same time alien. One of these strands was deeply familiar to me, but I had never seen it. It wound in and out of his entire being. It was the first time I had ever seen a part of my own Path.

As suddenly as it came, it was gone. My eyes could barely focus. What was once my bright kitchen was now ashen and dim. I leaned forward at the table breathing heavily, trying to get my eyes to adjust.

"Cassie, can you hear me?" asked Logan.

I nodded.

"What happened?" Logan asked.

"It--it was the Path. But not like usual, not like—" I took a deep breath and tried to organize my thoughts. "The Path, it opened on its own. It was different, . It poured over me. It was forceful. Stronger." At the last moment, I decided to leave out details of Logan and Vincent's Paths. I didn't want them to know how deeply I had seen them. "It was a jumble of colors and emotion, a complete assault on my senses."

Vincent's blank face gave nothing away, but Logan looked tense.

"This kind of thing shouldn't happen," Logan said. "You." He turned to Vincent. "Do you know what this is about?"

Vincent looked troubled, but shook his head.

"Maybe it was a one-time thing?" I suggested. "A side effect?"

"Things should have settled down overnight," Vincent said.

I rolled my head in a few circles to shake off the unsteady feeling the Path had left.

"Keep an eye on her." Logan got to his feet. "The sooner I go, the sooner I get back."

Once Logan left, it only took a moment for me to realize that I was alone with Vincent. Unease began to build around me.

Vincent broke the silence. "You don't look comfortable with this arrangement. I'll go."

"It's fine," I said. "In fact, it will give me time to catch you up on the case."

"If you are certain."

"I am."

"I gather you are looking for missing persons?" Vincent asked.

"Actually, we're looking for a murderer." I filled Vincent in on the details while I served up the roast that Gran had been cooking.

Vincent's complete lack of questions meant we spent the second half of dinner in awkward silence.

My mind raced over different questions ranging from delicate to rude, but I needed to know.

"You said you know me." I could feel my face going red. "What do you know?"

Vincent took a moment to respond. "I took in what makes you, you. I see your stronger memories and how these memories sculpted your personality."

"So you know my personality type and a few memories."

Vincent's brows furrowed. "There have been great upheavals throughout your life. The most recent was a few years ago."

My face grew red with embarrassment. He knew about Zander trying to force me into a mental hospital. Shit, why did I

SHATTERED SOUL

ask the question? Did I want to know what he knew?

Vincent continued. "The incident destroyed your trusting nature. You want to trust people, but inwardly you do not. This leaves me troubled. You appear to trust me enough to be in your home, but I don't understand why."

"I'm not sure I understand it myself," I said.

"You shouldn't trust me."

"Probably not," I agreed.

Vincent frowned. "I know what will affect your psyche, so I could manipulate your every emotion."

My insides tensed. "You're sounding creepy again."

He said nothing, but the tightness around his eyes dropped and one side of his lip bent up the slightest bit.

I narrowed my eyes at him and crossed my arms. "Which is exactly what you intended."

For a moment, Vincent looked surprised, but it didn't last long. All traces of emotion pulled away from his face.

I rolled my eyes and got up from the table. He had looked smug until I called him out.

"My intention was for you to understand," Vincent said.

A part of me wanted to call him a jerk and ask him to leave. Another part wanted me to tell him that I understood that he meant well, but he was a complete idiot.

"It's getting late," Vincent said. "I am going to excuse myself."

I cleared my throat in an effort to keep my voice level. "Do you know where you are going?"

"Hank gave me the address."

I nodded and led him out through the living room, grabbing the keys to the truck along the way.

"I'll see you tomorrow," I said holding the door open.

Vincent stopped on his way out. He stood there until I let out an impatient puff of air.

"Tomorrow, I hope to find a way to apologize," Vincent said. Then he walked away.

Standing in the open door, I watched him go. Had he straight out apologized, I probably would have yelled at him. It would have been completely irrational, but I know myself well enough to realize that I was still aggravated and wasn't ready to hear an apology. It was an eerie thought that he understood this about me after one day.

When he pulled away, I shut the door and went to clean up. Apprehension started to build and I began to pace. The itchy spot between my shoulder blades was back, but it was deep under the skin now.

Logan called on his way down south, but I kept the call short. After the call, my mind started racing through the past two days. Vincent, the fairy, my job, Gran, Logan, the case, my power, they all sprinted through my thoughts.

When Gran came home, my anxiety was on its way out, but it was leaving a hole sunk deep in my middle. I tried to hide the desolation that was starting to spread over me.

"Where's your phone?" Gran asked.

I forced a smile onto my face. "They gave me a new one today. It's an upgrade."

"I see that. It looks very nice." Gran gave me a quick hug. "Don't you worry about a thing. Go upstairs and take a hot bath. You'll feel better in no time."

I didn't argue. It never did any good to argue with a psychic.

My bath was short. I floated and stared at the ceiling while my skin turned pink. As the water started draining away, I did start to feel better. The anxiety was gone and the depression washed itself away down the drain. I threw my bathrobe on and went downstairs to talk to Gran.

She was hovering around the window next to the front door.

"Thank you, Gran, I feel much better." This time, the smile was real. "The bath was exactly what I needed."

"Don't be silly, dear. A bath can help ease the blues, but you need something altogether different for what ails you."

"What do I need?"

SHATTERED SOUL

Gran nodded out the window. Shaking my head, I gave Gran a quizzical look and peeked out the window shade.

My face fell. "No." Our work truck sat in the driveway. "No, no, no."

"I didn't think the man would be fool enough to sit in the driveway. Go out there and bring him inside."

"What?"

"It's good manners. Besides, what will the neighbors think if we left some man in the driveway all night?"

"They'll see Vincent, and think those are smart women in that house."

Gran crossed her arms. "Cassandra Heidrich, you get out there and bring him in. You're both being ridiculous."

I took another look out the window. "Did you invite him over? Do you know what's going on?"

"He was already nearby. I told him to come over and the only thing I know is that the two of you apart is not the best idea right now, for either of you."

"I guess I can make up the upstairs bedroom." I sighed and went to the door.

"Already done."

Stopping, I looked at Gran.

She gave me a sweet smile. "I fixed it up yesterday."

Resigned to my task, I slipped on a pair of shoes and went out. Approaching the truck, I had no idea what to say. I didn't see Vincent, so I knocked on the truck door.

"Yes?"

I jumped and spun around, my hand automatically going to my side. My heart pulsed harder when my hand landed on my thigh and not my gun.

Vincent stood unmoving at the back of the truck.

I took a steadying breath. "What are you doing out here?"

"Margaret told me to come over."

"And you listened to her?"

"She told me what would happen if I didn't."

My curiosity was piqued. "What did she say?"

Vincent didn't respond.

"Did she—" I started to say.

"She told me what I would do."

"What would you do?"

Vincent sighed and leaned his back and head against the truck. It was the first truly human thing that I had seen him do. I felt like I was intruding on something private.

Maybe I was.

"You feel better now though?" I asked changing the direction of the conversation.

"Yes." The relief was clear in his voice.

"Me too."

We stood in silence. Whatever this was, it sucked.

"It's getting late," I said, turning to head inside.

"It is."

"Come on inside." When I didn't hear footsteps on the gravel, I turned back around. He was standing straight and tall again.

"I'll stay out here."

"Don't be ridiculous. What would the neighbors say?"

Vincent didn't move. "You don't have to do this."

I put my hands on my hips. "What would my grandmother say?"

There might have been a sigh, but maybe it was just a breath of wind. Vincent walked stiffly to the truck, grabbed his bag, and then followed me in.

That night went easier than the last. Thoughts of what the hell is going on and what does this mean, kept me tossing and turning, but those were real things. I could name them and I knew where they came from.

By the time, I dragged myself out of bed the next morning and headed downstairs, Gran was already gone. She left me a note telling me to take the aspirin with me. Not a promising start to the day.

Vincent came into the kitchen and nodded. He looked

SHATTERED SOUL

completely put together and ready for the day. Something that I was not. I reached for coffee when the phone rang. I sighed before answering.

"Cassie, this is Kyrian. A situation has arisen and we have a job for you."

"What kind of situation?" I asked grabbing paper and a pencil and sitting at the kitchen table.

"We've had a report from over in Linn County. It's not far. People have been spotted around the area the fairies inhabit for the past few evenings. Normally, they wouldn't have thought anything of it, but the fairies are adamant that the people are getting closer. If someone has spotted the fairies, or has it in their head to catch one, we need to investigate. Can you and Logan check it out?"

"Um, actually, Logan's translating in the Ozarks."

"Oh, yes, I forgot Barry loaned him out. There is a new guy, Vincent Pironis. He's a transfer and hasn't been assigned anything. Are you up for it today?" It was a last minute question. Kyrian didn't have the full story on what happened yesterday, which surprised me. She was usually not one to be left in the dark.

"I'm fine," I replied. "Is there anyone else to ride along?"

"Everyone's out already," Kyrian said.

"Vincent's here, we can take it."

"I'll have the information sent to your phone." She disconnected.

Hanging up the phone, I looked over at Vincent. "Logan is going to kill me."

"I think you're safe. I'm pretty sure he'll aim for me." If anyone else had said this I would have laughed, but Vincent didn't sound like he was joking.

I ran back upstairs and finished getting ready in a hurry. My hands shook as I laced up my boots. Logan was my partner and mentor. I had never been out without him. Maybe I should call him.

Shaking my head, I dismissed the idea. Whatever he was doing sounded important. We could handle this. Within five minutes, we were headed out the door.

The drive would take almost an hour even if we pushed it. The first few minutes were completely silent. My anxiety level went through the roof. Steady calm waves came from Vincent as he drove. I tried to grab hold of the calm, but it didn't help.

Reading the reports out loud took up some of our time. After that, the silence started to stretch on. I made the mistake of trying to fill the void.

"I've never been in the field without Logan," I admitted.

Vincent didn't respond. To give myself something to do, I grabbed a gear bag from behind the seat and started rummaging, trying to think of what we might need. We'd probably need everything. Grabbing my phone, I read the file to myself again.

"Logan won't really kill you, you know," I said, reading the descriptions of the fairy clan in question for the third time.

In my peripheral vision, I saw Vincent grip the steering wheel tighter. "I'm not as confident about that as you are."

"That's ridiculous. I'm fine. Right as rain and all that."

If anything, he gripped the steering wheel harder. "If that was true, why did I spend the evening in the guest room?"

"Physically I'm fine. Mentally, I'm—"

"Shattered."

The words sat heavy in the air, threatening to weigh me down.

"Not your mind," Vincent said in a stiff voice. "Your soul."

Anxiety started to creep in, so I turned back to files on my phone. Mentally, I was fine, and I'd be damned if I let anyone tell me anything different.

Vincent's tension started swirling against my anxiety. Usually, I had to be reading the Path to feel the atmosphere this strongly. Now I was being swamped by the emotions swirling through the air. Shivering, I sat the phone aside, took a few deep breaths, and closed my eyes. A whirl of worry from Vincent

SHATTERED SOUL

meandered around the other emotions.

"You need to chill out," I said opening my eyes. "I'm fine."

Vincent looked like he was concentrating hard on the road and the air cleared a bit.

Deciding it would be best if I centered myself, I closed my eyes again and started emptying out my thoughts, concentrating on the feeling of my body. Sometimes I employed this meditation technique to center myself before using my gifts. Today my body seemed to fight me. Nothing seemed to flow correctly. After trying for a while, I gave up.

"We need to come up with a plan," I said.

Vincent stared hard at the road. I watched him, expecting an answer, refusing to let him slide by without a response. Once I folded my arms and started glaring in his direction, he took the hint.

"I'm not used to working with a partner. I've always worked alone."

"Company policy is that no one works alone."

"There are rare exceptions to that rule. Most would prefer not to work with a Walker."

Here I was, stuck with a Walker, alone, with no back up.

CHAPTER 7

WE ENTERED THE SPRAWLING STATE park and skipped the ranger station, instead, choosing to go straight to the location on the GPS. The temperature stretched toward eighty-five degrees. We passed cars parked on the edge of the road and people out enjoying a hike on the warm day. Once we parked, I hopped out of the truck and pulled a few items from our bags. Like most of our assignments, a handgun was out of the question with people so close by. Any shots could ricochet and hurt someone. The tranq gun and pepper spray would be adequate.

Vincent grabbed his gear and stowed the bags while I carefully went over the map on the phone. My mind worked furiously fast. Do we have everything we need? Do I take the lead here? What if I can't read the Path? Will I be of any use?

I pushed these thoughts aside. Putting forth my best was all I could do. Plunging into the woods, we headed to the fairy homestead. We decided to talk to the fairies and then scout the surrounding area. We'd see how close people came to the fairies and provide facts to the agency. The agency would decide if the fairies needed to be relocated.

We hurried to the fairies. The open spaces and fresh air worked wonders on my nerves. Vincent followed close behind.

"Do you get this type of job often in the North West?" I asked, slowing down to walk next to him.

Vincent's jaw tightened. "I've done many surveillance jobs."

"This isn't really surveillance though, is it? I mean, we're talking with the fairies, not staking them out."

He didn't respond, but I pressed on, determined to know what type of expertise my partner had. "Surveillance jobs don't sound too bad. We do more relocation and integration here. What other types of jobs do you do?"

Vincent stepped in front of me and faced me in one fluid movement. I nearly walked into him.

"Why are you pressing this?" Vincent asked. His voice would have frozen a pixie to the spot.

"Pressing this?"

Vincent was a head taller than I was. He loomed over me with eyes darker than I remembered them being.

It wasn't the best time to remember that I was alone with him, in the middle of nowhere. Instinct yelled at me to take a step back. I decided to screw instinct.

Crossing my arms, I glared at him. "Why do you think? We're on a job together. Like it or not, You. Are. My partner." I slowed down the words to emphasize them.

Crap, did his eyes get darker? I shook the thought out of my mind and continued, "In order to work with each other, we need to know what to expect from the other."

"I work alone," Vincent said, enunciating every word except 'I'. The air seemed to grow colder with each syllable. "I watch, I analyze, I deduce, and I kill."

I could tell that he was looking for a reaction, so I gave him one.

"Not a people person. This is me being surprised." I rolled my eyes. "Have you ever relocated one of the Lost? Do you have any experience working with fairies? Is there absolutely anything that you can do that is relevant here?"

His eyes narrowed a fraction, his jaw clenched, and every muscle I could see tensed. His body howled out his anger without making a sound.

The intensity of the animosity churned my stomach. The Path ripped open and a deluge of red, so deep that it was almost black, flooded over me. I stumbled back a step and fell. The real world was almost completely lost somewhere under Vincent's fury.

71

Then it became less. The Path of the world returned. My fear lessened as the inundation slowed enough for me to force the Path closed.

Breathing heavily, I watched the colors of the world turn mute. With each blink I took, a ghost of sheer black covered everything.

It wasn't supposed to be this way. What good would I be for AIR if my powers were out of control? I shouldn't be worried about Vincent. He should be worried about me. I was the liability here.

"It is getting worse," Vincent said from some distance away.

Depressed, I didn't bother looking around. "Not worse." I sighed, knowing that I needed to be fully honest. "But not better. And not as good as I tried to lead you and Logan to believe."

The expansive woods spread out in front of me. There were fairies in there. Maybe pixies too, I should have checked. What use was I to any of the Lost as a Reader that couldn't control the Path? The black overlay started to dissipate and the dullness of the forest colors faded to reveal a lush green wonderland.

I stood and turned my back on it. Vincent stood closer than I expected.

"I'll fix this," he said.

I nodded without meaning. "Yeah. For now, take this." I handed over my phone. "The GPS will take you to the fairies."

"You're too unwell to continue?" His forehead was creased with uncertainty.

"I'm putting us at a disadvantage. I'll meet you back at the car." Trying to distance myself from the situation, I walked away.

"We'll call another team in to take this," Vincent said, matching my steps.

"There isn't anyone else," I sighed. "Go talk to the fairies."

"We can't work alone, remember?"

"You already work alone, you'll be fine."

Vincent brushed past me and blocked my way again. This time, he wasn't looming. There was no anger. Maybe there was a bit of weariness, but that could have been my own reflected feelings.

SHATTERED SOUL

He was making me think about it instead of letting me walk away. "You're making this difficult," I said.

"We're either going in together or leaving together."

I shook my head.

He lowered his voice. "Do you really want to send me out to work with the fairies alone?" He didn't sound menacing or malicious. It was an honest question.

"You're not going to hurt a fairy. I know that." It was the truth. Something inside of me knew with certainty that he wouldn't harm an innocent fairy.

"How about being alone with the humans walking through the area?"

I hesitated, knowing I was on uncertain ground. I shifted gears, not wanting to answer that particular question. "I should have been honest up front and let you know what was wrong. I shouldn't be in the field."

"Do you think we didn't know? That I didn't know?"

"How could you? I didn't even know it would be this bad."

"We were with you in the kitchen yesterday. We knew it was worse than what you were telling us."

I looked at him, not knowing what to say or do at this point.

Vincent took my hand and closed it around my phone. It was the first time he touched me since yesterday's incident. Where his hand held mine, warmth spread out and wound its way up my arm. Vincent looked at his hand holding both my hand and the phone. I wondered if he too felt the warmth.

After a few breaths, he pulled away and stepped back.

Vincent cleared his throat. "I'll keep my emotions in check. There should be no issues."

Indecision threatened to root me to the spot. In the end though, I thought he was right. If he kept his emotions in check, if we kept our emotions in check, I should be fine.

Turning, the woods spread out before me. There were fairies in there. It was past time to see what was going on.

We continued on a trail for a while before heading in a

73

different direction, straight toward the fairies. Every now and again, we stopped to listen for others in the area. We didn't hear anything or see any signs of other people passing through. When we approached what looked like the fairy homestead, we carefully investigated the area for footprints before calling out to the fairies.

Fairy homesteads can vary greatly based on the area they live in. Sometimes, it's a group of trees growing close together. Other times, it's a rocky area with hidey holes. This area was a mixture. A gnarled old tree sat next to a tiny rock-bottomed creek. A large boulder sat next to the tree and a small rocky cliff was only a few feet away. To most visitors to the area, this was a pretty stretch of woods. The difference was in the air. It radiated a gentle, natural magic. The noises were a bit softer. The trees, bushes, and moss, seemed to pulse with life.

Once we deemed the area safe, we announced ourselves and waited for the Speaker to join us. Noise, like hundreds of irate bees began to move toward us. The Speaker appeared, but focusing on him was difficult. His agitation made him vibrate so fast he appeared as a blur.

Trying to take the lead, I talked to the Speaker directly, as I had seen Logan do half a dozen times. My existence seemed to be an affront to the fairies, though. The moment I started talking to the Speaker, he zipped toward me, and then away from me aggressively. Vincent stepped in to talk to the Speaker. The man calmed slightly and addressed everything directly to Vincent.

While they talked, I felt something drift down on the air and settle around my shoulders. Looking around, I saw a fairy flit around above me dropping a crushed mixture on me. I'm pretty sure it wasn't a welcoming present, but I hadn't started itching yet. As soon as the fairy was spotted, it hurried away after giving me a dirty look. As Vincent finished his conversation, I spotted another fairy throwing tiny rocks at me. The rocks were too heavy for the little creature, so they never actually hit me. It still seemed determined to try. Fairies usually didn't act like this around me, as long as I announced my intentions.

SHATTERED SOUL

Then again, we were both strangers and they've had people around their homestead. The fairies led us to the site where the people were last spotted. The Speaker sent the rest of the fairies back to the tree and advised them to stay close to home and travel together if they left the homestead. Vincent asked the Speaker if all the fairies were accounted for. Several of them were away from the area, gathering up food for the winter. They were all accounted for this morning, and he assured us it was normal for them to travel around the area to gather food at this time of year.

The speaker led us away from the homestead where the humans had last been seen. The people had been pretty close to the homestead. There were obvious tracks in the leaves. I started touching the ground where the leaves had been kicked. Without the Path, I sensed an aura of excitement along with something darker. Vincent prowled around the area looking for clues.

While we combed over the area, I asked the fairy Speaker to check for signs that a fairy might notice, but that we, as humans, might overlook. Intent in my work, I had forgotten their aversion to me. He shook his fist and yelled for a bit before flitting around the area. Vincent watched us closely as the fairy zipped away. His face was blank, so I shrugged and continued to look around.

Being nervous about opening the Path got me nowhere. Vincent was heading up a hill, far enough away that he wouldn't notice me or have an effect. Taking a few deep breaths, I opened myself. A storm of emotion raged through the area. Images flashed like lightning. My breath became rapid. I tried to sort through the chaos, but it was no use. There was too much. Retreating from the flurry of images wasn't easy. Closing my eyes, I tried to find my center, but I could see the Path as easily with my eyes closed. With some effort, I was able to push it away.

Leaning over, I tried to catch my breath. It felt like I'd been running. When I looked up, I saw that Vincent had moved further away, but watched closely. He didn't ask me if I spotted anything, so I didn't volunteer. It was too unsettling to see my gift so out of control.

The Speaker flitted to Vincent. Loud enough for me to hear, Vincent thanked him for searching. It wasn't long before he was flying away again.

"He didn't find anything," Vincent said, careful to maintain some distance. "We're not going to find anything this way either."

"You have an idea?" I asked.

Vincent looked around the woods. We were almost in a bowl. Trees with thick monkey vines stretched up and away in all directions.

"The people have been spotted for a few days in a row in this area. They have kicked up leaves and left boot prints all over the place."

"They seem to like this area," I said.

"A possibility," Vincent said. "I'm hoping they come this way this evening."

"You want to wait for them?" I asked.

"Watch for them. Up there," Vincent said, pointing to a low hill that had a pretty decent view of the area.

"That sounds like a good plan. I'll call it in once we find our position." I started to head in the direction of the hill, but Vincent stopped me.

"If we go straight up the hill, we'll leave as large of a trail as they did," Vincent said. "We go around."

It took forty-five minutes to walk what could have taken us five minutes. I could see his point though. From our vantage point, we could see traces of people that had walked through the area below.

I called into Hank to let him know our position.

"Hank speaking."

"Hey, Hank. Vincent and I are at the park. We've decided to stick around until tonight to see if anything turns up."

"You're where?" Hank asked.

"In Linn County. The Fairy homestead at the park."

There was nothing but the sound of shifting paper from Hank's end.

SHATTERED SOUL

"Where Vincent and I were sent this morning."

"Who's order?" Hank barked.

"Kyrian."

"Logan's still in the Ozarks?" Hank sounded strained.

"I doubt he's back yet."

"Coordinates?"

I looked at my phone and rattled off the numbers. "Everything okay, Hank?"

"I don't have your log."

I couldn't tell if he was worried or mad. I was feeling both. Not being logged meant no one knew where you were. It was my understanding that when the operation was unlogged, you knew about it going in. This was a giant red flag for any agent, even for an agent as green as I was.

"You've got us logged now?" I asked.

"You're logged."

"Hank?" I wasn't sure what was appropriate at this point.

"I'll know what happened by the time you get back."

"Thanks, Hank." I turned off the phone.

Vincent's stony face met my gaze.

"You heard?" I asked.

He gave a curt nod.

"Know what it means?" I asked.

Vincent's gaze was steady on the landscape below. "Someone mixed up the paperwork." His voice was expressionless, but the tightness of his eyes gave him away.

Two days ago, Logan mentioned a mix up of paperwork. That one almost left me dead.

The Path was shut, but I could sense the buildup of emotions surrounding us. "Why don't you stretch your legs for a few minutes?" I suggested.

He looked at me and back to the forest floor below. "We should stay in position."

"Of course we should," I muttered.

I situated myself to remain hidden from anyone below us.

77

Feeling more pressure being swung around, I glared at Vincent before going into stakeout mode.

"Huh," Vincent took in the view from all directions. "Stay silent and still. I'm going to check over the rise." Moving quickly and quietly, he walked down the opposite side of the hill.

He wasn't gone long, but he was certainly calmer when he returned. We didn't say anything, but got into position and waited.

The afternoon crept away in boredom. With Vincent lying not far away, I thought over how he listed his agent expertise. It was a pretty gloomy way of looking at your job. And yourself.

Knowing that sound could travel far in the woods didn't make it any easier not to talk, but we remained silent and vigilant. Vincent was better at both. He took attentiveness to a level I had never seen.

It was evening when we started hearing voices. It was difficult to make out what was being said. I couldn't even figure out which direction the voices came from. They came nearer, and then started to fade.

A sense of urgency jolted through me and I jumped up. Looking around didn't help. Chewing on my lip, I closed my eyes and forced my thoughts away. We had to act, and move faster.

I tried to feel for the Path instead of reading it. The sensation was unfamiliar. Air around us started to feel heavy, but with frantic flares tossed out. I wasn't sure I read it correctly.

Vincent was standing in front of me when I opened my eyes.

"What do you know?" Vincent asked.

"Something's wrong. Something happened."

"We need more."

"I'm not sure." I kept my voice quiet, and turned around on the spot. I felt around for the passage of people. My focus slipped and the Path opened up once again. Through closed eyes, I fought the torrential flood of information and focused on the sensations.

SHATTERED SOUL

It threw me off balance but I steadied myself against a tree.

"That way," I said, pointing down the hill behind us. In the distance, there was a streak of vibrant, eager purple.

Pushing the Path away, I started jogging down the trail. I could hear Vincent keeping pace behind me. Time seemed to slow and it felt like it was taking forever to reach the spot that I had seen.

When I reached the spot, I felt around, trying hard not to open the Path. "There were people here not long ago. I looked in both directions the trail had run and I was locked with indecision.

"Which way?" Vincent asked. His steady voice was reassuring.

"That way." Once again, we rushed off and it wasn't long before we reached an overgrown trail. It may have been an animal trail at one time, but the way the grass was worn down, you could tell something large had been through.

I pounded down the trail, trying to be quiet, but the pressing of intensive need urged me faster. The trail ended at a well-worn and maintained park trail. We had to be a few miles away from the fairies at this point. I didn't pause to catch my breath or guess the direction; the air remembered the direction of those we were pursuing. Even though I couldn't see it, I could feel the purple pulsing through the area. Being a Reader had never worked in this way before, but it felt familiar and I trusted it.

Before long, I could make out voices ahead. Slowing down, I listened intently. It could be two people out walking; I didn't want to jump out at innocent people.

"Two months of this shit and we finally have something to show for it." It was a male voice.

"We better get a good pay out for this," came another male voice.

"This fucking fairy is going to get us richer than you can imagine," the first guy replied.

I'd heard enough. I ran forward, not caring how much noise I made.

I rushed around a bend in the trail and spotted the two men who had been talking. One of them was carrying a box, the other an empty cage.

"Stop where you are!" My voice shook with anger. "Federal agents."

The two men turned toward me, dressed in camouflage like hunters. One man was large and hairy with a large mole on his face. The other guy had narrow beady eyes and a nose that was much too long for his face. Mole was startled and Snake was pissed. Clinging to their possessions, they both took off running. Why didn't I have my gun out? There was not much I could do but run after them.

They ran down the trail, which was lucky for me. They were out-of-shape, so I was gaining. The bad news was I could no longer hear Vincent behind me. Where the hell did he go? It didn't matter. The men didn't run for long. They hesitated at a fork in the path and made a wrong turn. They followed the trail straight into a box canyon. There was only one way in and one way out, unless they were planning on climbing rock walls that quickly soared high. The entire area was less than half a football field in size, but there was no getting out unless they came back through me.

Both men turned to face me. In one hand, I held a tranq gun, in the other a can of Mace. It wasn't a lot, but it was enough for the out of shape men.

"Put the box and cage down and step away!" I yelled. Mole man put the box down, but Snake sneered at me.

"What's got your panties in a twist?" Snake's face was red from the exertion of running. His mouth turned down and his eyes were dark and menacing.

"Put the cage down and step away," I repeated.

"The way I see it, it's two to one. Two men, one little woman," said Snake.

"One woman federally trained to take your ass down," I replied with hostility.

SHATTERED SOUL

The man's sneer faded. It looked like he was thinking over my words and it looked like it took effort. He put down the cage and frowned. "It's just an empty cage," Snake said, sulking. Then the man half grinned and took a step forward. I took a step forward, meeting his stupid grin with a hard glare.

I felt the hard metal of a gun pressed to the back of my head. I didn't move or drop my hard stare, but inside, my mind had gone blank.

"Drop your weapon," came a deep voice from behind me. I didn't move, but the numb coldness of fear started spreading through my body. Then I heard the distinct sound of a hammer being drawn back. "Don't be stupid. Killing you won't bother me in the least." I dropped my weapons, but made no other move. The Mole man looked nervous, but Snake looked pleased. Snake took a few steps closer.

Fear coursed through my body along with a surge of adrenaline. My mind kicked into gear and fought furiously to find some way to get out of this. Where the hell was my partner?

CHAPTER 8

The air became thick with dark excitement from Snake. He took another few steps closer.

"I am a federal agent." With a gun to my head, my brain was having a hard time coming up with a plan. "Put your weapon down and step away."

"I have no doubt you are a federal agent," came the steely voice behind me. "But I do doubt your ability to do anything. Maybe it will be no surprise to others that you never make it home."

Taking a few deep breaths, I called to the energy of the area. I tried to calm the situation. Since I was far from collected, it took extra effort. I was surprised at how far my influence ranged. Snake became a little dazed and Mole seemed to relax.

The man behind me was calm to begin with, which was troubling. After a few moments, the gun moved from the back of my head. I'm sure it was pointed at me, but I sighed in relief that it was not pressed against my skull.

The relief was short lived. Hard metal crashed against the side of my head, slamming me into the ground.

Pain shot through me. My eyes blurred. I clutched at my head, but realizing I was prone, I knew I had to move. With some effort, I kept one hand pressed to my head, rolled over to my knees, and tried to get to my feet. My fingers clutched my head and started to feel slick. As I made it to my knees, a foot struck me across the ribs. I cried out as my body rolled over, putting me straight on my back. I couldn't tell if it was tears or blood running down my face.

SHATTERED SOUL

Snake's angry sneer came into view. "Shouldn't have tried to stop us. Stupid woman." He started to bring his foot down on my stomach. Grabbing the foot, I softened the blow to my stomach, but not by much.

There was a commotion off to the side, but I kept my focus squarely on the man's foot in my hand. Using a burst of adrenaline, I twisted his foot, forcing him to fall back.

Still on the ground, I turned and caught my first look at the man who had held a gun to my head. He was well built, all muscle where the other two were flabby.

Unfortunately, he was standing, once again, with a gun to my head. However, he wasn't looking at me.

"Enough!" The man with the gun grabbed my shirt collar and pulled me up. My stomach rolled and my vision blurred again. For the second time today, I had cold metal pressed against my head.

"Federal agents aren't supposed to be here." The man's voice was deep and calm. "You, step back next to the rocks."

The blurry shapes began to take form. The man with the gun had his attention focused on Vincent. I didn't know where he had come from, but Vincent had the Mole on the ground. His knee dug into the man's back. Mole appeared to be unconscious. Vincent looked up at me. His eyes had turned almost completely black. Only a small band of white remained. It lasted only a few seconds before he looked away and walked slowly back to the rock bluffs.

The gun was removed from my temple. "You, pick him up and let's get out of here." The steely voiced man put an arm around me and dragged me backwards. Snake moved between us and roughly tried to pull his partner up. He had some difficulty, but after one look at me and the man with the gun, he dragged the man away.

We waited silently until all noise the other two made had disappeared into the coming night.

"We don't need to take long here," my captor said.

I didn't say anything. I was at a complete loss for what to do. Do you make someone talk in this situation or attack? Thoughts seemed to be running through murky water in my mind. Somewhere, I knew the answer was there.

As the sun started to set, I decided it didn't matter. I was probably dead either way. Tensing, I got ready to push his gun arm away.

Metal brushed against my cheek. "Don't make me pull the trigger."

I shut my eyes and tried to get my muscles to relax. In the distance, we heard a horn blaring.

"I have to admit, I didn't expect federal agents."

I felt the man's breath on the back of my neck and cringed. He forced me to walk with him to the entrance of the box canyon.

"You especially," the man gestured to Vincent, "intrigue me. I'd love to know what you did to knock my employee unconscious so quickly." We stopped moving. I could barely make Vincent out in the shadows of the cliffs.

A few silent moments passed. Did the man expect Vincent to answer?

"Ah, well, I can't allow you to follow me."

My stomach churned as I sensed Vincent move subtly. The frustration rolling from him was palpable.

"I've never killed a person," the man continued. "Luckily, I have another option."

The gun moved out in front of me directed straight at the box lying forgotten on the ground. I heard the crack and saw a flash as the bullet left the gun, but my ears went silent and the expected echo didn't follow. The hole in the box registered in my mind. I tried to step forward, but the ground rushed up to meet me.

Stunned, I lay there, afraid to move. Why did I leave the house today?

Through the ringing in my ears, I heard Vincent's voice. "Cassie? Are you okay? Cass?" His anger swept over me. My

SHATTERED SOUL

stomach churned harder and I instinctively pulled back as he approached. Taking in deep breaths of air, I tried to push back the turbulent emotions and calm myself.

"Are you okay?" Vincent's voice demanded.

I nodded, which was a mistake that caused a rushing in my ears. Trying not to move my head too much, I looked toward the box. "The fairy?"

Vincent went over to the cardboard box on the ground. I held my breath and watched, hoping like hell the person inside was safe. Whatever the man thought, if he had killed the fairy, he had murdered a person. Most of the Lost were people, maybe not human, but if you started thinking of sentient Lost as animals or creatures, your perspective became skewed.

Very carefully, Vincent opened the box. A small shape darted out. It moved so quickly that I had trouble following. Disappearing into the forest, the fairy was gone.

Vincent turned his attention back to me. He didn't come closer, but watched me intently. I could feel that much of Vincent's anger had left, and harsh sadness had taken its place.

"We should go after them," I said. My head pounded, but my stomach started to settle as the adrenaline left my body. I also ached all over. It didn't mean the bad guys weren't getting away.

"They're gone," Vincent said.

Knowing he was right didn't make it any easier.

"Do you need my assistance?" His voice sounded stony, but after the short time we've been together, I knew he was trying to rein in his emotions and hide behind indifference.

Hiding behind lies can be a safety net. I should know since I do the same thing by trying to convince others and myself that I'm whole after meeting Vincent.

I wanted to lie back on the ground, but instead, I motioned Vincent over to me. He slowly came, as though worried I might lean away again. I reached out and used Vincent's arm to pull myself up. Dizziness threatened to swamp me, so instead of standing, I chose to sit on a nearby rock.

85

"You should let me take a look at your head," Vincent said. I turned toward him. He wore an aura of uneasiness, but the rest of his emotions seemed settled.

"Okay," I said.

Putting his hand under my chin, he inspected my eyes first. Since he wasn't a doctor, I wasn't sure what he was looking for. His eyes, which I had mistaken for black earlier, were green with lines of gold darting through them. After a few moments, he turned his attention to the side of my head.

A pronounced frown settled into his face and his anger flared so suddenly that it made me gasp and wince. It wasn't pain, like the pain in my aching head. It was more like being slashed across the body by some invisible force. I shuddered. Closing my eyes, I tried to force the anger away, but that only made my head hurt worse. Vincent moved away quickly, leaving me alone on my rock.

My mind was a jumble of thoughts. What the hell was happening? Emotions from other people don't affect me this way. Feeling weak and depressed, which I despised, I watched as Vincent gripped his hands tight. He took a few deep breaths and relaxed his hands. When he returned, he inspected my head. His expression and his touch made him feel detached and void of emotion.

"I'm fine," I lied, pushing his arm away from my face.

"You were threatened, kicked, and pistol-whipped. You are distinctly _not_ fine."

"I'll _be_ fine then," I said. He was right though, I hurt like hell. "Where did you go on the trail? You were right behind me."

"I heard another person, so I pulled back," his voice was hesitant. "It did not go as I planned."

"You need to work on your partnering skills. But next time, you can practice on someone else."

"Do you think you can stand?" he asked.

Sighing, I opened my eyes. My own partnering skills were lacking right now. Critically, I inspected Vincent.

SHATTERED SOUL

"I should have asked if you are all right," I said. "I didn't see what happened."

"You're avoiding the question," Vincent said.

"Maybe, but I didn't see what happened. Are you okay?"

"It was a mistake," Vincent said angrily, "I thought I could circle around fast enough."

"Good plan," I said.

"No," Vincent said roughly, "I shouldn't have left you alone."

I shrugged. "You're not used to having a partner, and I've only had Logan as a partner. It's not a great combination."

Vincent didn't reply, so I let it drop.

"There has to be another road nearby. They came to the fairies from a different direction," I said. "We need to call this in and check on the fairies."

"I'll check on the fairies and bring the truck to this side of the park."

"And you leave me behind without a plan?"

Vincent hesitated and turned. "You're going to—" he stopped. "One of us should stay here and make sure no one enters the area, and call this in."

"That sounds like a plan. I'll call it in." Moving my head as little as possible, I looked around. "I need my tranq gun though."

Vincent grabbed the dropped weapon and handed it over with my missing Mace.

"That'll work," I said.

"I'll hurry." He disappeared.

Darkness crawled through the box canyon. I gripped the gun tightly in my hands. Usually, I was not an introspective person. Since joining AIR, I had been more a 'jump in and get it done' kind of person. I usually didn't look back or think twice about the decisions I made, possibly because Logan had been leading me.

Now things were different. We weren't only relocating Lost, we were working against killers. Then there were the reactions I had been getting from others. The fairies hated me. They threw

87

things, dusted me, and wouldn't talk to me. I had met loads of fairies, and none of them ever treated me that way before.

Thinking about the Path was worse. What the hell was wrong with my power? Why was Reading so different? What use was I if I couldn't handle the Path?

Then there was Vincent. Beyond the fact that he was dangerous, I knew very little about him.

Darkness grew around me. Keeping the gun gripped tightly in one hand, I pulled out my phone. Time to stop dwelling and get to work.

Hank picked up right away.

"Reporting in," I said.

"Good. I found your log."

I didn't have the willpower to interrupt, so I listened to him continue.

"It hadn't made it to my desk yet, but it had been made. It had been rerouted since Vincent's transfer hasn't officially gone through. We're all on the same page now."

I sighed. It was good to know, but after the afternoon I had, I couldn't muster any enthusiasm for the found log.

"What do you have for me?" Hank asked.

Beginning from our position on top of the hill, I started going over the events. I avoided everything about the Path using the terms, 'I knew' or 'we discovered' when necessary. I kept my voice steady and kept the pace slow. The sound of furious typing sounded through the phone.

While I slowly took Hank through the afternoon, the pain became less intense. When I came to the part where the third man joined us, I started stumbling over the descriptions. Hank let me finish. A few times throughout the conversation, Hank covered the phone and shouted instructions to someone in the office.

His voice was calm when he probed deeper with questions, starting with my injuries. After explaining each one, I assured him I didn't need an ambulance. He reminded me that I was

SHATTERED SOUL

required to see the doctor the moment I returned. After agreeing, he continued the inquiry. Each question was answered as clearly as I could.

When he asked me to send pictures, I was able to stand. Once my head adjusted to the higher altitude, walking became easier to handle, so I was even able to send him crime scene pictures from my phone. Hank assured me that a crew was coming to collect evidence before he signed off.

The night seemed denser among the cliffs. Noises from small nocturnal animals came from out of sight in all directions. It wasn't long before I felt uneasy. Knowing Vincent was around somewhere made it feel like pixies were determined to tie my stomach into knots. I decided to call Gran.

"Hi, sweetie."

"Hi, Gran." I hesitated. "Did you have a good day?"

"Had a great day," Gran said, "but I know that's not why you called. You called about Vincent."

CHAPTER 9

I LET OUT A SIGH. IT wasn't all bad living with a psychic. The mess that I felt inside funneled from Vincent. "He's safe, right?"

"That man is not going to hurt you. I didn't say he was safe. Far from it. But you and I have nothin' to fear from him."

"Do you know what he does?" I asked, my stomach clenched, not sure I would be happy with any answer.

"No, I know that you're as safe with him as you would be with Logan."

"Thanks, Gran."

"You didn't grab the aspirin."

"Did you know why I would need it?" I wondered how much Gran saw about today.

"Nope, knew you'd have a headache."

"Yeah, I'm regretting I didn't take the aspirin. I'll pick some up on the way home. I'll be late. Love you, Gran."

"Love you, sweetie."

My wait for Vincent's return seemed less grim after talking with Gran.

When I heard someone approach on the trail, I stood at the ready, gun still firmly in hand. I was certain it was Vincent, but I did feel better once I was able to confirm.

"The fairy wasn't harmed," Vincent said as he neared me on the trail.

"That's a relief. There's another crew on the way to collect evidence."

Vincent brought out the first-aid kit and by the light of a

SHATTERED SOUL

flashlight cautiously cleaned up the gash on my head. It wasn't bleeding anymore, but I felt awful. When the forensic team arrived, I was more than happy to head back to the Farm.

The trip back to the office was ceaselessly interrupted by Hank's calls. He spoke with Vincent to get more details. Vincent's answers were short and to the point.

I wanted to sleep, but Vincent interrupted each attempt I made.

At the Farm, the doctor looked me over and bandaged me up. Head wounds bleed a lot, so I really looked worse than I was. No stitches were needed, but butterfly sutures were placed over the cut. My ribs were bruised, but nothing was broken. Hank seemed to have endless rounds of reports. Eventually, we were allowed to tear away from the Farm and head home.

I wanted to sleep on the way, but Vincent had other ideas.

"There are some things we need to talk about," Vincent said.

I sighed. "Sure. What did you have in mind?"

"The fairies. You seemed surprised at their treatment of you."

"I was. Sure they try to dust me, but today, yesterday I guess, they seemed really to hate me."

"Have you ever had interactions with that homestead?"

"No, but then, neither have you. They talked to you. Is that normal for you?"

Vincent took some time before he answered. "It's not something that I would have expected. Fairies in general have no aversions to me that I've seen, but they do prefer to talk to others if the possibility is available."

I shrugged and looked out the passenger side window. "Everything about me feels off. Maybe they sensed it." The thought wasn't comforting.

That night, sleep didn't last nearly as long as I would have liked. When the next day came, my head pounded as I dragged myself out of bed. My ribs were covered in bruises, which matched the dark circles under my eyes.

The moment I stepped out of my room, Vincent showed he

took the partner thing seriously. He stuck close to me. Since I didn't leave the house, it got annoying fast. Trying to get him to talk took so much effort that I gave up quickly.

Logan returned late in the afternoon. He walked in with a smile on his face, but it disappeared after one look at me.

"Called into work?" he asked.

"Yeah, the fairies in Linn County." Vincent and I filled Logan in on the details. We left out some information. We already knew working as a team didn't go well, and we didn't need to hear Logan's opinion on our less than stellar efforts.

"Hank didn't mention it when I reported in," Logan said, almost to himself.

"I'm sure he has his hands full," I said.

"No truer words spoken. Two more Lost are missing from the Ozarks," Logan said. "We found footprints and tire tracks after hours of searching the woods, but no witnesses. Too remote an area."

"Why would someone kidnap the Lost?" I asked. "Is someone trying to take them public?"

"Not an ideal scenario," Vincent said.

"It would cause chaos for the world," Logan added.

I nodded. "Does the total missing stand at six?"

"That's all we know of," Logan said. "The agency is checking on everyone, but it's a lot of checking up to do. Anyone at the office have any theories yet?"

Vincent shook his head. "We haven't been into the office today. No one said anything when I called."

"Anyone at the office have any more information on the fiend, or why you were attacked?" Logan asked.

Vincent answered. "There are no leads in that area. My contacts on the west coast stated that no one else has been sent here. After the incident with Cassie, the office has dropped the contract and they are working with this branch to investigate."

I crossed my arms not liking the terminology. "The contract?"

"For the fiend."

SHATTERED SOUL

"Your contacts have enough reach to know for sure?" Logan asked before I could say anything else.

"He's certain. There are also new safeguards and redundancy plans being put into place to prevent any further incidents against agents," Vincent said.

"That should mean Cassie is in the clear then," Logan said.

"That is probable, but it is too early to rely on new protocols," Vincent said. "It is still possible that someone believes that Cassie is a demon."

The idea set me on edge. It didn't help that they had started talking about me as if I wasn't there.

"We can keep an eye on her at work," Logan said. "At home might be trickier."

"I'll be here." Vincent said.

To me it sounded suffocating.

Logan's expression didn't change, but he looked ridged. "You'll be here?"

"We didn't have a chance to tell you," I said. "It worked out better for him to stay in the spare room."

"Margaret agreed to this?" Logan asked.

"It was Gran's suggestion," I said.

The news appeared to settle over Logan. He stared hard at Vincent. Uneasiness from both men seemed to swell in the room, swamping my own senses.

"Knock it off," I said through gritted teeth.

Vincent moved away and Logan's confusion became evident.

"It seems I've missed much more than you're telling me," Logan said.

"Vincent can fill you in." I needed to get my mind wrapped around my heightened emotions and damaged abilities. That wasn't going to happen here. "I'm going out." Logan and Vincent both got up, ready to follow. "Alone," I added.

"If you're uncomfortable with him here, we can send him away," Logan said.

"It's not that." And it was true. I wasn't sure what to think

93

about Vincent anymore. His presence brought confusion, but I wasn't uncomfortable.

"It would be unwise to go to the office," Vincent said.

I glared at Vincent. "There are places outside the office. Besides, if anyone from inside the agency wants me gone, they're going to have a harder time trying now. You said so yourself."

"That doesn't mean they won't try." His voice was low and monotone. Signs of discomfort showed on his face. "Are you going far?"

Frustration rose at the thought of being tethered down. I shook my head. "I'm going to the Sanctuary. It's not as far away as you were staying."

Vincent didn't say anything.

Logan seemed more puzzled, but he was at least willing to back me up. "You strapped?"

"I'm only going for a walk, but I'll take it."

"Don't rely on tranqs and check in," Logan said. "In the meantime, Vincent and I have a few things to discuss."

"Right." That didn't sound reassuring. I thought about telling them to keep the blood off the carpet. When I looked from one man to the other, I decided it wasn't a good plan to put ideas into their heads. "I'll call in later."

I took my car. There was some discomfort the further I got from the house. *From Vincent*, I corrected. Knowing it was temporary made it easier to contend with.

Pulling into the Sanctuary drive, I could see that there were already several cars parked in the lot. Very few knew about the Sanctuary, but the Lost, and those in on the secret, could access the park. Still, I didn't expect there to be many people.

Travis gave me a warm smile as I walked up to the small group of people.

"We have a few agents in from Arizona tonight." Travis nodded to the group. "Are you here to join us?"

"I'm actually here for a walk," I said returning his smile. "I need to clear my head."

SHATTERED SOUL

"Getting in touch with nature does wonders for a person's psyche. James Long," Travis pointed, indicating an older man, "is a Shaman who lives in the area. He helps many keep their balance between nature and life."

James looked intriguing. He was marvelously tall, with long white hair smattered with a hint of gray that fell well below his shoulders. His beard was the same color and almost as long as his hair. Nestled in the middle of his beard was a long thin braid. I shook his hand and noticed that the smell of sage lingered like perfume. The amazing part was that as soon as I shook his hand, I felt calm.

James looked at me for a long time before saying anything. "You are broken."

Anger made my cheeks flush; so much for calm. "Excuse me?"

James didn't bother with a response. Travis, on the other hand, looked livid.

"Cassie is going for a walk to help pull herself together," Travis said, straining to keep his voice calm.

"She needs it." James walked away.

Travis watched his retreating back. "I'm so sorry. I've never seen James behave this way."

"Don't worry about it." I tried to shrug off my anger. "I'm off." Nodding to Travis, I headed toward the trail that would lead me along the riverbank. Before moving too far away from the gathering, I turned back, and saw that James was watching.

When I started out, I didn't think about my predicament. The path hugged a stream and when the trail curved into the woods, I decided to stay next to the water. Downstream I found the perfect spot. Several large rocks stood on the bank. Climbing onto the largest boulder, I got settled.

Meditating to the sound of rushing water, I let its energy wash over me. Once I centered myself and felt calm, I opened my eyes and watched the ripples of the stream and the trees waving in the breeze. I started to mull over my situation. It helped being calm and having a clear head.

It hardly seemed possible that a little over forty-eight hours earlier, I was almost killed. Thinking someone was purposefully trying to bump me off was too egotistical to comprehend. I wasn't important enough for someone to try to kill. Maybe it really was an accident.

My would-be killer had since taken up residence in my house.

Tossing that idea around, I thought more about Vincent. Getting a feel for the guy was difficult. Emotion was one thing, but intentions? It didn't help that he appeared even more guarded with Logan around. His claim of wanting to help resolve his mistake was going unfulfilled. Admittedly, we've been busy, but still, can a soul be fixed?

He claimed to know me.

That seemed true enough. Several times, he started to say things and changed his tactic. Last night I was sure that he was going to tell me to sit where I was. The moment that 'you're going to,' came from his mouth, I was ready to tell him off, but then he stopped and made a suggestion instead. Thinking this over only led to more questions. Was he trying to avoid an argument, manipulate me, or was he trying to be nice? It would be nice to know where Vincent fell in the scheme of things.

"Do not move," the gruff voice came from the woods.

Startled, I attempted to spin around and fell from my perch. A man was on top of me before my brain caught up with the situation. He pinned me to the ground.

"I said, do not move."

Panic and adrenaline gave me the strength to pull an arm free.

"I am trying very hard to fight my instinct to kill you right now." His voice strained.

It was Rider Wolfe. In the dark, he looked pained, but my mind was behind my reaction speed. My free hand had already pulled my gun. Attacking me was the wrong thing to do, but at the last moment, I changed my aim away from center mass.

SHATTERED SOUL

I pulled the trigger. The bullet sliced through his side and he rolled away from me.

Shit! I shot somebody!

I rolled up and put the rock at my back, facing Rider. I breathed heavily, trying to will the panic out of my body.

"You were not who I expected." His speech was staggered by panting.

I didn't answer and kept the gun firmly in hand. He no longer showed signs of aggression toward me, but I wasn't taking any chances. I also wasn't going to take a chance on him getting away. He walked up and had warned me not to move, for all the good it did either of us. Thinking of the strain on his face, it had really seemed like he had been trying to fight instinct.

"Why did you attack me?" I asked at last.

Rider considered the question. "You smell different."

"And that's a bad thing?"

Rider shrugged from his spot on the ground. "You smell like prey. Like dinnertime." He was silent again.

"Let me get this straight, you want to eat me?"

He did not look in my direction. Was this a werewolf thing? I really needed to read up more on the people I worked with. I gripped my gun in case this wasn't a cultural misunderstanding.

"I think that would be a bad thing," Rider said.

"Damn straight, that would be a bad thing. Can I move now? Have you gotten yourself under control?"

"I will not attack you."

The gun never left my hand, but I took my finger off the trigger. Rider didn't move from the ground.

"I shot you," I said, stating the obvious.

"Yes, thankfully, you shot me."

"Thankfully?"

"It would have been bad for both of us had you not." He sounded calm now.

I wish I could say the same thing. "I should call a doctor for you." I dug in my jacket pocket for a cell phone.

97

"No need," replied Rider. "I only have a scratch."

My first thought was that I should check out the injury. My instincts decided my brain was stupid. Instinct won out and I stayed with my back planted firmly against the rock.

We sat in stark silence for a while. Rider still didn't move.

"What do you mean I smell different?" I asked.

"You smelled one way. Now you smell another."

"Is it normal for someone's smell to change?" I asked.

Rider hesitated. "It usually takes something drastic. But then, I am new here, maybe it is normal."

"Someone sucked part of my soul out the other day," I said. "Maybe that's the difference."

Rider's response was not what I expected. From the ground, he laughed long and hard. My arm was getting tired and I felt like an idiot pointing my gun at a man laughing on the ground. I put my hands in my pockets, with one of them still resting on the gun, and looked over at him, feeling a little uncomfortable. I was clearly missing something.

He caught his breath. "That was one of the last things I thought I would hear coming out of your mouth." He laughed a bit more.

"Really?" I asked. "What did you expect?"

"Nothing quite so exciting."

"That's me, full of excitement," I mumbled.

"Honestly, I was not expecting anything that exciting to happen here. My dad said it was tame when he lived here."

"Is that why you came over? Because your dad lived here?"

Rider was quiet again for a bit. He moved into a sitting position and pulled away from me. At first, I didn't think he was going to answer. Maybe I asked the wrong question. Who knew what was appropriate with a werewolf? Thinking back to what Logan said about werewolves didn't give me any indication of what might be considered ill-mannered. Then again, he had attacked me and I had shot him. We were probably well beyond being worried about courtesy at that point.

SHATTERED SOUL

"He lived here for a while," Rider finally admitted. "My mother is from here. She left the house to me when she passed away."

We let the silence go on for a while. Finally, feeling it appropriate to do so, I replied, "Sorry about your mother passing away."

"We all have our time."

"What brings you out here tonight?" I asked.

"Travis invited me. We are getting to be friends, so I thought I would try meeting a few other people."

"Travis is a good guy." Remembering what Logan said, werewolves have a unique view on friendship. It was hard to become their friend, but once you are, they were a friend for life.

"He is, and he knows who I am. There was another fellow tonight that somehow knows, too. Travis called him James. He looked me over and called me a shifter right away. Thankfully not in front of others."

"I met James tonight. I don't know anything about him."

"Hmmm, he does seem to—" Rider stopped and stood. Freezing, I listened hard, but I didn't hear anything.

"Rider?" I asked.

"Something on the air," he said quietly. He twisted and turned silently across from me.

Without thinking, I opened the Path, trying to sense if anything was with us. Rider took a sharp intake of breath. In the Path, he had a vibrant twist of colors that moved throughout his body. The rest of the forest flowed through the path before us. The trees shot from the ground, grew to their length and died, only to be replaced by others. My eyes watered. I didn't dare blink, because I was seeing the past, present, and future of the area. The rarity of the event and the beauty of the passing of time made me not want to let go, even though it felt like I was drowning in the river of the Path. Sitting on that spot, I saw the river rise, and the sun rose and fell a hundred times. All the while, Rider's bundle of flowing colors did not change. I had no idea what it meant.

"What are you?" Rider asked in a whisper.

It was enough to shatter my attention and I snapped back to seeing only the present. I would have followed that vision until the end of time, even if I withered and died while watching. Pushing the Path away was a struggle. I wiped my watering eyes and pressed the torrent back.

"There's no one close to us." I looked at the trees. The world was so dull now. Without the colors that spun around inside him, even Rider looked diminished.

"It is on the air. I smell blood."

"Blood? I shot you, it's not surprising."

"This is different. Troll blood, I think. Stay here and I will find out."

"Excuse me?" Sit here while he runs off? I don't think so. "The troll is my responsibility. If he's hurt? Well, I'm going with you."

CHAPTER 10

RIDER REGARDED ME. IN THE dim light cast by the moon, Rider nodded. He started going into the woods, and raised no objections when I followed. Rider was almost silent as he walked through the trees. He avoided sticks and branches as he made his way through the underbrush. I found every last one of them, but to his credit, Rider didn't say anything.

My heart thudded hard in my chest. Maybe Rider was wrong, or maybe the troll had injured himself. Until we checked out the area, I had to stay calm. We finally emerged near the cave where Logan and I had placed the troll days earlier.

An acrid smell filled the air, forcing me to cover my nose and mouth with my sleeve. Usually, my night vision is good. The cliffs glowed white in the night, but at the base was nothing but darkness. I could see nothing, but there was no way I was going to try to open the Path here. Instead, I tried to get a feel for the area. The air vibrated at a menacing frequency.

"Rider, I can't see anything." The negative energy of the area seemed to push in on me. "There's something not good here." The last came out in a muffled whisper, but I knew he could understand me clearly.

"He is dead," came Rider's voice softly. I could see his outline in front of me against the wall of rock. "Torn apart."

"Torn? Can you tell what did it? Or smell it? Is it still here?" I hated the anxiety that I let slip out through my voice, but the abhorrent feeling in the air seeped into everything around me.

"I cannot tell what it was. The smell is unfamiliar. It seems to have gone off in that direction." Under the darkness cast by the trees, I could only tell the general area where he was pointing.

"I need to get Logan out here." I kept my voice low. "I don't think we should track it."

Rider turned to me. "We should go back to the entrance and warn Travis and the others. You can call Logan from there."

"Warn them-- oh no, Essy. Rider, did that thing go off in the fairies' direction?" I didn't wait for an answer. "You have to go warn Essy!"

Rider hesitated.

"Look," I said, "you're quicker and quieter than I am. If you run into whatever did this, run away. Go!" He turned and was gone.

I took a few steps backward. I couldn't see where the dead troll lay. My imagination started getting the better of me. For all I knew, I could be standing in an area surrounded by pieces of dead troll, torn apart by something that could be roaming these woods. I took another few steps backwards. The air felt coated in an oily residue.

It became very hard to breathe. The air pushed in on me and the smell was nauseating. I couldn't stay here. I tried to figure out where Rider and I had arrived through the woods, but I was disoriented in the dark. Instead, I followed the cliff, back away from the area.

Maybe Gran would know to send Logan, I thought wildly. However, I couldn't count on that. Pulling out my phone, I pushed up against the cliff face yards away from where Rider and I had stopped. The air was not as thick here. Trying to collect myself, I breathed in and out steadily and tried to focus on what was around me. I dialed Logan. Safety, I thought. I need to make sure I'm safe. The call wouldn't go through. I jabbed the numbers again and again in futile effort.

There was nothing else I could do but open the Path. I had to know. Concentrating hard, I tried to open myself a tiny bit to the Path. The air rippled then started rushing around with great strength. Not quite the deluge I'd experienced before, but it was close.

SHATTERED SOUL

Inky blackness choked the Path. Against the darkness, I pulled out feelings of safety. I was able to build a shimmery shell of safety, pushing back the defilement around me. I tried to sense anything alive that was close to me. It wasn't until I searched up and reached the trees that I sensed anything.

I looked up into the trees directly in front of me. Something large loomed above me. With as little movement as possible, I tried to make myself smaller by pushing myself further into the cliff at my back. Terror washed over me in waves. My concentration broke and the Path grew stronger around me, but I held onto my bubble of safety. I let the Path pour over me, afraid to expend the effort to push it away. With all the murkiness, I couldn't make out what was watching me. The Path showed me only the present, for which I was thankful.

I could sense the creature waiting. *Enough*, I thought fiercely. Would Logan sit here and tremble if he was left alone? Rider took off without any thought of what he might face when he rushed to warn Essy. If something was going to try to kill me, I wasn't going to sit here and let it happen. Very slowly, I pulled out my gun. I didn't move my eyes away from where I thought the creature perched.

"You are standing near an AIR crime scene," I said. I was surprised my voice came out so steady. "I order you to come down for questioning."

There was an odd screeching noise in front of me and the air chilled. A swooping noise filled the night. Something thudded on the ground close by. I couldn't see it, but pointed my gun in its direction. My bubble of safety was thrown back at me, followed by cold, dense darkness in the Path.

Once again, the atmosphere became thicker and oily. I could see a dark outline of something in front of me. Was this thing causing the unnatural taint in the air? Needing my eyesight instead of the contaminated Path, I concentrated and pushed the Path away. The creature didn't move, but I felt something flex. Something as solid as a wall slammed into me. It pushed me up hard against the cliff. The force disappeared and I bounced off the cliff, only to be lifted by nothingness and smashed again into the rock face.

The air rushed out of my lungs as I hit and my feet were no longer touching the ground. The strength of the force did not dissipate, but instead, tried to grind me into the cliff face. I tried to scream, but had no air to do so. Every bruise and cut I'd gained the night before screamed pain throughout my system.

The solid wall suffocated me. Death waited for me.

The wall of energy vanished and I fell to the ground. Another swooshing noise filled the air. I sat up and swung my gun out in front of me, ready to fire at my attacker, but I found nothing to shoot at. Anger coursed through me. I looked at the sky, but still caught no sight of my attacker.

"Cassie!" Rider called from the woods.

"Cassie," mimicked another high-pitched hissing voice. The air grew lighter. I didn't drop my weapon.

Rider came running out of the woods. "Where is it? What is it?" Rider put himself in front of me. He crouched down and then leaned forward, ready to pounce on anything that moved.

Trembling, I moved my finger off the trigger and slid down to the ground. I'd already shot Rider once tonight, not that he seemed to care, but I certainly didn't want to shoot him by accident. I was having a hard time catching my breath.

"Gone." My voice wasn't as clear as before. Rider stood ready to attack anything that approached. He stayed like that for several minutes. I didn't move. As I sat there, I discovered tears running down my face. The adrenaline rush faded and I felt like I was falling apart. Silently, I wiped the tears off my face hoping Rider hadn't seen them. Rider began to relax his stance. He stepped beside me and leaned down to get a good look at me, never putting his back to the woods.

"Are you all right?" he asked.

"Was Essy okay?"

"She and the others are in hiding until I let them know it is safe."

SHATTERED SOUL

Sighing with relief, I leaned my head back against the cliff face.

"You are bleeding," Rider said.

"I was tossed into a cliff wall and then ground into it. Of course I'm bleeding."

"We should leave."

"Give me a second." I steadied myself. I made sure the Path was pushed firmly away. I thought I might drown in caustic darkness if I slipped back into the Path here. "What's the quickest way back?" I asked.

"Can you walk?" Rider asked.

Since there was no way I was going to let someone carry me out of the woods, I said the only thing I could. "I'll be fine."

"This way," Rider motioned.

The shortest way back didn't involve a trail. It was straight through the woods, across a field, and through more woods. We ended up taking several breaks. Twice Rider heard something moving through the thick foliage, but both times, he decided it was animals moving around. A few times, we stopped so I could rest and catch my breath. When we finally emerged behind one of the buildings, it looked like the gathering was over. Only Travis and James lingered. They headed toward us after we stepped out of the woods. I leaned against the building and slid down, sitting hard on the ground. Rider stood close to me.

When Travis was close enough, I asked him to call Logan and get him out here. He didn't ask any questions, which was a relief. The ordeal in the woods was too fresh to relive.

James moved closer to me. Rider made a low menacing noise, and James stopped.

"I'll bring no harm to anyone here," James said.

Rider took a step back to stand beside me, but didn't relax. James walked forward and crouched in front of me. "I'm sorry for earlier. I'm not sure what came over me."

I nodded.

Travis ended his call and came to join us once more. "Logan

is already on his way. Cassie, are you okay? James sensed something in the area and we sent everyone away."

I was getting sick of everyone asking me if I was okay. Maybe if I didn't give people reason to be concerned, they'd stop asking? "I'm good, just worn out." I glanced at James, and then back at Travis. Travis took the hint.

"James is safe to talk to, Cassie. He has clearance and I'll vouch for him."

Nodding, I looked up at Rider. He kept his eyes on the woods. After rolling my head on my shoulder to let some of the tension loose, I followed Rider's gaze. I let the Path fall over me without resisting it and felt through the area around us. Rider shivered, but didn't take his eyes off the woods. Checking the entire area around the building, and above for good measure, I didn't sense any of the oil slicked energy that resonated around the creature that attacked us.

Before I felt overwhelmed by the force of the power, I pulled myself away from the Path. James looked at me appraisingly. He didn't ask any questions and I didn't offer anything.

"Let's move inside, out of the open air." I pulled myself up and we entered one of the buildings. I cleaned up while we waited for Logan. He arrived with Vincent in tow.

Logan's face looked more angular. It seemed wrong to me that the elf hadn't smiled much in days. He didn't say anything as he came over, giving me a cursory glance. He glared at Rider, Thomas, and James. "Who are you?" he asked gruffly to James.

"He has clearance," Travis said.

"Show me." Logan looked over the card that James produced. After careful inspection, he passed it back. "Fine. Explain."

I didn't need to see the Path to feel how infuriated Logan was. His fury engulfed the entire room, bouncing off walls and people. Rider filled Logan in. Looking around, I saw that Vincent stood a bit away from the others. His hands were balled into fists. From here, his eyes looked solid black. His arms trembled slightly.

SHATTERED SOUL

As soon as Rider finished, filling in my part of the story for me, Vincent turned around and headed out the door.

"Now, wait a minute!" Logan called after him.

"No." Vincent's voice was shaking. He walked out.

"Stay away from the Troll!" Logan yelled as Vincent retreated. He turned back to the room. "I've gotta go out and take a look at the site. Travis, would you mind if I used one of your ATVs again?"

"I should go with you," Travis responded. "It's dark and I know the way well. James, would you mind staying here with Cassie?"

"I'm going," I stated.

"Cassie," Logan started.

I glared at him and stood up. Without looking back, I walked outside.

CHAPTER 11

THE TRIP THERE WAS SHORT compared to the journey that Rider and I took. Travis stayed with the ATVs, ready to lead us back out again. Logan handed out flashlights and then grabbed his bag. Rider led us along the cliff toward the area where the murder occurred. The oily residue still clung to the air. Logan stopped at one section of the cliff and flashed the light around. It took me a minute to realize that this was where my encounter with the creature took place.

Shining my flashlight through the trees, I tried to search out the area where the creature must have stood. There was no evidence that it had been there. We went further toward the cave until we found what remained of the troll. My stomach clenched and threatened to rebel. The acrid smell, which must have been the troll's blood, filled the air. Rider was right. It had been torn to pieces.

The turbulent energy in the area lingered. Between the smell of blood and presence of that horrible residue in the air, I was beginning to feel ill.

"This is a mess," Logan said. I could hear the sadness in the elf's voice. "I'll call it in." He turned away and called the office asking for a code four clean up at the Sanctuary.

He turned back to us when he hung up. "Let's go back to where you were attacked."

"Sure," I said, thankful to get away from the smell.

It didn't take long to reach the spot.

Rider stopped and inspected part of the cliff. From his position, I could tell that was where I had been crushed into the

SHATTERED SOUL

rock face. Rider was a mixed jumble of energy, so it was hard to get any clear reading of him without entering the Path.

"We're going to send you back to the entrance with Travis," Logan said to Rider.

"Thanks for your help tonight, Rider," I said, looking at the cliff.

He nodded. "Do I need to wait for anyone at the entrance?"

"No. We'll stop by if we have any questions," Logan responded.

Rider nodded. With another glance at the cliff, he went back to Travis. Logan waited for them to drive away before pulling out flares for the area. We only had a few in the bag. Logan placed them all around the perimeter.

"You know," Logan said, "that hole in Rider's side looks an awful lot like a bullet hole."

"Oh, yeah," I said, "it was the strangest thing." I had forgotten about how Rider and I met up that evening. I relayed the story.

"He attacked you?" Vincent asked. Jumping, I turned and almost fell as Vincent walked out of the woods. Logan, however, didn't seem the least bit surprised when Vincent joined the conversation.

"He said it was instinct," I said, relating the information again. I shrugged. "He made up for it here anyway. If he hadn't shown up, I would probably be dead now."

"Where'd you go?" Logan asked Vincent.

"I attempted to track the thing, but had no luck."

"It flew away," I said. "Hard to track that."

Vincent shrugged.

"Look," Logan pointed at Vincent, "you can't wander away on your own. You're either a part of our team or not. Make a choice and stick with it."

Vincent's surprise mirrored my own. To cover the awkwardness, I started to go over what happened at the cliff. I flashed my light once more into the trees above me. As I finished my part of the story again, the enormity of the night started

109

catching up to me. I pushed it back down. Being scared about it wasn't going to help.

Logan scaled the tree the creature sat on, but didn't find anything. The ground wasn't wet, so there were no footprints.

"Anything in the Path?" Logan asked me.

"I can try it, but I'm adjusting to how much I see now," I admitted. "I'm not sure how much use it'll be."

"It's been a few days. Things aren't back to normal?" Logan asked. I looked up at him just in time to catch a glare he shot in Vincent's direction.

"Perhaps you could explain the change," said Vincent. If he noticed the glare, he ignored it.

"The Path is different now. There was so much of it hidden before. I see things—" I broke off, trying to think of a better way of explaining. "I see floods of information when I saw only a trickle before. I'll adjust." Before they could say anything more, I closed my eyes and opened the Path.

Like earlier, I tried to let only a little through. Opening my eyes, I looked around. Ignoring the glowing centers that were Logan and Vincent, and the vestiges they left behind, I started feeling for the remains of emotional residue from the creature. Once I found the traces, I tried to follow them back into the past. It was a struggle. The deluge of colors roaring by and the constant shimmer in the air didn't want to go back; it only wanted to move forward. It was almost as if the Path itself wanted to get rid of the creature's presence.

Something in the air caught my eye. Streams of blues and white swirled around. Currents ran into each other, mixed, and swirled apart. Fascinated, I watched as it moved through the trees, making them sway. Was I seeing the wind?

Feeling a hand on my shoulder, I turned. Vincent's feelings of concern fell over me. His Path was firmly in the present. His whirl of color mixed with others, much like the waves of air. Inside, he fought against waves of other energy crashing against him. There was one current wrapped firmly around his own. He wasn't fighting that flow. It didn't take long for me to realize that current was my own.

The realization struck me like a blow. Distracted, the Path swamped over me. Closing my eyes, I saw its flux of color, but with some effort, I managed to push it away. When I opened my eyes, I looked at Vincent.

"Did you see anything?" Vincent asked. He was detached, and could have been asking what I saw inside him or what I saw in the area.

It was better to take the easy route until I thought through what I had seen inside Vincent. "I couldn't see anything about the creature," I replied.

His eyes searched mine. In the flare light, I could see small signs of relief as the tightness of his face relaxed.

We moved the flares around the murder site. The smell was horrendous, but Logan managed to find some vapor rub in the bottom of our bag. We put some under our nose, which helped a little.

"Take a look at this," Logan said, indicating something on the ground. As I leaned in closer, I realized he was inspecting a piece of the body. I swallowed hard a few times to keep from retching. "Look at the joint," Logan continued.

Vincent joined us and then moved to another area. "It's the same with this piece as well," Vincent said.

I hated knowing that I was missing something. Blaming it on fatigue was an option, but not a good one. Instead, I cleared my head and tried to detach myself from the situation. I looked at the finger joint, and then moved over to Vincent. The joints had the same type of damage.

"He was literally torn to pieces," Logan said.

"At each joint," Vincent added.

Repulsed, I had to keep my mouth firmly shut in order to keep my lunch down. What was happening with my job? Overnight, I went from relocation to homicide investigation, and, let's face it, I'm no detective.

"Do you think the creature you saw would be capable of something like this?" Vincent asked.

I swallowed hard. "It pulled me off the ground without touching me. Whatever it is, it's powerful."

"You remember anything else about it?" Logan asked.

"Nothing," I replied. "Why would it tear apart the troll? I mean, it doesn't look like it ate anything. There's no way the troll would have attacked it."

"Hard to say what the thing eats," Logan said. "Maybe it tasted the troll and didn't like it?"

We searched for any sign of missing parts. Opting to examine the smaller pieces, I let Vincent inspect the torso. I'd never say it out loud, but I didn't think I would be able to examine the troll's insides. How I was coping with the smaller parts was a mystery. Every time a morbid thought crept up, I pushed it back down. When I remembered that this troll was alive less than twenty-four hours ago, I locked the thought away. If for one moment I really thought about what happened, I would be done. Logan and Vincent probably thought the same thing. If they could keep going, so could I.

"Looks like all the parts are here," said Logan.

"Lot of blood, too," Vincent added. "It's not a blood drinker."

"Food wasn't its motivation," I said. "We can start by trying to track its motivation."

"You up for seeing more?" Logan asked. I stared at him blankly for a moment. Realization dawned slowly. He wanted me to read the area. The thought churned my stomach.

"I'm not sure I'll have much luck," I said. "The other spot didn't give anything up."

"I understand if you don't want to try," Logan said.

Vincent's eyes narrowed at Logan, although I'm not sure he noticed. My partner knew which buttons to press. When he put it like that, I had no choice.

Instead of attempting to pin down the darkness of the creature's energy, I concentrated on the troll. The atmosphere

SHATTERED SOUL

didn't fight me like it had earlier. The troll's imprint didn't want to leave. This was its home, and it wanted to stay, not be lost and forgotten. The wilderness seemed content to keep his memory.

Pulling through the Path, I went back. I saw the troll alive. He walked back toward his cave. The shimmer of the path dulled. The darkness swelled. I caught movement in the Path, but it blurred. The Path struggled to wash away remnants of the darkness. I struggled against it, trying to pull back the darkness and see, but it was no use.

The energy of our victim was there. I watched as our troll was torn apart, the darkness hid some of the details, but I had seen enough. It was too much. I threw back the Path.

I fled away to the edges of our scene and my stomach contents ended up on the ground. No one came near me, for which I was thankful. Slowly, I pushed back the emotionally charged images I had witnessed. Once I got myself under control, I joined the others. In the distance, I could hear an ATV. Our clean-up crew was almost here.

Taking a deep breath, I plunged in. "There was no reason for it. It appeared, tore-- er, did what it did," pushing back the images took a bit of effort, "and left."

"What was it?" Logan asked.

I shook my head before his question was fully formed. "No idea. It was hidden, but I saw what it did. I couldn't see any motive."

"Where did it come from?" Vincent asked.

"It came in following the cliff face from that direction," I said pointing.

"Where did it go after? Or did it stay here for a time?" Vincent asked. This was a harder question. I was pulling myself out of the Path when it was leaving.

"It went into the woods," I said.

"You bring up an interesting question," Logan said. "Where did the creature come from?"

"Wouldn't we have known if something like that lived around here?" I asked.

"How often do you get Portals?" Vincent asked.

"We get six or seven natural portals a year in the Mid-West." This was the type of question I could answer. "That's why we only have a handful of field teams. There are more down south, which is why we have a hub in the Ozarks."

"Same locations each time?" Vincent asked.

"Each time. Our techs let us know when one is getting ready to open. They can monitor the buildup of energy," Logan said. "Sometimes we don't get a lot of warning though. Natural portals can be unpredictable."

"We're there when one opens to keep anybody from wandering through. In either direction," I added. "We have a few standard created Portals on the farm."

"Nothing from a dimension that might have a creature like this?" Vincent asked.

"Nothing," said Logan.

The ATV noise was gone, and voices approached. We held our discussion as Travis led the other team through the woods. Travis looked weary when he approached. We handed the crime scene over to the crew. They were armed with bags, lights, and coolers. I didn't want to think about what they were going to use the coolers for.

CHAPTER 12

HIDING UNDER MY COVERS ALL day was tempting, but wasn't really an option. The workday loomed ahead, so I dragged myself out of bed and got ready for the day. When I walked through the living room, Gran's cat hissed at me and scratched my leg. Luckily, I was wearing jeans. I shooed the cat until it slunk away into Gran's room. Gran had left some ibuprofen for me on the counter with a note saying she was over at Morgan's house today. She had also made a pie for Logan and his family.

Grabbing a drink, I downed the pills. I heard the shower turn on upstairs and knew that Vincent was up. I grabbed leftovers that Gran had left, eating them cold. Wondering what the weather was like, I wandered into the back garden. This was Gran's domain in the summer. She and Cici, the stray fairy that Gran adopted, tended the garden, which produced vast quantities of veggies and herbs throughout the summer and early fall. Cici kept the garden free of insects, except the bees of course, and Gran took care of the planting. The plants were clinging to life. We might even get a few more tomatoes before the end of the season. I wandered out near the tree in the central part of the yard. I wrapped my arms around myself, trying to push back the sadness that threatened to swamp me from the day before. I heard a high-pitched buzz and squeal. Looking around, I spotted Cici flitting around the tree.

Instead of the usual warm welcome I received from Cici, she cried out in alarm and started pelting me with acorns.

"Ouch, Cici!"

She fluttered around and started sprinkling a fine powder down on me. Assuming it was some sort of poisonous plant, I retreated into the house.

Feeling dejected, I called Logan. It was past time to get the day started.

"Busy day planned, we'll need to split up. The cleaning crew is working on the site. One of us needs to go out and check on the progress in person now that the sun is up." Logan said.

"Sounds like a job for Vincent."

"I was thinking the same. Hank is running through old records, checking to see if any portals popped up in the last month that might have been overlooked. I'm meeting with him this afternoon. I'm going to have dinner with the family tonight. Jonathan wants us to meet his girlfriend."

"It looks like Gran left you a pie for dinner. One of us also needs to check on Rider today."

"It would be a good idea after last night," Logan agreed.

"I'll do that," I said.

"The doc will have my ears if you don't take things easy today."

"Dropping in won't exactly be strenuous."

"I'll be by shortly. If you see Margaret, let her know we appreciate the pie."

"Where are you dropping in?" Vincent asked as I put the phone down. I jumped. How did he always manage to sneak up on me?

"Uh, Rider," I said. "I'm checking up on him after yesterday. There are leftovers in the fridge if you want anything."

Vincent shook his head.

"Logan will be over soon," I said.

Vincent didn't respond.

"Everything okay?" I asked, and then caught myself. "I mean, I know everything isn't okay, after yesterday. But—"

"You gave me quite a scare last night."

"When?"

SHATTERED SOUL

"I'm guessing it was about the time you shot the werewolf."

"What are you talking about? You weren't there."

"And yet, it felt as if I were."

It was too early to wrap my brain around what he was trying to say, so I didn't bother replying.

"It felt unpleasant," he said.

"Well, you made me feel unpleasant when we met." I meant for it to be sarcastic, but nothing but anger came through. "I guess that makes us even."

"I don't know that we will ever be even," Vincent said miserably. "What I did—"

"Is in the past," I interrupted, thinking Vincent wallowed in his own self-pity. "This is a hell of a way to start a day. Can't this wait?"

"No, there are things you don't understand." He paused, "I'm not sure that I understand them. I think I made what happened last night much worse than it could have been."

"Because everything is your fault?"

"No," Vincent sighed. "But I should have warned you. Rider is a werewolf. They are predators."

"Rider saved my life," I said fiercely.

"He also tried to kill you. Besides the predatory nature that exists in Rider, I have no objections to him. Please let me explain." When I didn't interrupt him, he continued, but he vibrated with anxiety. "Your essence is shredded. That I was able to return it to you was a miracle, but it is in pieces inside of you."

"You really want to do this now?" I asked.

He nodded, but his anxiety didn't fade. I had been avoiding this since we met, but there was no avoiding it anymore. We'd barely begun talking and I already felt my blood pressure rising.

"I've never seen this happen before, so I didn't understand the consequences," he said. "I'm starting to see some of them now. Things are falling together in a frightening pattern. Logan is unsettled and angry, which clashes with his general nature. I don't want to upset you, but it's more evident when you are present."

"He's upset because everything is in turmoil right now," I replied. "He's upset because you blundered in."

"That's part of it I think, but then I heard the Shaman's reaction to you. I'm not sure precisely what happened between you and Rider. But it sounds like Rider fought his own natural instincts. He wanted to harm you."

I started to protest, but it was feeble. Rider himself said he wanted to eat me, whatever the hell that meant. Maybe it was literal.

"You were attacked by something in the woods. Something that had left, but sensed your presence and returned." Vincent stopped. He clearly looked uneasy about where this conversation was going.

That made two of us.

"So putting that together, where do you think that leads?" I asked. I was pretty sure I didn't want to hear his answer and he seemed equally unsure if he should give the answer.

"I've made you a target," he finally said. "People sense your change."

"Why would shredding my soul make me a target?"

Vincent flinched. "Predators, like Rider—"

I made a small noise of protest. Vincent sighed, which only aggravated me more.

"You're one to talk about predators. It was your job to come in and kill me. You tried your damnedest to do just that." Vincent started to say something, but I wasn't through yet. "You didn't even question what you were told. You came in and tried to kill me. How many others have you killed?"

"What I do saves lives." Vincent started to get angry now. "This is the first time an accident like this has happened."

"Do you even care that what you do saves lives?" I asked. "You walk around trying to look expressionless most of the time. You didn't even seem too fazed by the troll last night. The only thing that seemed to bother you was that you didn't get to catch the thing that did it."

That caught Vincent off guard.

"I was doing my job," Vincent said, "which wasn't at the murder site."

"Of course not. You ran off to create another." His eyes started to grow dark, but I didn't care. I pushed forward. "Do you know what happens after you kill someone?" I asked. "After you suck their soul out of them?"

"Everything that I pull out gets thrown between the worlds. You have no idea what I do." His voice grew softer, but held a sharp edge.

"You're right. I have no idea what a Walker does. Logan thinks your race is cursed. Want to know why you're cursed?" I leaned in and watched, as his eyes turned to a flat black. No white remained. "Not everything you take in gets thrown out. You keep a piece of every soul you take away from people."

Vincent's hands were clinched. "Nothing stays with me."

"Really? Because the evidence is coiled around inside you. It pulls together and becomes part of you. Tell me, Vincent," I spat. "What makes you kill? What do you have living inside you?"

He didn't move or make a sound. Those flat black eyes bore into me. Realizing I didn't have my gun on me made me think that I might have pushed things too far.

"Aren't you two glad you got that out of the way?" Logan asked, coming in from the backyard. Logan took a few steps into the room. His movement was fluid, and he wore a smile. "I'm surprised it didn't happen sooner, but things have been busy." Logan rocked back and forth on his heels and started humming.

I recognized the tune '*The Sun Will Come Out Tomorrow*'. Logan had been humming the tune the first day we met. It did the trick; my anger deflated. I don't say it often enough, but I have the best partner in the world. When I wondered if I could make it to my gun, Logan saved the day.

Looking up at Vincent, I saw that he struggled with his anger. He had unclenched his fists, but his eyes were stark. He closed them and took a few deep breaths. When that didn't work, he shook his head and walked out of the room.

"Thanks," I said. "How did you know?"

"I hesitated walking in, but it seemed like good timing."

"Your timing couldn't have been better," I said.

"Good to know. I'd let him cool off before trying to talk to him again."

I nodded in agreement.

"I'll call him once he's had some time," Logan said.

I nodded to the pie on the counter. "Gran left this for you."

"I'll give her a call too. That little lady is something else. Can I borrow some sugar, too? Gerald ate our last bag."

Elves have a sweet tooth that Gran loves to feed, so she always keeps loads of sugar on hand.

"Thankfully, the department has dental insurance," I said. The last vestiges of anger and resentment faded away.

"It's best to make good use of these things. Check in later." Logan tipped an imaginary hat and left.

I didn't try to look for Vincent. He might have been in the guest room, or he might have left. Either way, I thought it best if we both had some space.

Before I left for Rider's house, I strapped on my gun and put the tranq gun in my purse. Better safe than sorry. For good measure, I used a bit of body spray. With Rider always talking about how I smelled, I was getting a little self-conscious. Grabbing my keys, I headed to Rider's house.

"I am surprised to see you today," Rider said when I arrived. "I thought you would be over at the Sanctuary."

"We were there through the night. Other agents are there now."

Rider nodded.

"I wanted to stop by and see how you are," I said.

"Kind of bored after last night. That was the first excitement I have had in this world," Rider said.

"Your side isn't sore?" I asked.

SHATTERED SOUL

"My side?"

I stared at him in disbelief. "Your side. Where I shot you."

"That was a scratch," Rider said. "It healed quickly."

"Good to hear." There was an awkward silence for a while. He was fine, so I figured it was time for me to go. Standing up, I said, "I wanted—"

"Do you want to go do something?" Rider asked.

"Um, what did you have in mind?" Going home didn't appeal to me, so I was up for almost anything.

Rider shrugged. "I have no idea. After yesterday, I feel cooped up here."

"There are a lot of great state parks and hiking trails around if you want to go walking. Would you be interested?"

"That sounds wonderful," Rider said. "Is Logan joining us?"

"Nope, just us." I hesitated, "You're not going to try to kill me again, are you?"

"I think I can avoid that."

"That's reassuring," I said, heading out the door.

The nearest state park was a large one, so I headed in that direction. When we stepped out of the car, I breathed the fresh warm air rustling through the area.

"Which way are we going?" Rider asked.

"Let's head this way," I said, stepping onto a trail. "There's an old tunnel up here that's pretty neat. Ghosts haunt the area above the tunnel. Sometimes when you're inside the tunnel, you can hear phantom noises."

"Ghosts?" Rider asked.

"Ghosts are spirits of the dead." Rider still looked puzzled, so I went into detail about specters and old ghost stories from the area as we walked. Rider wanted to see one, so I explained that most of the time they can't be seen, and that was kind of the point.

It was turning out to be a pretty good day. We reached the tunnel and walked through it slowly, listening for phantom noises. I didn't hear anything, but Rider jumped and turned around a few times. He looked a little freaked out, but he also looked like he was having a really good time. Before we left the tunnel, I started making ghostly noises. Rider laughed and chased me out of the tunnel. We kept on walking.

"What else do you do in the area?" Rider asked.

"If you like to watch sports, there are games at the University."

"You watch them? Would you not have more fun playing the sport?"

"I guess. I'm not really into either. Work keeps me pretty busy."

"I met a bunch of the Lost at the Farm. Fairies, centaurs, gnomes, and pixies, but no other werewolves."

"Logan mentioned that he met a few," I said.

"My dad lived here for a while, but he did not mention any other Werewolves," Rider said.

"When did your dad live here?" I asked.

"He came over about thirty-five years ago. He stayed for a while. He met my mom and they had me, but my mom died soon after I was born. Dad and I went back to our world."

"I'm sorry about your mom."

"My dad talked about her some."

"Is that why you came to this world?"

"One of the reasons." Rider started to look uncomfortable about the shift in topics.

"My dad passed away when I was really young. I remember him a little, but not much," I said.

"What do you remember about him?"

I grinned. "For some reason, I remember our last Halloween together. He dressed up with me and we went trick-or-treating for hours. I was dressed as Tinkerbelle. I had my hair done, make-up, everything." I reflected on the memory. "You know, Halloween is coming up."

"What is Halloween?"

"It's my favorite holiday. People dress up in costumes and kids go door to door for candy."

SHATTERED SOUL

"Why do they dress up?"

"It used to be to confuse the spirits. Or ward off spirits. Now people dress up to scare other people, or as a chance to pretend to be something or someone else for a night."

When the sun started to set, we swung around and headed back. The thought of being out after dark made me a little nervous, but I felt safe enough with Rider. He was intrigued by the idea of Halloween, and it led to discussions about other holidays. Easter thoroughly confused him.

It was nearly full dark when we reached the tunnel. Once again, we walked slowly through, listening for noises that we couldn't explain.

Rider grabbed my arm. "Cassie, I think I see something!"

CHAPTER 13

WE CREPT FORWARD SLOWLY. "I see it!" I whispered.

We stopped and watched a form move to the edge of the tunnel entrance. Rider broke into a run. I ran after him, laughing and excited about the prospect of catching up to one of the fabled ghosts. I had never seen one, but the company was sometimes called in to relocate ghosts and poltergeists.

We ran out the opening and turned to the left, trying to spot where the figure had disappeared. Only it hadn't disappeared. Rider was thrown back. He slammed into me and we both thudded to the ground. Fear pulsed through my veins. I struggled to push Rider off me to reach my gun.

The thing was tall, emaciated, and pale, with skin that hung around it as though it were an ill-made suit. This was no ghost.

Fumbling a bit as Rider jumped back to his feet, I tried to unsnap the holster to get to my gun. I felt a strange new power rush over me. Lurid and rhythmic energy pulsed through the air. It held me enthralled and the pulsing went through to my core. I could feel it in every inch of my body.

Rider's fury nearly threw me back, snapping me back to our situation. The pressure in the air increased. Rider lunged.

Hurling Rider away, the figure turned to me. Unblinking eyes stared, glowing with an inner light. The crushing fury that belonged to Rider shifted.

I managed to get off two shots before the creature lurched forward and struck me. Sharp pain tore through my body, as I flew back and smashed into the tunnel wall. I rolled over and took aim from the ground.

Rider sprinted forward, struck, and retreated, before the creature could retaliate. My heart thudded in my chest as I waited to get a clear shot. Rider took a blow to the face and fell back. The pale skinned being darted towards me. I was struck again by rhythmic thumping. The sensation wrapped itself around me. Entranced, I could only stare.

"Stop!" Rider's yell was a command.

The slack pale skin stopped moving. The pulsing stopped and I started to come to my senses.

Shots echoed through the tunnel as I emptied my clip. Each bullet struck home. The monster screamed and charged towards me again. Rider came at it from the side.

Staggering to my feet, I rushed toward the creature. I dove to the ground and snatched up my purse. Within seconds, I had a second clip in hand and jammed it into place.

Claws slashed across my back. Where each nail ripped through skin, fire erupted from my flesh. Rider yelled as I lifted off the ground. It had me in hand. Agony poured through me and it pulled me up to its face. It drew me close. The peculiarly lit eyes were inches from my face.

I pushed the gun into the folds of skin under its face and pulled the trigger. A shriek tore from the creature's throat. It dropped me.

Rider used the distraction to grab the creature's prone throat. The scream was short. Blood from the thing pooled on the ground around me. When the body was limp, Rider pushed the corpse aside.

So much blood. How much of it was my own? My back felt scorched. Rider pulled me up, but the pain grew too intense. For a while, there was nothing.

I started to become aware of what surrounded me. The air brushed by, light and warm before energy whipped around me in a flurry. Then I felt detached and floated away.

As I rose up, my restraints fell away. The noise died away, but my eyes opened to increased activity. Rider was on the ground. He appeared to be injured, but no one was coming near him. Tears ran down his face. Something was cradled in his arms and he rocked back and forth. It wasn't until he yelled out that others approached. Vincent was there. Anguish, pain, and anger marred his features. He seemed unable to speak. Logan was there. There was no fluidity to his movements and he looked grim.

Rider moved his bundle carefully onto the ground and I stared down onto myself.

This is wrong, I thought, so wrong. I couldn't be dead. Yet, here they were, standing over my body.

No! I thought vehemently. This wasn't going to happen today.

Closing my eyes, I concentrated hard. Something was missing. I could feel parts of me that were torn away. It was like a puzzle that needed solving, only someone kept removing pieces. Sensing bits of energy around me, I concentrated harder, pulling it into myself. It became easier to spot the parts of me that were no longer attached and I pulled each one in. More pieces emerged and I wrapped them together. Parts began flying toward me on their own.

The air felt tangible once again. Noises flooded back, although they weren't recognizable. Intense pain flared as the last pieces of the puzzle slammed into me. I cried out and it grew quiet.

The ground trembled with hurried steps. Fierce agony shot through me when someone pulled me up. Tears began running down my face and I opened my eyes.

Logan's was the first face I saw. He looked older, yet more real to me than he ever had. He said something and pulled me close to him. Individual sounds were amazingly clear, but they each came at me at such a rush that I could not distinguish one from the other. The entire world seemed to be on fast forward, while I was stuck in slow motion.

SHATTERED SOUL

Fighting through the pain and the assault of sound, I struggled to pull up the important facts: Logan, Vincent, and Rider. My mind was a tumble of half coherent thoughts. As I grabbed at them, I discovered the one I needed.

"Logan," My voice came out quiet and scratchy. Clearing my throat, I continued. "Is it dead?" There was a lurch as the feeling of slow motion died and the world sped up.

Logan started laughing, though tears ran down his face. "It's dead." He hugged me close to him, which made me wince in pain.

"Is Rider okay?" I asked.

"He's going to be fine," Logan assured me, without pausing to check.

Rider and I didn't get to go home. The doctor arrived on scene and insisted that we be taken to the Farm. An oxygen mask was thrust over my face before I could object. Not that I would have objected. My back felt scorched. After managing to push the mask away long enough to tell Logan to take Gran to the Farm, I settled in, face down on the bed.

It wasn't an ambulance we went back in, but a work truck fitted so our beds wouldn't roll around. Several times on the ride back, I tried to fall asleep. Each time, the man that sat next to me made me wake up. He wasn't nice about it either. It would be nice if I could say I made some witty or sarcastic remark, but I was too exhausted for witty, and in too much pain for sarcasm. I endured the trip in silence.

Rider was silent on the bed next to me. Logan and Vincent didn't ride with us. Too many bodies, not enough space. When we reached the Farm, we were ushered onto the property in record time.

Once again, I found myself in the medical ward at the office. Dr. Yelton had us wheeled into separate rooms. The doctor came in and kept talking to me, but I gave up listening. The words stopped making sense. There was too much pain and I wanted to sleep.

When I woke up again, the discomfort was almost gone. The room was dark, but I had no idea if it was the same night or the next.

"You're awake." Vincent came into view, although slightly out of focus.

"I think so." My tongue felt thick in my mouth, but I felt pretty good. When I tried to wipe a stray hair out of my eyes, I discovered why. An IV pumped something into me. Whatever it was, I hoped they kept it coming.

"How are you feeling?" Vincent asked.

"Not bad, actually," I responded. "How's Rider?"

"He'll be fine soon. Werewolves heal quickly." His voice was coarse.

"Where is everyone? Gran and Logan?"

"Logan is checking on his kids. Your grandmother went with him to pick some things up for you."

"And you stayed behind. You're not going to blame yourself for this, are you?" I asked, remembering our last conversation.

"This wasn't my fault. This one's on you," His voice had a sting to it, even though his face was a blank mask.

"On me?" I asked.

"All on you." His anger lingered in the air, even though it didn't show on his face.

Trying to wrap my brain around what he was saying was like trying to catch dandelion seeds in the wind. The drugs were making my mind too muddy. His words had a ring of truth to them.

"What attacked us?" I asked.

Vincent shrugged. "They don't know yet, but there are tests that need to be run."

"What was it doing there?" I asked.

Vincent's anger broke, marring his features. "You know why it was there." His voice came out cold.

I felt confused. The medicine was making my mind slow. Lifting my arm, I focused on where the IV entered. I looked

128

SHATTERED SOUL

it over as carefully as my sluggish brain would allow. Then I plucked it out.

"What the hell?" He raised his voice, but he didn't sound as angry as he had a few moments earlier.

Vincent grabbed my arm and put pressure on the spot where I had pulled out the IV. I took a few deep breaths and looked at him.

"I know why it was there?" I asked.

Before Vincent could reply, the door opened. I wasn't in a position to see who came in, which made me suddenly uncomfortable.

"What are you doing?" It was Rider's voice.

Vincent's features went stony. "Go back to your room."

"Not with you in here yelling." Rider came into view. He had a few bruises, but otherwise, he looked okay. Relief spread over me.

"We were having a conversation," Vincent said.

"No, you were yelling," Rider said.

"Never mind, Vincent. How are you doing?" I asked. Vincent glared at me, but I ignored him. Well, I ignored him as much as I could, considering he was holding my arm.

"I am well, but the doctor wants to run more tests." Rider looked back and forth between Vincent and me. Finally, he turned to me and said, "Do you need assistance?"

I shook my head. "I'm fine." I tried to shake Vincent off my arm.

"She ripped out her IV," Vincent said.

"The medicine tubes?" Rider asked.

"I said, I'm fine," I repeated. My mind was less muddled, but some of the pain had returned. Vincent carefully released the pressure on my arm. Once he had assured himself that I wasn't bleeding, he stepped away.

"Do we know anything about what attacked us?" I asked.

"Nothing," said Vincent. "But you can count on more of them." He turned and left the room.

129

"Does that mean there are more in the area?" Rider asked.

"I'm not sure what he means," I said.

I looked at Rider. The full impact of what Vincent said hit me. The entire attack was my fault. Without backup, I took one of the Lost who I was supposed to keep safe on a hike. Even after knowing that I had a target on my back. I didn't know anything about the thing that attacked me, but I knew there was a different monster in the area, and I went out anyway.

"I'm really sorry about what happened," I said.

Rider was quiet for a bit. "Is that what he was yelling about?"

"No, but that's what he's mad about."

"This caught both of us off guard. There is nothing to be sorry about."

"Actually." I hesitated. "You know how you thought of me as dinner?"

Rider nodded.

"Well, you aren't the only one who thinks I should be on the menu. I knew that, and I took you out."

Rider looked confused. "Are we friends?" he asked.

The question came out of nowhere. "Yes," I said without thinking. "Up until the attack we were having a great time."

"I thought so, too," Rider said. "As your friend, I did not think for a minute that you would not hold up your end of the fight. If you want to stay friends, you have to know that I will always hold up my end." Without another word, he left.

I closed my eyes. Even with my mind less muddled, I wasn't sure who was right and who was wrong anymore. The door opened again and I sighed.

"Miss Heidrich," Doctor Yelton said. "You are not permitted to pull these tubes out again."

Vincent followed the doctor in, but said nothing.

"Sorry, Doctor," I said.

"You're going to do yourself more harm than good." He inspected the IV before pulling out a new one and inserting the needle. "This is not to be removed until I remove it."

SHATTERED SOUL

I nodded.

Soon the medicine did its job and the doctor left. The pain that had flared up died away and I started drifting off.

"I can't fix my mistake if you get yourself killed," Vincent said.

I probably should have been pissed, but the medicine lured me into sleep.

When I opened my eyes again, Gran was sitting next to my bed.

"Mornin', Sugar," Gran said. "How are you feeling?"

"Better," I said. "I'm surprised actually."

"You have a few stitches in your back. Not as many as they first thought you'd need. Whatever got ya had poison in its claws, so I imagine it felt worse than it looked."

"It felt pretty bad."

"Well, they found somthin' to counteract the poison. It took a while, but seems to have done the trick. Your back is lookin' better already."

"So, I'm already on the mend."

"Dr. Yelton is runnin' more tests, but he thinks you'll be out soon."

"Have you heard anything about Rider?"

"That young man is somthin' else. He's fine, but gettin' more tests run to make sure. Looks like he should be out tomorrow."

"That's great to hear," I said.

"You've had a string of co-workers come through here. I kept track of all their names for you." She read, from the back of a deposit slip, the names of everyone that stopped by, including Barry, Kyrian, and Hank, along with other field teams.

When the doctor came by, he checked some vitals and took away the pain meds. My mind started feeling less fuzzy, which was a nice change.

"Where's Logan?" I asked Gran after the doctor left.

"He's at home. He's been tryin' to convince his kids to move out here to the Farm for a while," Gran said sadly. "Jonathan flat out refuses. Susan and Gerald aren't keen on the idea either."

"Has anything happened to them?" I asked.

"No, they're all fine. Logan just worries. We talked about it this mornin'. With what's been going on, he doesn't want his family targeted. I tried to reassure him, but it wasn't any use."

"Have you picked anything up?" I asked.

"I can't see anything from here. This place is somethin' awful. I can't see in and can't see out." Gran wasn't talking about seeing in the normal sense. It must be uncomfortable for her here at the Farm, not being able to see into the future. It was as much a part of her day as waking up in the morning.

"It's probably the portals. Or maybe because there are so many Lost here." It's hard to believe that, once upon a time, Logan came to our world through a portal. Then he went back and brought his children to this side. "The portals in the basement use a lot of energy. That's probably what keeps you blocked."

"Maybe," Gran said.

I dozed half the day. Sometime after Logan returned, I was able to convince Gran to return home.

Staring into nothingness, I thought about the case. The murders and apparent kidnapping attempts swam through my brain. The strange creature attacking me didn't seem to connect with the rest of the picture. When the doctor returned, he agreed to let me put on the clothes Gran brought me, and he detached me from the IV completely.

As the medicine wore off and my mind cleared, I itched to get downstairs. What was happening while I sat in bed? Where the beast that attacked me fit into the picture didn't become any clearer. I needed to do some research. After some time spent fidgeting, I got up and poked my head out of the room. It wasn't long before I spotted Dr. Yelton and waved him down.

He wanted me to stay in bed, but after he examined me further, he didn't put up much of a fight when I told him I wanted to go downstairs.

Rider's room was next to mine. I looked in to check on him, but he wasn't there. My back ached, but it wasn't too bad. I could feel the stitches stretching my skin closed, but I didn't

SHATTERED SOUL

dwell on it. The idea that threads were sewn into my flesh, and that's what was holding it together, freaked me out, so I put it out of my head.

When I entered the control room, Vincent was the first to spot me.

CHAPTER 14

VINCENT STALKED OVER AS I settled into an empty desk near the door and booted up the computer.

"Did you pull off your IV again?" Vincent accused.

"Hello to you, too," I snapped. "The doctor disconnected them earlier today. He said I could be here." Not quite the truth, but close enough. It seemed to mollify Vincent at any rate.

"You should at least have taken a day off," he mumbled.

"Bring me up to speed," I said, ignoring the remark.

Vincent stared hard at me, apparently undecided. Then he grabbed a nearby chair and pulled it up across the desk from me.

"Two more Lost have gone missing. A minotaur and a pixie," Vincent said.

"A minotaur? But they're huge!"

"Yes, this was a farmer in Northern Missouri."

"*Is* a farmer," I corrected. "Or have we found evidence that the Lost are being killed?"

"All the killings appear to be accidents," Vincent said.

"No wonder Logan is worried about his family. If a minotaur has gone missing, none of the Lost are safe." Vincent held up his hand, and then motioned toward Barry and Kyrian. I hadn't noticed the whispered argument going on nearby.

"—didn't authorize the removal of the agent overseeing the Sanctuary," Barry said. He sounded pretty upset but he managed to keep his voice low.

"We needed the agent in the field, not on guard duty," Kyrian responded, keeping her voice level.

"We're working on getting more agents, but you've

134

overstepped your bounds. It's not your decision to make."

"I did what was necessary. The other issue is Hank," Kyrian said, guiding the conversation away from her mistake. "He's been spending time after work digging into records from the past few months."

"What type of old records?" Barry asked.

"Satellite imagery, electromagnetic readings, portal activity."

"Sounds sensible," Barry said, "I'll talk to him about his findings. Make sure you keep me updated on all activity." Barry started to walk away.

"There was one last thing, sir," Kyrian dropped her voice significantly. Barry raised his eyebrows, waiting for her to talk. She hesitated for a moment. "I heard a rumor about Special Director Hadley. He might be retiring at the end of the year."

Barry burst out laughing. He didn't bother to whisper. "That rumor floats around every three or four years. I think he floats the rumor himself to see what he can stir up. Take your mind off his job. At least for a few more years."

Barry walked away. Kyrian looked furious for a moment, but then put on her business face and nodded at Logan as he entered.

"Did you see anything?" Vincent asked, tapping his forehead. It seemed strange to see him referring to my gifts the same way as Logan.

"I didn't try," I admitted. Shifting around on my chair, I clicked the mouse a few times to make sure the computer was waking up. "There's too much electricity and vibration here. Reading the Path here is difficult to begin with. I'm not even going to try."

Glancing up, I saw Logan in conversation with Kyrian.

Vincent frowned. "We really need to work faster fixing what I've done."

"I wasn't aware we had started working on the issue." I didn't look at Vincent.

"I've been quietly reaching out to other people. No one has ever heard of putting a soul back into someone once they've started to remove it. I've started checking old records as well. It's been an all or nothing thing in the past."

"And it usually kills the person?" I asked.

Vincent flinched at the accusation. "It kills the person. Sometimes not immediately, but it doesn't take long."

"Maybe if I understood things better, about what you do, I mean." There was some small comfort knowing that Vincent was working on putting me right again. I couldn't live this way forever.

He looked unsettled. "The agency collects information on all the Lost and all the gifts they discover. Walkers don't make it a habit of adding to the agencies collection of knowledge."

I blinked at this information. "Do we really keep that much information on people?"

"As much as they can dig up."

"I've never really looked anyone up. Not even information on Readers. I'm sure there are others." I had Gran to talk to about my gifts, but what would it be like to talk to other others who share the same aptitude? "Why do you work for AIR if you don't want information to get out?"

Vincent shrugged. "Others that work here are the same way. Our talents are put to good use, but it's an agency that compiles information. The more we share, the more control the agency can exert. Logan is the same way."

Realization struck me. Logan was cagey when I brought up something he did. Even though we were close, I was an AIR agent first, his friend second. He must have been afraid that I would give the information up.

There was a catch as I let out a deep breath. "I never really thought about it that way," I said. "I've never monitored or censored anything I've said around here." Damn, was I naive? Or were they overly paranoid? I decided it wouldn't hurt to be cautious from here on out.

"You already know enough about what I do. Every soul I take is from dangerous things that shouldn't be here. But they are things that others can't easily get rid of."

SHATTERED SOUL

"That sounds like it could be difficult to deal with."

"It gets easier with time."

"Is that because you keep a part of each soul you take?" I asked.

Vincent narrowed his eyes at me. "We don't—"

"Kyrian said Rider's applying to be a field agent," Logan said. Startled, I pulled away from Vincent and went back to pressing buttons on the mouse.

"So that's why he wasn't upstairs," I said. Pulling up an incident report related to our attack, I started adding detailed notes.

"I guess he had a good time rough housing and wants to continue," Logan said.

"I'd prefer a little less action," I said.

"You have this much excitement on the coast?" Logan asked Vincent.

"It's usually pretty active. We have more people, which causes more issues, but fewer Lost. It's more active here than I was led to believe," Vincent said.

"It's been more active around here, that's for sure," I said.

"We've run into some powerful Lost. Have we had any clues about where they came from?" Vincent asked.

"Kyrian was asking the same question," Logan said. "So, my guess is no one's discovered anything yet. We should talk to Hank to see if he's found anything in the past month or so."

"I think Barry is going to have him closeted up for a while," I said. We filled Logan in on the overheard conversation.

"Kyrian is keeping a sharp eye out," Logan mused.

"I think everyone is," I said. "If Hank found anything for us, he'd let us know. It's frustrating to sit still, though. We have to start helping."

"Do you have anything in mind?" Vincent asked.

"Do the same thing we do for any other Lost that slips through," I said. "Weed through the news to find stories or rumors that match up."

"You all don't stand there and wait when they slip through at a portal?" Vincent asked.

137

"There are lines of natural energy in the land here like we said before. Sometimes we can tell early when one is about to open, but old power boils up at times," Logan said. "We don't always get a lot of warning. We usually find those that slip through portals soon enough, though."

"If that's the case, wouldn't you know if you may have missed something?" Vincent asked.

I shook my head. "Some things get pushed here, or have been here a while."

"What Cassie is referring to is the old ones," Logan said.

"The old ones?" Vincent prompted Logan.

"Been portals here for longer than anyone knows. The human race wiped out most of those Lost that slipped through when they pushed west. Some of the Lost are good at hiding, and let's face it most humans aren't good at looking. They see what they expect and nothing more. The old ones are the Lost that came through before all the electronics and gadgets could notice them."

"I don't think we have much of that problem on the West Coast," Vincent said.

"It's a population difference," I said. "The West Coast is more densely populated, as is the East Coast. We tend to sprawl here in the Midwest. Old ones have had a chance to breed and adapt to us. Every now and again, we hear rumors of something, or odd news stories and we find a Lost that we've never seen before."

"Essy's family is like that," Logan said. "Her family was here before we were."

I tried to hold back my surprise, but I failed. Essy's family had been here that long? Not Essy herself of course, fairies had a shorter life span than humans did. But I had met with them repeatedly. It was my job to watch over them. Why had I never looked up the history of the tribe? Am I just along for the ride on this job? Am I letting myself be used without jumping in and learning more?

SHATTERED SOUL

"We had a spook light in southern Missouri," Logan said. "Rumors started in the 1800s about a strange light down there. It took us until the 1980s to figure out it was actually a Lost. Little guy only pops out at night because he's sensitive to light. It likes the moisture of a foggy night but it'll pop up whenever it's curious enough. That spook light had quite the little following for a while."

"What was it?" Vincent asked.

"Will-o-the-wisp," Logan said, looking around the room. He was done with the subject and ready to move on. He waved and went to meet the doctor as he walked in.

Knowing it would be better if I made the decision to go back upstairs on my own, I sighed and shut down the computer.

"Will you ask Logan to grab me a laptop?" I asked Vincent as I stood.

"I'll grab it. I want to try something anyway."

The question must have been visible on my face.

"I want us to meditate together," Vincent added. "I don't think the doctor will object."

Meditation had fought me since Vincent attacked my soul. It wasn't a process I enjoyed. Instead of arguing, however, I nodded and went upstairs. It was time to stop dodging the problem and start fixing it.

The doctor arrived on my heels.

"We need to do another round of tests," he said. I frowned and sat back on my bed. "Just as a precaution since you are going home soon." He took a blood sample and looked over my back. He declared it almost as good as new.

"How is that possible?" I asked as he started popping out stitches.

"We were lucky. Rider healed pretty quickly, despite having the poison in his system. Something in his blood counteracts the poison."

"How does that affect me?"

"We did a blood transfusion using Rider's blood."

My skin turned cold. "Is that safe?"

"Normally, we wouldn't try it, but Rider is part human. We received his permission and discussed the issue with your grandmother. Something in his blood also worked well with yours and increased your healing rate exponentially."

The doctor pulled the last of the stitches out. "You can lie back now. We'll be able to send you home tonight. Rider too. I'll run a few more tests. Get comfortable, and we'll let you go as soon as we can."

Vincent walked in as the doctor left. "What's wrong? Bad news?"

"What? No." I had been watching the door after the doctor's retreat. Pushing back the thought of Rider's blood coursing through my system, I smiled. "I'm going home, actually."

"Already?" Vincent asked.

"The stitches have been removed and everything. Thanks for the laptop. I'll use it at home instead of the office."

Once we were released, Vincent drove Rider and me to my house. We kept quiet the whole way.

"I'll take Rider home," Vincent said.

Rider curled up his nose at Vincent before turning to me. "Mind if I stop by tomorrow?"

"Sure." Some of my tension drained away. "See you tomorrow."

Once in my bedroom, I opened the laptop, fully intending on doing work, but my bed was too inviting to pass up.

Two flower arrangements greeted me in the kitchen the next morning. I read the card attached to a vase of vivid sunflowers and saw they were for me.

"Susan dropped those off this mornin'," Gran said. "They're from the whole family."

It was nice having Logan's family live nearby. I had assumed that Gran had picked up the other vase. Daisies, my favorite flower, filled the container. I leaned in and took a deep breath before reading the card. Vincent's name was written neatly on the tag. A smile tugged at my lips.

SHATTERED SOUL

I was consuming my second muffin of the morning and eyeing the daisies on the counter when the doorbell rang. From the other room, Gran shouted that she had the door and returned with Rider in tow.

"Nice flowers," he commented. "Why are they in here instead of outside?"

"Logan sent these and Vincent sent the daisies on the counter. These flowers were meant to be indoors."

Rider blinked and looked at each of the vases of flowers and back to me. He cleared his throat. "I missed some sort of social convention."

"Don't you worry about it, Rider. You don't need flowers to let Cassie know you're happy she's home." Gran placed a plate in front of him. "People give each other flowers for a variety of reasons here: the death of a loved one, when someone gets sick, holidays, birthdays, anniversaries, to cheer someone up, or to let them know that you care. All those are reasons to give flowers.

"It's also a part of courtin'," Gran continued. "If a man is interested in a woman, he'll give her flowers before a date, or because he wants the woman to know he's thinking of her."

Rider looked thoughtful, but his muffin had been torn to pieces instead of consumed.

"What would you do, if you were interested in a woman?" Gran asked. If she weren't an old lady, I'd probably kick her under the table.

"Gran! Rider, you don't have to answer that," I said.

He shrugged. "We do it differently." He didn't elaborate.

Rider spent most of the day asking questions about AIR. Since he was one of the Lost, I felt comfortable answering most of them. I hedged a few answers, but Rider didn't lose enthusiasm. The phone rang late in the afternoon.

"Cassie, it's Hank. Logan and Vincent are on their way to pick you up. We have a portal opening south of the city, outside Brookville."

CHAPTER 15

HOW SOON 'TIL IT OPENS?" I started to pace.
"You won't make it in time."
"Is anyone closer?"
"No. It's a new one too. Luckily, it's wooded, away from people. There are some quarries nearby, but they haven't been worked in years."

"Right, new portal." I started chewing on a nail. New portals are rare. No telling what might come pouring out of it. "Do we have a satellite in the area?"

"It should be coming up as you reach the area."

"Anything else?"

"Good luck and come back safe."

Rider wanted to come with me to help, but he hadn't been authorized yet. I asked him to stay with Gran and check in on Logan's kids. He didn't seem convinced, but agreed.

Logan, Vincent and I, didn't waste any time getting on the road. We didn't use sirens, but Hank had already radioed ahead. Sirens alerted people. Speeders got nasty looks from other drivers. With the call in, the highway patrol would avoid pulling over our government vehicle. You'd be surprised how often this kind of thing happens with police. It's not only our agency that uses this service.

Even with the extra speed on the highway, we weren't there when the portal had gained enough power to open. By the time the GPS led us to the anomaly, the portal closed. If someone crossed over, there would be no way to send them back.

We piled out of the truck. Having no idea what we would

SHATTERED SOUL

be facing, we were loaded down. We each had a backpack of supplies. We had tranquilizer rifles slung over our shoulders and guns holstered on our hips. I really hoped we didn't need our guns.

The sun went down and a chill seeped into the air. We went through the forest as quietly as possible, listening for anything that might alert us to the presence of something that didn't belong in this dimension.

I held tightly to the straps of my tranquilizer rifle. Logan motioned for us to stop, which made me grip harder, ready to pull the rifle from my shoulder at a moment's notice. His ears were unfurled, listening intently for any noise.

He motioned Vincent and me toward him.

"We aren't alone." His voice was soft but intense.

"What do you hear?" I whispered, hoping my voice didn't carry to sensitive ears.

Logan shook his head. "Not sure if it's a Lost. I hear two people, maybe more, to the southwest." He looked on the verge of saying more, but stopped and shook his head. "You two stick together. Make your way straight through the woods to the west, southwest. I'm gonna circle around to the south side. When you see people, Vincent will circle around and cover the direction they're walking. We can converge from three points. No flashlights."

I had decent night vision, so with the bright moon, I could see the shapes of the trees and branches. Logan's night vision was about as good. Vincent was an unknown.

Logan slipped silently into the night. Vincent and I crunched our way forward. I felt a bit better knowing that there was at least one other person who walked normally through the woods.

A few minutes into our walk, I noticed how very alone Vincent and I were. I bit my lower lip.

I took a deep breath. "Thank you for the flowers." I thought that would be a good place to start.

Vincent cleared his throat quietly. "You're welcome. I

haven't asked. Are you feeling better?"

"I can hold up my end tonight." My voice contained a bit of heat.

"You know that's not what I meant."

I deflated. He was being nice, and once again, I tried to turn it into something else. "Sorry. You put me on edge sometimes."

He put out his hand and grabbed mine. Warmth spread out. I pulled in a breath. When I looked at Vincent, he held a finger to his lips and dropped his hand away from mine. He looked ghostly in the dim moonlight. He pointed and I followed his gaze.

In the trees ahead, lights flickered.

I nodded and leaned in. "Time to circle around."

Vincent took my hand once more and squeezed it before dropping it and disappearing into the darkness.

I watched the spot where he disappeared, my chest tight. What the hell was I supposed to do with that? I watched for a few more moments before pushing the incident out of my head. I'll agonize over it later. It's time to work.

Time seemed to slow as I moved forward. After what seemed like hours later, I could make out the voices of two men. I stayed back, giving the others time to get into place. After five minutes, I crept forward again, staying out of flashlight range, but close enough to hear what they were saying.

"We're almost back to the truck. Quit your whining." The man's voice sent ice through my veins. It was a familiar voice. The voice belonged to the same man that had held a gun to my head not a week ago.

"It's not whining. I'm telling you the way it is. I'm out, after this job. I'm not dying 'cause some rich bitch wants a pet."

I crept forward further and pulled my rifle.

"Shut up." The man with the familiar voice was in the lead.

He stopped. Had I made a noise? The other man struggled to pull a large bag behind him. He looked as if he were running out of steam.

"Come out now!" The man in the lead said.

SHATTERED SOUL

"Seth, don't—"

"You asshole." Seth pulled a gun and moved in close to the other guy. I didn't have a shot.

I cocked the rifle as quietly as possible and took aim. Not quiet enough. Seth pulled the trigger. I froze. He missed me, but my teammates didn't know that.

Vincent appeared out of the darkness and moved forward, opening fire on Seth. A tranquilizer dart lodged directly into Seth's chest, and another in his arm.

Logan charged the area. He announced himself as a federal agent and told the men to drop their weapons.

Seth's partner raised his gun at Logan. The sound of my own shot was lost among the others. Seth's partner fell.

Logan fired at Seth as I emerged from the woods.

Seth lunged forward going for Logan. He was going to use him as a shield, same as he used me.

The tranquilizers started to take hold. Seth fell to the ground before reaching Logan, but brought his gun around. He wasn't going out without a fight. I ran forward, knowing I would never make it, but I had to try. No time!

Seth's gun fired. Logan dropped. My world threatened to shatter. My partner was down.

Vincent reached Seth and had him by the arm. It was only a touch, but Seth was unconscious in moments.

Vincent didn't let go.

"No! Vincent, stop!" I continued my charge into the area. Vincent looked up, eyes dead black. He had a death grip on the man. I had been on the receiving end of that grasp. I didn't want a piece of that man's soul inside Vincent.

"We need to interrogate him," Logan said. "Let him go."

A tightness in my chest released at the sound of Logan's voice.

Reluctantly, Vincent let go and stepped away. Seth's body fell like dead weight.

I ran to Logan. "Are you okay? Where did he shoot you?"

My breathing was coarse and loud in my ears. Over and over, I thought, please don't be hurt, please don't be hurt.

"Dodged most of the damage." Logan's voice was strong, but he didn't get up.

When I reached him, I started pulling his equipment away. I grabbed a flashlight from his gear and shined it over him. Blood dripped down Logan's side.

"Vincent, I need you!" I cried out and Vincent was there. He put pressure on Logan's side, as I fumbled off my backpack and grabbed the first-aid kit.

My mantra changed. He's okay, I can do this. I can do this. I've been through the training, so I could take care of my partner.

Vincent held the pressure while I checked Logan's pulse. It was strong.

"It's not a deep wound. A graze. Bandage me up already, we've got a job to do."

"I'm checking the injury first," I snapped. I can do this, I thought wildly. I can do this.

Logan tried to get up and winced. "I've been stabbed worse than this."

"It's deep enough that you're going to need stitches. Logan, you're bleeding out."

Logan tried to laugh, but it turned into a groan. "Girl, you have to calm down. We have a Lost out here somewhere."

That made me stop. Med kit in hand, I turned to look at the bag on the ground. Whatever lay inside was motionless. Could they have a Lost in there?

"You first, Logan," I protested.

"Vincent's got this, don't you, Vincent?" Logan asked.

I looked up at Vincent, pressing down on Logan's wound. From the discarded flashlights, I could see that his eyes were back to normal. His skin however, looked pale.

"He's never had a partner, Logan. I've got this. Vincent, cuff those men and see to the Lost."

"The men will not wake in the near future."

SHATTERED SOUL

I didn't argue, but was still glad to see Vincent pull out zip strips for cuffs. I turned my attention to Logan and put pressure on his side. The blood flow was already slowing.

I pulled back Logan's shirt. The wound slashed straight across his side. "You're definitely going to need stitches." I poured alcohol over the wound, wincing as Logan sucked in a shuddering breath. I set to work putting on butterfly sutures to hold the skin together. I maybe went a little overboard bandaging his side. "I think that's the best we can do out here."

"Nice work. I can get to my feet."

"Maybe you should wait till we're ready to leave."

"Vincent's going to need our help." Logan nodded toward Vincent.

The bag the men had been carrying lay open on the ground. Vincent checked the pulse of the creature inside. At least that's what I think he was doing. There were no arms, only legs. Four legs and a long tail. The creature looked like a large cat, except his head. The head was mostly feline, but had some cranial aspects of a person.

Logan sighed deeply. "Poor kid."

"Kid?" I asked.

"Go take a look," Logan said.

Spellbound, I moved forward. The creature was larger than a bobcat, but smaller than a mountain lion. His coat was a sandy color. His eyes were closed, but his chest rose and fell. Alive, but unconscious.

Knocked out and dragged around in a bag. I wanted to kick the men on the ground. Looking over at Seth, it was hard to see if the man breathed.

"That guy's alive, right?" I asked.

"He'll survive." Vincent's voice was monotone. All emotion pushed away. "The other man did not." He had the creature's paw in his hand and checked his watch.

"He's dead?" I asked.

Vincent didn't answer.

147

"Is the Lost okay?" I asked.

"He's going to make it. He's been drugged," Vincent said.

"Do you need any help with him?" I asked.

"We've done as much as we can from here," Vincent said. "I'll continue to monitor."

Turning my attention to the other two men wasn't easy. Vincent had both men cuffed with zip strips. I checked the pulse of the man nearest to me, but I knew what the result would be. His face was purple and the body was already starting to turn cool. My nose curled when I checked on Seth. I was loathe to touch the man that had held a gun to my head. He had a pulse and he wasn't shot.

"How long will this man remain unconscious?" I asked Vincent.

Vincent didn't look up from the Lost. "Not as long as I would like."

"Will he stay down for transport?" I asked.

"Yes," Vincent said. "We need to find a way to get this kid back to the truck."

"I'll carry him." Logan moved to his feet.

I started to protest, but the elf started stretching without wincing. Still, we needed more than one elf to take care of this mess.

I pulled out my cell phone and called Hank.

He cut out any preamble. "How'd it go?"

"We've got a—" I paused and looked at Logan.

"A sphinx." Logan had a half smile.

"We have a sphinx and two guys down. One dead, the other, well, the other is down. Logan's injured."

"Define injured." Worry crept through Hank's voice.

There had never been a day in the office that I didn't see Hank and Logan talking. I should have thought about that before I called.

"Just a graze, but he was shot."

I could hear Hank's strained breath through the phone.

SHATTERED SOUL

"Another team is en route. They should be meeting up with you in twenty."

The sphinx began to stir.

"Give them our location," I said. "Our newest Lost is waking up."

CHAPTER 16

THE SPHINX MEWED LIKE A kitten. Immediately, my heart melted. I wanted to cuddle up to the cat and let it know that everything would be okay. Then his claws opened wide in a stretch. They were long and sharp. His eyes popped open. He looked stricken. Terrified. Before he could talk, Logan touched his paw, spoke a few words, and injected the kid. He fell asleep in no time. The terrified look sank away into a peaceful purr.

The new team loaded the sphinx into the back of our truck. Vincent and I managed to get Seth into the back of the second truck. We left as the second team started to sweep the area to locate where the portal had opened and check for evidence of other Lost. We made our way back to the Farm.

Hank met us at the door. Once he confirmed that Logan was on his feet, he went back to work. Logan's wounds were superficial, but I hovered outside the room while the doctor stitched him up.

He stretched on the way out the room, showing no concern over his side. "You should be downstairs."

"I was heading that way," I lied.

We met up with Vincent and Hank in the main control room. Our case had finally gotten a break. We had someone in custody.

"Have they gotten anything out of the guy we picked up?" asked Logan.

"He won't be up for a few more days," replied Vincent. He shrugged. "They're trying to revive him, but they won't have much luck."

SHATTERED SOUL

Logan said. "Does anyone at the office have any theories yet?"

"Everyone is waiting for the guy we picked up to regain consciousness," Hank said. Hank seemed about as concerned as Vincent did. "They'll have to wait a bit longer."

Logan glared at Vincent. "Did you have to knock him out for so long?"

"It felt necessary," Vincent said.

Logan looked at me and I shrugged, not wanting to add details. It would be nice if we could interrogate him, but the man was brutal. He was ready to use my partner as a shield, so I wouldn't be shedding any tears for him.

"How's the sphinx?" Logan asked.

"He's sleeping off the shots," Hank said. "There's a natural portal that opens in Egypt. The Egyptian government is being contacted now."

I breathed a sigh of relief. "They'll be able to get him home?"

Hank smiled. "It'll take some time, but he'll make his way back home."

Hank pulled us into a nearby conference room.

Logan sat down at the table. "We have a few more details to work with now."

We all joined him.

Hank booted up his laptop. "Talk me through what happened."

We walked him through our night in the woods. When we made it to the conversation the men were having, Hank paused, his fingers no longer flying over the keyboard. "He said that someone wanted the Sphinx as a pet?"

Vincent cracked his knuckles, his face unreadable. "His exact words were, 'I'm not dying because some rich bitch wants a pet'."

Hank shifted in his chair. "This changes our approach to things. We've been expecting an organization ready to expose the Lost to the world. We've had other theories, but that was our most probable lead."

Logan looked disgusted. "Sounds like they're selling the Lost."

"But tonight was different," I said. "As far as we know, they've been picking up Lost that live here up to this point. Tonight, they were at a portal."

"They've stepped up their game," Logan said.

"With so many Lost missing—" I started.

"And from such a wide area," Vincent interjected.

"The operation must be large. There has to be a way to track them," I finished.

Hank cleared his throat. "We can start with infrared satellite sweeps. If the Lost are being kept together, we might be able to pick them up. We'll start locally and spread out our search from there."

Logan smiled. "I like your optimism."

"That'll give us some place to start," I said. "While we're waiting for that, Logan and I can talk to the sphinx. I'd like to know what took place before we got there."

Logan agreed and we broke apart. Logan and I entered a viewing area and found the sphinx pacing in an interrogation room whipping his tail around in agitation.

"Before we go in there, we need to go over a few things," Logan said.

I nodded, watching the sphinx.

"Most importantly, sphinxes tell riddles. It's like a sign of intelligence and good breeding in their world. If the kid is highborn, he may try a riddle. If he does, do not respond. Do not acknowledge that you heard the riddle."

"Why wouldn't I acknowledge it?"

"Since we're outsiders, most sphinxes will kill the person who doesn't answer their riddle correctly. That usually doesn't apply to juvenile sphinxes like our friend in there, but it's better to be on the safe side."

"And if we know the answer?"

"Then he may feel compelled to kill himself for being outwitted by an outsider."

SHATTERED SOUL

My eyes widened. "He'd kill himself for that?"

"The young ones usually don't, but again, better safe than sorry."

"Anything else I should know?" I asked.

"Remember that he's scared. Kids can lash out without thinking and this one is almost as big as you, and has bigger claws and teeth."

"Will he recognize our language?"

"He may not know much of it. If he doesn't, concentrate on reading his Path." Logan walked into the interrogation room.

After taking a few deep breaths, I followed. Concentrate on the Path. Easier said than done.

We entered the room. The sphinx stopped pacing and sat down in one corner of the room. His agitation was evident by the twitching of his tail. Logan sat in one of the chairs and I followed suit.

"I'm sorry you got wrapped up in the mess," Logan started. "We're working on a way to get you home."

The tail slowed for a moment. At least he could understand Logan. Logan smiled his infectious smile. I folded my hands on the table in front of me, trying to feel at ease in the room.

"Can you give us your name?" Logan asked.

The sphinx stood up and started pacing once again.

"We need something to call you by. We could call you kid."

I winced. Most young people did not like to be called kid. The sphinx was no different; his tail started to swing faster.

"We are trying to help you," Logan said.

The sphinx pawed at the ground and sat back down. His face scrunched up. He looked much younger than I first thought.

"Iuput," the sphinx said at last.

"It's nice to meet you, Iuput. The men you met out in the woods, they were bad men. They shouldn't have done what they did."

Iuput looked like he was going to cry. I breathed deeply a few times and did what I could to help the situation. I pulled on a feeling of safety and trust. Once that feeling welled up inside me, I let it pour through the room. I blinked a few times. The feeling filled the room. I could feel it stretch past the walls. The influence had never been so wide spread before. Another side effect, but it did the trick. The sphinx's tail stopped twitching.

"What goes on four feet in the morning, two feet at noon, and three feet in the evening?" Iuput asked.

Thankfully, Logan provided the warning against answering a riddle. The answer, man, was on the tip of my tongue, ready to spill out.

Instead, we waited. We sat in silence, ignoring the riddle that Iuput gave us.

Iuput pawed the ground a few times. He began to speak. Unfortunately, I had no idea what he said. Logan nodded and made encouraging sounds. Since I couldn't understand him, I concentrated on the Path instead, letting a trickle of power through. The room grew a little brighter. It was closer to how the Path had looked before I met Vincent.

Logan and the sphinx continued their conversation. The calming effect I produced swirled around the room. The sphinx produced similar shades of blues and yellows. Logan's Path was the usual blank slate. It would take more power to see his Path.

The sphinx stood and came over to Logan. Logan took his paw in a sort of handshake. I beamed. I wasn't sure what happened, but I thought it was a good sign. Logan led the sphinx out. After giving Iuput a short tour of the office, Logan led him upstairs.

Vincent joined me in the control room. I beamed. Vincent's blank face loosened into a brief look of happiness. Before I could say anything, Logan joined us.

"We had a good talk with Iuput. The men appeared in the sphinx world. They went through the portal, found him, shot him, and he woke up here."

My good mood drained away. "Iuput seemed to understand English. He even gave his riddle in English. Does he know if the kidnappers said anything?"

SHATTERED SOUL

Logan shook his head. "Not a word. The kid was out before he knew what happened. He did say there were three men, not two."

"No one else was found in the area," Vincent said. "The second team finished their sweep. The satellite showed only two men and the sphinx."

"They left a third man in the other world?" I asked.

"Hank said something else showed on the images." Vincent said. "It was moving too fast to be a person and it was well away from the others. We assume it was some sort of animal; a deer or something."

"Let's take a look," Logan said.

CHAPTER 17

W E WENT OVER TO THE main consoles in the room. Large displays filled the wall. The night tech brought up the recorded images. We could clearly see the bright energy as the portal snapped closed. Two men dragged a body behind them. In the far corner, an image flashed out of sight. It appeared to be an animal, as Hank suggested.

We watched the images again, slower. Nothing new was revealed.

Logan yawned and stretched. "It's almost morning. I think we call it for the day."

"Is there someone else who can talk to Iuput?" I asked.

"Someone's coming in. The kid knows a few languages. Hank found someone from the city that's going to help us out."

"Another agent?" I asked.

"Ex-agent. He runs MyTH now," Logan replied.

MyTH is a non-profit that works with Lost. It advocates for those who need it. It would have been interesting to meet the man, but the reminder that the next day was getting started made me realize my exhaustion. Too many late nights and not enough sleep. Getting back on a regular sleeping schedule seemed impossible at this point.

As the three of us made our way home, the sun broke over the horizon.

I was surprised to find Rider crashed out on the couch. He woke up as we entered. Logan gave me a look and went to talk to Gran in the kitchen. Vincent frowned and immediately headed upstairs. I watched him go before turning to Rider.

SHATTERED SOUL

At first, I was puzzled as to why he was there, and then I remembered that he kept an eye on Gran for me.

Rider beamed at me. He was definitely a morning person. I apologized and thanked him for watching over Gran. We chatted for a bit. I yawned and Rider decided it was time to leave and let me sleep.

When I entered the kitchen, Logan was already gone.

"Is it weird that Vincent's staying with us?" I asked her.

"In the beginnin', I think it was a necessity, but he wants to fix up his mistake," Gran said. "You should eat something before you head to bed. You look worn out, but I bet you haven't eaten all night."

Gran gave me a plate of warm toast and eggs. She joined me with a plate of her own.

"Vincent thinks meditating might help." I yawned.

"It might be nice if you two meditated together."

I raised an eye at her. "Do you think it will help me get my power under control?"

"I can't say for sure, but it wouldn't hurt to try."

Sleep that day didn't last as long as I would have liked. When I woke up later that day, Vincent was waiting for me in the living room. His stoic face gave a hint of a smile.

"Is Gran around?" I asked.

"She went out."

"Did work call?" I asked.

"I talked to Logan a few minutes ago. Hank said that Seth, the man we caught, isn't awake. He also said they couldn't find anything on him in the system."

"He didn't have any identification on him?"

"We think he's a professional kidnapper, but he has no record. For now, we should return our attention to you."

"To me?" I asked.

"We need to start meditation."

I took a deep breath. "We've been putting off meditation for work, but I guess there's nothing standing in the way now. Let's get this mess fixed."

Vincent's hint of a smile disappeared. His eyes tightened slightly. "This may not do anything to help."

"At least it may help me get my power under control. I need to be useful in the field again. I've had limited success in the past few days. If I only use a trickle of power at a time, I can manage to read and affect the Path."

"Are you able to do that all the time?"

I shook my head. "The slightest distraction makes things spin out of control. It feels... It feels like I'm drowning."

"Have you told anyone at the office about this change?"

"Only you and Logan know," I admitted, "and Gran of course. Do you think I should let them know?"

"No." Vincent's voice was sharper than I thought necessary. "I don't suggest telling them anything about what you are capable of."

I nodded thoughtfully. "Let's give meditation a try."

We found comfortable positions on the floor facing each other. I looked at Vincent and immediately closed my eyes. Once again, I became aware of the fact that we were entirely alone. It wasn't an uncomfortable realization.

Vincent led me through the meditation. At first, I struggled to empty my mind. I even opened my eyes a few times to see if Vincent had his eyes closed as well.

He did. I sighed and closed my eyes again. I took a few deep steadying breaths. Thoughts of the case rose. The murder of the fairy, the kidnapping of the centaur I had never met, the troll, the sphinx. Having my soul ripped out.

My eyes popped open on the last thought.

"You're too anxious," Vincent said. "Put thoughts of the case out of your head."

"Easier said than done," I mumbled.

Closing my eyes, I thought of the Path. I remembered the gentle ripple that flowed through the world. The genial mix of colors and emotions that swirled through the landscape. I sighed, content on the memories.

SHATTERED SOUL

"Describe how you enter the Path." Vincent's voice was calm, low, and soothing. Something I never expected.

"Most of the time it takes no effort at all. I could slip into the Path because I was so used to doing it."

"What do you do when it does take effort?"

I thought for a moment. "It's kind of hard to explain. I would do a short meditation on what I know the world to be. Our world. Then I reach for the edge of that knowledge. Where the knowable world stops. Then my mind stretches beyond that knowledge. Something snaps into place and I can see the Path."

"How long does that usually take?"

"It used to take a few seconds. Always less than a minute."

I heard Vincent swallow hard, but he kept his voice steady. "And now?"

I sighed. "It's unpredictable."

We sat quietly for a while, meditating. I thought over pulling a small piece of the Path instead of the whole thing. It didn't always work, but I itched to try again.

I reached for the Path, slowly and carefully. I imagine a stone wall that only let a sliver of Path peek through.

It worked.

I opened my eyes. "It worked," I said. "I thought of a way to block most of the Path."

Vincent watched me. I looked at him and he shifted uncomfortably, so I moved my gaze around the room. A dim light of the Path filled the area. Filled the world.

"It's not as strong as it used to be," I said.

I took a deep breath and tried to pull a thicker stream through.

It didn't work. The stone wall broke apart. The dim glimmer became a raging river storming over me. My breathing increased. Vincent reached forward. His intense concern crashed into me. I pulled myself back. When I closed my eyes, the bright light of the Path was still there. Concentrating hard, I pushed it away.

The effort left me panting. Fatigue rolled over me.

"Maybe we shouldn't try that again." Vincent's voice was

flat. I didn't need to look at him to know his features would be expressionless.

"It was only our first time. I expected it to take longer." That was a lie. I wanted a magic wand to be waved and for me to go back to normal. I yawned and stretched.

"Do you want to try again?" Vincent asked.

I nodded.

"This time, feel for the power, but don't open yourself up to it."

That sounded like an easy concept, but the moment I tried, it was a struggle. I closed my eyes, felt for the Path, and tried to feel what the power was.

"It's there," I said, "but it twists out of reach."

"Don't try to force it, let it move to you."

Once I allowed myself to relax, the flow moved toward me. "It's like a ripple of water and silk."

"Is there anything else there?" Vincent asked.

"I don't sense anything else," I said.

"What happens when you slowly take hold of the Path?" Vincent asked.

Mentally, I stretched out toward the Path. Right before I reached it, I saw something.

"There's a glimmer," I said, "before I take hold."

"Describe it," Vincent said in a calm voice.

"The power is there, but when I reach to it, the Power is reflected back. It shines."

"Is there only one glimmer?"

"No, it's like small diamonds glittering."

"I think this is the root of the problem."

"What do you mean?" I asked, feeling the reflected power of the Path.

"Your essence is the core of your power. It's been torn to pieces. Each of those pieces is reflecting the Path. It's amplifying your Power."

There was a quaver in the Path, as excitement broke my concentration. I was engulfed. Trying to use what little I had

SHATTERED SOUL

learned, I tried to step out of the Path, but it didn't work like that. The power coursed around me.

My breathing increased. Vincent was talking, but I couldn't make it out. Battling back the Path took all my concentration. The Path clung to me, but with extreme effort, I pushed it away. My newfound excitement had already died.

"That didn't work." I was leaning against the couch trying to catch my breath. "Maybe we can try again later."

"I'm unable to find another solution. I've been talking to a friend, another Walker, and we've gone over and over what I've done." Vincent stood up. "We hypothesized about what it would mean to pull out a soul and put it back. What it might mean if we repeated the process."

I shivered but said nothing. That sounded like the worst idea ever.

"So far we've come up with nothing that might work," he said.

"Maybe it's something that will fix itself over time," I suggested. "It's all there. Well, except for the piece you kept. Maybe it will pull itself back together?"

Vincent's eyes darkened. "Why do you insist on the idea that Walkers keep a part of what we take from others?"

I shrugged. "It's there inside you. I can see it. Surely, you can feel it."

"I—" He cut his words off and shook his head.

I rolled my eyes. If he wanted to avoid the issue, that was fine by me.

I stood up, stretched, and then headed for the kitchen. I needed food. I needed sleep. We all needed another break in the case.

Gran arrived while I was throwing together sandwiches.

Once he had food in front of him, Vincent concentrated on that, but the tightness in his eyes told me he was annoyed by our conversation. After dinner, he excused himself for the evening.

Gran and I stayed up to talk for a while. She talked about her garden, playing bingo, and Dee Dee's new boyfriend. It was a welcome reminder that the world was moving on around us while we worked the case.

Gran looked amused when I made my way downstairs. "Vincent's out. I told him it would be better if he stuck around, but he didn't listen."

Everyone listened to Gran. Vincent would learn in time that her suggestions were always dead on.

"He'll learn or he will live a life of regret." I was surprised I hadn't noticed that he was away.

Gran laughed. "I was about to make breakfast."

If Vincent and I can be apart, maybe things were starting to settle down for my soul. That put a spring in my step.

"I'll cook this morning. Pancakes? Eggs and bacon?"

"Pancakes sound perfect."

We chatted while I pulled out our pancake recipe and whipped us up breakfast. Gran did most of the cooking, but I learned how from her and Mom while growing up. Cooking skills ran in the family as much as unnatural abilities did.

"I should call the office before we eat," I said, putting the plates on the table.

"They'll call after a while." Gran winked at me.

Smiling, I dug into my breakfast.

"Logan's having a family meeting this morning," Gran said. "Did he call?"

"He didn't have to."

"Pick up anything new on Vincent?" I asked.

Gran hesitated.

"Gran?"

"I think that young man is having a difficult time. He's easier to read when the two of you are together, but even then it's difficult."

Thinking over the last week, it wasn't surprising he was having a hard time. "I can understand that," I said.

SHATTERED SOUL

Gran looked like she wanted to say more, but it was hard to tell. We cleaned up and Gran started another pot of coffee brewing. She brought down three travel mugs.

"Any idea what we're up for today?" I asked.

"Nothing specific yet."

"I'll get my gear ready. Just in case."

Gran's cat slunk into the room. He hissed at me as I walked by. My mood sank a little, but I tried to ignore the cat. What did he know anyway?

When I got back into the kitchen, Gran poured coffee, sugar, and milk into the tumblers. The phone rang and I sighed. Time to get the day started.

"Cassie," Barry was on the other end of the line, "I couldn't reach Logan on his cell, and I've got a job for your team."

CHAPTER 18

"OF COURSE, WHAT'S THE JOB?" I replied.

"We requisitioned an infrared scan of the area. Hank discovered property about an hour's drive from the Farm. According to tax records, the buildings are derelict. There is a mass of heat registering in one of the outbuildings. We're sending a team with you, but you all are going to take point on this."

"How many buildings are in the area?" I asked.

"I'll send the images to your phone. The area is isolated. It could be a meth lab, so we're trying to get more satellite imagery before bursting in." Last thing I needed was to be blown up in a meth lab. "Keep me informed. Back up will be heading your way. Get Logan and Vincent and get out there."

Barry hung up and I disconnected. The realization that I was in way over my head wasn't lost on me. We were either breaking up a methamphetamine lab or a kidnapping ring. Not exactly the relocation work that I was used to doing. I called Vincent back home, letting him know that we had a job, and then I walked over to Logan's house.

Sounds of crashing came from inside before I had a chance to knock on the back door. Wishing I had my gun, I rushed in.

Gerald was at the kitchen table reading, and barely looked up when I entered. "Hey, Cassie, Dad's in the living room."

"What's going on?" I asked, keeping my voice low.

"Jon doesn't want to leave his girlfriend and go to the Farm. I think he and Dad are coming up with a compromise of some sort."

"Does that mean you all are heading out to the Farm?" I asked.

"Uh, I don't think so."

I headed toward the noise, thrown off by his lack of concern. My hand itched for my gun, but I forced myself to peer around the corner into the living room.

Logan had Jonathan shoved into a wall. Each of them had a death grip on a spear. Jonathan tried to shove Logan off. He nearly succeeded, so Logan switched tactics. Instead of crushing the spear shaft across his son's chest, he pulled it forward, throwing Jonathan off balance. Before I knew it, Jonathan was pinned to the floor.

"Dad, I'm heading to class," Gerald called from the kitchen.

"Sure thing," Logan said, never taking his eyes off Jonathan.

Gerald took off, but I was frozen to the spot. I'd never seen Logan fight with his son. I'd never seen anyone fight with a spear. Who the hell fights with a *spear*?

Logan said something I didn't understand, and both men stopped struggling.

"Nice work," Logan said, pulling Jonathan to his feet.

"You disarmed me," Jonathan said. I looked around and noticed a spear sticking out of the wall next to the stairs.

"Yeah, but I've had more practice. Unless you run across an elf, centaur, or some big guy, you'll be good. You see a minotaur, you run the other way." Logan turned to me while Jonathan dug his spear out of the wall. "Howdy."

"Sorry to interrupt," I said.

"We were finishing up," Logan said.

"We have a job," I said.

Logan nodded and looked around the room. "Let's go ahead and leave these out," Logan said, motioning to the spears. "Tomorrow, we'll go to the range and start gun training." Logan turned to me again. "Let's saddle up."

"Vincent's on his way. Grab your stuff and I'll meet you at my house."

Surprisingly, when Logan got to my house, Jonathan was in tow with a spear in hand. Gran raised an eyebrow at Logan and he winked at her.

"We'll talk on the way," I said, gear in hand. "Gran, anything for us?"

"Check the corners and hide behind something," Gran said.

"Any idea what we're hiding from?" Logan asked.

"None at all," Gran said.

Logan took a serious look at Jonathan when he said his goodbyes. They had a short exchange and we were out the door. Vincent arrived while we were checking inventory of equipment, and without a word, he joined us and we headed to the Farm.

At the front gate, the other team met us. We put on our ear bud communicators, pulled up the location, and led the team out.

My stomach flip-flopped as we moved closer to our destination.

"Have you all done this before?" I asked. "I've never been involved in the lead team of a tactical group."

"Well," said Logan, "I've led warriors into battle and I've led small groups of people around in the field. I don't expect this to be much different."

Looking at Logan, I tried to see if he was joking. He led people into battle? My Logan? Logan moved his head and upper body to the beat of a nonexistent song.

"I've led many teams out west. Not that they've enjoyed taking directions from me," Vincent said. "We'll do fine."

"Sure," I said, "I'll follow your lead."

The trip was forty minutes of stomach-wrenching nerves. My hands started trembling. Vincent suggested that we try to meditate again on the way. It was a distraction that worked. My mind was so preoccupied with fighting that I forgot to be nervous.

Logan pulled us out of our reverie to discuss tactics.

"Let's bring up the aerial imaging again," Vincent said.

Pulling out my phone, I scrolled out to get an aerial view. Vincent and I leaned over it.

SHATTERED SOUL

"Only one road in," Vincent said. "Both vehicles will go straight in. We'll have the guys following us to the right of the building with the heat signatures. We'll pull to the left. Some can search the other outbuilding. We'll take a few agents to cover the back of the building with the heat signatures. We go in through the front. Any objections?"

"Should be four men in the back of the building," Logan added. "Two at each corner to watch the back and sides. Two men should look over the front in case something slips out."

Sitting back and listening is not my strong suit, but I knew nothing about this type of operation. I didn't even watch crime shows on TV anymore.

"That leaves four men to search the remaining buildings," Vincent said.

"There were no heat signatures from the other buildings. Someone might be in the old house, so they could concentrate in that area, and then fan out," Logan said.

"Sounds logical," Vincent said. He started doling out orders through the coms unit as we hit the gravel road that led to the area we were infiltrating.

We pulled to a stop and jumped out of the truck. My heart, already beating rapidly, started trying to break out of my chest.

Moving toward our positions was eerily quiet. Only rushed footfalls and the beating of my heart could be heard. The moment I was in place, I signaled Vincent, who was steps away from me. I tapped my forehead. Concern tightened the corner of his eyes, but he nodded and I opened the Path.

The Path came with an ease that I hadn't felt since I met Vincent. I didn't open myself up all the way to it, but what I saw finally made me useful again in the field.

Anxious traces from our team flowed around, as older traces were interlaced. I could see a well-worn path between the house and the barn that Logan, Vincent, and I were about to enter. I quietly relayed the information and Vincent redistributed a few people.

There were other traces, but they were older and harder to explain. Too many Paths flowed through the same area. Some of the Paths held fear, others anxiety, and still others hinted at a twisted dark excitement. The barn itself felt wrong. The wood that enclosed the barn was saturated with despair.

I felt trepidation as I relayed the information and dropped the Path. I didn't want to press my luck and become a liability if the Path overwhelmed my senses.

I didn't want to be in the barn. The feeling was so strong that I almost said it aloud, but where my partners went, I went. I pulled my gun. Vincent did a quiet countdown and the uncertain silence lost out to the yells of agents identifying themselves. I chambered a round and Vincent kicked in the door before the announcement cleared his lips.

Logan and I did a tactical entry, the person to the right of the door inspecting the left arch of the room, the person on the left side sweeping the right arch. Once it was clear, we entered. Vincent was behind us.

Despair leached into my skin the moment we stepped inside. We each moved around the dim barn looking for signs of life. This part of the job I had practice with. It's sometimes hard to root out a Lost from a building. I took in my surroundings, looking for possible suspects or captives. I covered the horse stalls while Logan and Vincent started for the few enclosed rooms.

We were virtually silent. I wanted some noise to push back the bleakness of the barn, but I didn't dare break the silence. I went stall by stall. A few were empty, but in others, I discovered empty cages or chains, along with a horrid stench. By the last stall, I pushed back tears. The Lost were held prisoner here. Kept locked in cages like animals. I was sure of it. Kept locked in cages like animals.

Pushing back the revulsion from the barn was difficult, but it left me with enmity, which propelled me into action.

"Clear," I whispered. The earpiece would pick up my voice without jarring the others out of their search.

SHATTERED SOUL

Joining Logan on the other side, we made quick work of the front of the barn. The rooms were similar to the stalls, mostly empty, but with cages and chains latched to walls. Logan's fury increased with each room. In the last one, there were only chains that had been pulled out of the wall. There was also blood smeared across the floor. There weren't many things that I could think of that would be able to pull chains out of the wall like this. It was probably jumping to conclusions, but I hoped that the minotaur took one of the people behind this travesty down and not the other way around. Logan's rage stormed around him and his emotion was intense, but I felt no need to move away. His anger fed my own.

"Clear," Logan said. He didn't bother to whisper. I don't think he could at this point.

Vincent was at work in the room at the back of the barn. We checked in with him. There was a lot of hay to look through, but it was clear so far. After reminding him to check the corners, as Gran advised, we set to work.

I took deep breaths to try to calm myself before starting a more thorough search. One of the teams from behind the barn came to join us, bringing gloves and evidence bags. The other team joined the search of outbuildings. We took swabs from the bloodied room and bagged them. The cleanup crew would do a better job, but we wanted as much information at our fingertips as we could get. I didn't want to wait around for details.

Searching the cages more carefully, we found them all empty. Logan pointed out a few to be hauled to the truck. We searched one room and found a few scraps of newspaper, which we dumped into evidence bags.

Logan went to search another room and I went to help Vincent.

The room was filled with loose hay and a rusted-out tractor stood to one side.

"I can try to make your search easier," I said as I entered the room. My power had come easily earlier in the day and I was

169

willing to take the risk now that the building was clear.

"Are you sure you want to try?"

"I need the practice."

"Well, your search would probably be more thorough than mine." Vincent had hay in his hair and clothes.

The Path opened as easily as it had earlier. It sent a small thrill through me to feel my power working the way it should. Stronger perhaps, but that wasn't a bad thing. It didn't take long for the despair of the barn to settle in around me. Miserable blues and anguished blacks wrapped themselves around everything. They seemed to reach out to me, wanting to be acknowledged. I took a steadying breath and gently pushed this aside. I was looking for something fresher, a Path made by a living creature that was still here.

At first, the darkness stubbornly refused to be dislodged, but with soft nudges, it receded enough for me really to study the Path. It didn't take long to pick up the traces of something small hidden in a corner of the room.

I pointed, "Over there. Small. Could be a survivor."

Vincent headed directly to where I sent him. Our coms had gone silent. Everyone was waiting to hear more about the possible survivor.

I was so wrapped up in the living readings of the Path that I almost overlooked the inanimate. There were heavy remnants of bad intentions that hung around the object.

"Vincent, wait!"

He didn't listen.

Nothing that dark around an object could lead to anything good. It was a trap and we were falling for it. Vincent reached down. Stupidly, I lunged forward.

"Out of the barn!" I yelled.

The words had barely left my mouth when Vincent lifted a small creature off the ground, but overlooked what it had been standing on. Still deep in the Path, I reached out to the dark energy surrounding us and formed a tight ball of energy around the object on the ground just as it exploded.

CHAPTER 19

VINCENT WAS KNOCKED BACK, BUT somehow he remained standing. The bomb strained underneath my hold, trying to find a way out.

Vincent ran toward me with something small in the crook of his elbow. "Everyone out of the barn!"

"We're clear," Logan said through the coms.

My grip on the bomb wavered and I looked around wildly. Sweat started to build from the exertion of holding back the explosion. There was only one thing in the room that might be strong enough to survive the blast.

"Behind the tractor!" I yelled.

Vincent grabbed my hand and hauled me behind the tractor. The moment I lost sight of the bomb, my tenuous hold fell away and the explosion ignited the room.

Tightness built in my chest and I looked at our surroundings. A hole had been blown in the side of the barn, which I could only just make out over the flames that engulfed the remains of the room.

Logan's frantic voice came over the coms. "Cassie!"

I wasn't sure what to say. Exhaustion weighed me down from the attempts to hold off the blast. The heat of the flames was pressing in on us. Our exits were blocked by fire.

"Cassie!" Logan yelled again.

"We're here, Logan," Vincent said in an even voice.

"Get out here!" Logan yelled.

Vincent gripped my hand. The creature he held in his arms shifted. There was fire everywhere I looked.

I couldn't lose Vincent, and we couldn't lose the small survivor he held.

"We're surrounded by fire," Vincent said in a steady voice through the coms. He looked at me and I could see distress in his eyes. "There's a way out, Cass, but it won't be pleasant."

I knew he was talking about walking between the worlds.

"That's not an option." Logan's voice sounded fierce.

Smoke started to fill the area. I coughed and Vincent squeezed my hand. Trying to make my overwrought mind work, I looked around, trying to think of another way out.

"It's okay," I said trying to push back the fatigue. What worked for the bomb might work with flames. "There's more than one way out. Do you have a good hold of our survivor?"

"I've got him," Vincent said.

"Trust me and stay close." Still clutching Vincent's hand, I plunged into the fire, heading straight for the barn door.

The trick worked a second time. Who knew that a monster picking me up and grinding me into a cliff face would save my life later? Twice today, I was able to mimic the creature's trick by manipulating the Path. Twice it had saved our lives. The bubble of energy surrounding us dropped the moment we were out of the fire. Using one arm, Vincent had to half hold me up as we exited the smoke filled barn. In the other, he still cradled our survivor. The Path fell away. I wasn't strong enough to hold it open anymore.

Agents ran up as we moved away from the fire.

Logan grabbed the bundle from Vincent. Vincent didn't protest. He did seem surprised however, that another agent clapped him on the back before grabbing my arm. The agent let me lean heavily on him, helping me to the back of the truck where Logan stood. It felt like all energy had been wrung from me. At the back of the truck, the doors were opened. I sat to one side, out of the way, and leaned to support myself.

As stoic professionals, the other agents finished searching the other buildings. I could sense the unsettled feelings twisting through the area.

SHATTERED SOUL

Now that all were accounted for, we started assessing the damage. Logan had a first aid kit opened and was checking over the survivor.

A pixie stared up at us. He was about a foot tall with a head that looked too large for its frame. Iridescent wings sparkled in the light, but didn't move. Skin sluggishly tried to camouflage itself against Logan. The pixies protuberant eyes were wide, but he didn't try to run away.

"It's going to be okay," Logan said. "You're safe now."

No movement came from the pixie. The last time I had an encounter with pixies they tied my shoelaces and hair into knots, dumped honey on me, and tied me to a tree. Despondence was not in their nature. One of his wings appeared battered, but he was alive.

"You," I pointed at one of the other agents, "make sure the doctor is on his way." He nodded and relayed the message. He gave a thumbs up and continued to relay details as the all clear came from the final outlying building.

Logan called someone else over and told them to take care of the pixie.

"I'll take him from here," the agent said. "We can continue first aid treatment."

"He has a broken wing," I said as Logan passed the bundle over, "and he isn't responding."

"Could be hearing damage," the man said. "We'll check it while waiting for the doctor."

Logan turned his eye on me, assessing damage, and I turned mine on Vincent. He had cuts, bruises, and a nasty looking burn on one arm, which was being wrapped by someone. Once the man was finished, he looked me over, nodded to Logan, and then went to help with the pixie.

"What happened in there?" asked Logan.

I turned off my coms unit and turned to Logan who did the same.

"It was a trap," Vincent said. "Cassie pointed out the pixie.

173

He was alone. I thought he was trying to hide at first, but he wasn't camouflaging himself. I didn't notice that he was sitting on a bomb. The moment I lifted him up, the explosion went off."

Logan lowered his voice. "There's no way you could have survived a bomb explosion. Last I heard, Walkers aren't immortal, and I sure as hell know that Readers aren't."

Vincent looked at me. I slumped down further into the back of the truck.

"Remember that thing that attacked me at the Sanctuary when I was there with Rider? It threw me up and ground me into the rocks using its power. It was the first thing that came to mind. I tried it and it worked."

"That got us out too," Vincent said.

Logan looked at me with an unreadable expression. "Have you told anyone at the office about your power changing?"

I shook my head and stifled a yawn.

"I think it will be better for everyone if we leave this out of the reports. At least for now."

I was too worn out to disagree. Besides, if Logan thought it would be better, I'd follow his lead.

"Someone knew we were coming. The heat signatures were here this morning," Logan said.

"They cleared out fast," I added.

"They didn't want us to find anything," Vincent said. "We wouldn't have if that pixie had moved."

"They probably thought we'd find the survivor sooner," Logan said. "Pick up the survivor, trigger the bomb."

"Possible," Vincent said. "They could have expected the pixie to jump off as soon as they left."

"Brave pixie," Logan said.

"Your grandmother is something else," Vincent said. "Things would have been a lot worse if not for her and a lot better if I had listened to you."

We looked at the barn. Flames covered half and smoke billowed through the air. It looked like it wasn't going to last much longer.

SHATTERED SOUL

"We lost a lot of evidence in there," I said.

"We all got out," Logan said, "and that's the most important thing. What's our next move?"

"It's obvious that someone knew we were coming," Vincent said.

"It's also obvious they are keeping the Lost alive," I added. My thoughts turned to the room streaked with blood and a tremor ran though me. "Maybe not under the best of circumstances, but alive."

"They couldn't have moved everyone too far. There are a lot of missing to account for. If the plan was to expose the Lost to the world, they would have done so by now," Logan said.

"Why would these people be gathering them together?" I asked. "If they're trying to sell them, why would they have so many together? Wouldn't they sell them off as they picked them up?"

"We can guess they aren't studying them," Vincent said, "unless you all found some medical equipment?" Logan and I shook our heads. "The people that did this aren't trying to help them in any way. People treat animals better than the Lost were treated here."

Logan balled his hands into fists and nodded. "What do you do with animals you are trying to break?" Logan asked.

"These aren't animals, though," I said.

"What do you try to do to humans you are trying to break, then?" Logan's temper flared and the Path heated up around me to match the air of the burning barn.

I didn't want to answer, but Vincent spoke up. "They are breaking them to control them before selling to the highest bidder."

I pressed my hands against my stomach. I didn't respond for fear that I would lose my breakfast. I could feel the storm of the Path around Logan, as he took a few steps away and pulled out his cell phone. I could hear him talking to Jonathan, making sure everything was okay at home.

"Call everyone you can think of and tell them to be on alert," Vincent said.

I started making calls, starting with Gran. Gran agreed to call Morgan, and I contacted Rider and Travis before contacting every other Lost that I had a number for.

A call came in. Without even looking at the caller ID, I answered.

"What the hell is going on out there? Your team was supposed to report back to me as soon as you finished wrapping up there."

Vincent raised his eyebrows. Even several feet away he could make out Barry's ranting.

"We're wrapping up now," I replied, trying to keep my voice even.

"Then why are half the Lost in the state calling and asking for protection or wanting to move back to The Farm?" Barry's voice could grind stones. Unfortunately, I was the stone. "I want to see you three in my office before this day is over." Barry hung up.

It felt good for the three of us to be referred to as a team, but the thought was fleeting. Most of the agents were slowing down as the adrenaline high wore off.

"Should we have waited to contact the Lost?" I asked.

"If we don't do what we can for the people we're protecting, we shouldn't be doing this job," Vincent replied.

Sounded like a good philosophy, but I didn't think I'd mention it to Barry.

The doctor arrived. He took one look at the Pixie and left with emergency sirens blaring.

The cleanup crew was close behind, along with a civilian fire truck. Most agents kept their distance as the fire crew put out the fire. Logan, Vincent and I, went over the items we had recovered, making sure everything was tagged. As the sun started to dip, we closed up our truck and headed toward the office.

"They cleared out because they had been warned," I said. "It's like what you said earlier, Vincent. They knew we were coming."

"That bothers me," Logan said. "No one outside AIR could have known."

"And the information was precise enough that we could have suffered casualties," Vincent said.

"Someone at AIR caused this damage?" I had a hard time wrapping my brain around that type of betrayal. "Did they want us dead, too?"

"I think it's both," Logan's voice could eclipse the sun. He took a deep breath. "We already know someone wants Cassie dead, but Hank hasn't been able to find any traces of that."

"It could be any number of people at the office," I said. "Who arranged this, I mean, not who wants me dead. I don't know anyone who would want me dead."

"Vincent did at one point," Logan said, not taking his eyes off the road. "You survived where most people would have died."

"I thought we were past blaming Vincent," I said.

"Logan's not wrong," Vincent said. "I can take it for granted that I'm not guilty, but you two can't afford to do that."

This conversation was not going where I intended it to go.

"Don't go jumping ahead," Logan said. "I said at *one point*. I've watched Vincent pretty closely the past week. I think he's in the clear."

"But there are other possibilities," I said, trying to push past the idea of Vincent being wrapped up in this mess. "Who else could arrange this?"

"Pretty much anyone with computer access," said Logan.

"Possibly, but they would have been working fast. The place hadn't been abandoned long," Vincent said.

"The Paths weren't that old," I agreed.

"So, either we were told to investigate and they left in a hurry, or they cleared out and then we were told to investigate. Someone probably planted the bomb while we were on the way, although it could have happened before we left."

"That leaves most of AIR as suspects," I said. "Anyone could have overheard Barry or Kyrian discussing today's operation. Or maybe even overheard Hank report about the hot spots detected by radar."

"Leaves a lot of people," Logan said, "even ourselves."

"Barry and Kyrian weren't shy about their discussion the other day," Vincent said. "They kept it quiet but didn't go behind closed doors. As busy as the office is, I wonder if they've had other conversations that could be overheard?"

We pulled up the gates and used our card key to get through. Silently, we made our way to the office building and straight into Barry's office. As we went across the main control room floor, I took a closer look at everyone there. Who could have overheard the conversation? Who could have set this up?

Barry was alone in his office. As he talked, his face grew dark and his voice rose. In the end, his face was red and he was nearly out of breath. He made it clear that everything must go through him in the future. Not someone else in the office, but him. I managed to look properly chastised. Vincent's face was blank. Logan was rocking back and forth on his feet humming softly. I knew that Logan wouldn't have done anything different.

After being dismissed, Vincent went up to the doctor to get his arm re-wrapped. I wanted to go with him, but I wasn't sure if it was because he was my partner, or because I was starting to feel something more. It had been an intense afternoon, but I still remember the crushing feeling I had when I thought I would lose him.

That only brought more confusion. In the end, I stayed downstairs.

The day had been a long one. The items in the truck weren't going to log themselves, so after a large helping of coffee, I started schlepping everything into the office. I took careful notes, cataloging each thing. Vincent helped and even Logan poked around the contents. By the time I was done, the office was dark and only a few people sat at desks.

We had narrowed down our suspect list to AIR agents. I took note again of each person around the room. The list of suspects

SHATTERED SOUL

might be narrowed, but it was still a substantial list.

The house was dark when we returned home. Logan ghosted around the side of the house, headed for home.

Vincent and I headed straight for the stairs. The smell of smoke hung around us, and I was desperate for a shower and my bed.

On the landing, Vincent grabbed my hand before I could open my door.

"Cass, wait," he said, "I made a mistake today."

My heart skidded and I was suddenly more awake than I had been a moment ago.

"What do you mean?" I asked.

"Today at the barn. I almost killed some good agents today, including you."

"You didn't know."

"I didn't listen."

"Look, it's not your fault."

Vincent clutched my hand. "If anything had happened to you..."

Thankfully, it wasn't likely he could see my blush in the dim light.

I squeezed his hand in response. "I felt the same way."

The words were barely out when he kissed me. There was no tentativeness. It was a hard, unrestrained kiss.

CHAPTER 20

I WAS WIDE AWAKE AS THE heat built up in my body. I pulled myself into Vincent, meeting his force with my own. Deep inside, I felt connected with him as I had with no one else.

He pushed me against the wall. I pulled him against me roughly, making sure there was no space between us. We were caught up in the passion of the moment.

At least I was.

Vincent squeezed my shoulders and pushed himself away. We were both breathing heavily.

"I've wanted to do that for a while now," Vincent said.

I grabbed his arm. "Then why stop?"

"We should wait," he said. "I don't want anything to get in the way of fixing your soul. If we get distracted by this..."

The fact that he was right didn't make it any easier to walk away. Something inside me wanted connection with Vincent.

"Cassie, hon, you gotta wake up."

Startled from sleep, my eyes snapped open and I flung myself away. It took about two seconds before Gran's voice registered. It was still dark, but the light from the hallway illuminated her shape.

I glanced at the clock. Since I had been startled, my mind sluggishly turned, trying to catch up. "It's 3:30 in the morning?"

I'm not sure if I was asking a real question, but I think it came out that way.

"I know, sweetie, but you've gotta get up and get to work."

"Work called?" I asked, getting up to speed. After being chewed out by Barry last night, I wasn't looking forward to an early morning disaster.

"No, no, work didn't call, but you gotta go to work." My eyes were starting to adjust to the dark. Gran rubbed her hands together anxiously. "I've already called Logan and he'll be here in a jiff. I'll meet you downstairs."

"Gran, wait," I said, starting to move around the room, "do you know what it is?"

"I'll meet you downstairs," she said again, and shut my door behind her. After throwing my clothes on, I nearly ran into Vincent in the hall. For a moment, we stared at each other, the only light coming from downstairs. He touched my arm briefly before we headed downstairs. We made a beeline to the light in the kitchen. Logan was already there.

"Margaret, is everything okay?" Vincent asked.

Gran poured black coffee into a tumbler and shook her head.

"I just don't know," Gran said. "I don't know." She stirred up coffee with milk and sugar. "Maybe someone left the coffee maker on at work, or maybe it's something else." She poured another steaming cup into a tumbler and added a generous amount of Hershey's syrup. "It feels like something else. Something bigger." Gran filled a third tumbler with straight black coffee.

Logan looked in my direction. I combed my fingers through my hair as a means of brushing it. I stopped. The usual happy, always smiling Logan had a cloud over him. That made me draw up and really think about what was going on.

My clumsy early morning brain protested at being put to work. I closed my eyes and drew in a few deep breaths of air. The air tasted static. Concentrating hard, I tried to open only the smallest hint of the Path and I looked around the room. The air

181

around Logan was empty, which was a relief. This is how his Path had looked before my soul had been damaged.

Looking over at Gran, the Path rippled and showed me a charged storm cloud clinging to her. It resisted the usual ripples and flows of the Path. Keeping a vice like hold on my concentration, I walked over to Gran. I hesitated, not wanting to get to step into the turbulence that surrounded her.

Her eyes were wide and her hands were trembling. Taking a deep breath, I took her hand, gripped it for a moment, and then held my hand a hair above her own. The atmosphere around Gran's hand presented some resistance. I pushed my energy out through my hand, expecting it to flow into Gran's aura and chase away what lurked around her. It felt like my Path hit a glass wall. Without saying anything, we both held out our other hands, this time Gran putting her hand above my own. I forced energy out with my right hand as I tried to pull in with my left. Usually, this would have created a circuit of energy flow. Anyone can create a circuit like this. It's a great way to share energy. This time, however, there was no flow.

"Gran?" There was real fear in my voice. This made Logan and Vincent pull nearer to us, but they dared not touch us.

Gran sighed and lowered her hands.

"Gran," I said again, "you're being blocked." I tried and failed to pull the fear out of my voice. I had never been blocked before, and to my knowledge, neither had Gran. It was as if someone had put a bubble over her.

Logan frowned and moved in. He put a hand on Gran's arm. He rested it there a moment, then squeezed her arm and pulled away.

I looked up at him, hopeful. Maybe some of his hidden elfin magic could fix things.

He frowned and shook his head at me. "I thought maybe—but no, I don't feel anything."

"Vincent?" I pleaded.

Vincent came over and put a hand on my arm and a hand on Gran's. He shook his head and backed away.

SHATTERED SOUL

"You've gotta go," Gran said. She moved back over to the counter and fitted lids on our to-go cups.

"No, Gran, we have to fix this. This is—" My words tumbled away. Gran shook her head.

"It's like an itch I can't scratch, but I'm fine, sugar. You and Logan have somewhere you need to be."

It felt wrong. Deep in my heart and head, it felt wrong to leave her like that.

"We can work on this, it won't take long." There was a tremor in my voice.

"You should know better. Neither you nor I even know what this is. It could be nothin'." Gran shook her head as my words once again died away. "Look at the three of you. It's not like my hand has been cut off. I'm not standing here bleedin'. Scat, all of ya. What I do know is that you, Logan, and Vincent have to be on your way into the office." Gran smiled at our stubbornness and shooed us out.

She said it wasn't like her hand has been chopped off, I thought as I followed out the door. I wasn't so sure about that.

When we got into the truck, Logan took his usual place in the driver's seat. We were quiet.

Logan usually would have tried a pep talk at this point. He was very adept at noticing when something was dragging me down, and his determination for happiness was something that could not be conquered. This morning, he wasn't smiling and there was no cheerful humming to fill the silence. Missing the cheerful noise wasn't something that I expected.

"You heard her." I tried to fake a smile. "It could be something small."

"She's blocked," Logan said.

All attempts at putting a good natured spin on things vanished. I sniffed.

"I don't know what to do. I've never felt anything like it." Panic welled up inside of me. "I shouldn't leave her like that."

"Is there anything you could do?" Vincent asked.

183

He reached out and took my hand. If Logan noticed, he didn't say anything.

"Maybe the doctor?" I suggested.

Logan shook his head. There it is. That sinking feeling of coming up to something and falling way short. I didn't bother to reply. If I had never felt anything like it before, how could I hope to combat it? Maybe it was something natural, but no, I was fooling myself into thinking that way. I took some comfort in the warm hand wrapped around mine.

"Have Susan check in on her, will you? Or Jonathan?" I asked Logan.

"I'll call as soon as we get to the office," Logan said.

After passing through the checkpoints, we parked in the office lot next to the other work vehicles. The night field crews were out, so there weren't many cars. It was only with reluctance that I let go of Vincent's hand.

Walking into the building, we saw no signs of life. The place looked exactly like it should look at five in the morning. There was no excitement and no one running around screaming fire. Nothing to indicate what Gran might be worried about.

Logan called Susan and asked her to check on Gran. For good measure, I called Gran as well. She repeated her 'I'm fine' mantra, which did nothing to soothe my uncertainty. Logan nodded at me and we headed to the control room.

When we entered the room, there was a complete lack of activity. Lost that only came out at night tended to keep the shift as busy as we were during the day. And we had only been gone a few hours. Only a handful of the night crew, either bent over desks, or hovering around the small coffee table, was present.

There was nothing to indicate why Gran would be alarmed. People looked up when we entered, surprised that someone would be coming in at this time. Some returned to work with a nod in our direction and a few raised their hands in hello with puzzled looks on their faces. Vincent went over to a desk and booted up a computer. The nighttime technician waved Logan and me over.

SHATTERED SOUL

"A little early for you day timers, isn't it?" he asked as we walked up.

"Decided to get an early start on things," Logan said. "Everything quiet tonight?"

"Quieter than it was when you left a few hours ago. You've had an eventful week," he said.

Logan, settling in to talk, looked a little lighter and livelier. I mentioned meditation and slipped away. When I entered the room set aside for such endeavors, I was surprised to see that Vincent was already there. He was quiet in his own meditative state, so I joined him.

Feelings of agitation and depression welled up once more as I sat down, but I prodded them away. I found my center and emptied my thoughts. Once I concentrated on my energy, I started to pull it in, creating a bright ball in my mind. It was one of the many exercises I did to keep me aware of my own influence on the Path. I once again sent out a small rope-like tendril of energy to get a feel for the atmosphere surrounding me. Like home, the surrounding the area held a buzz, like static. I probed it a little, only to get pins and needles sensation.

Something else was in the air, something that called to me without words. Tentatively, I moved a tendril of energy toward the whisper in the Path. When my energy met the echoing piece in the Path, it was a near mirror image of itself, but hooked elsewhere. The tendrils wrapped warmly around each other before pulling apart. I opened my eyes and stared at Vincent. I felt lighter.

Vincent's eyes were wide. "What was that?"

"I think…" I stopped and tried to wrap my brain around the sensation. "I think I was able to sense the piece of me that you have inside."

"It felt…" Vincent shook his head and stood.

"What?"

"It felt familiar." Vincent shifted and didn't look me in the eye. "Like a part of me was anchored somewhere else."

I stood up. "I wonder if that means that I have a piece of your soul—"

"No."

I jumped at the harshness in his voice.

Vincent took a deep breath and his voice came out much softer. "Sorry, Cass. What I mean is that I wouldn't— No, I think we'd know by now if you had some of my essence."

I wasn't convinced, but I could tell he didn't want to continue the discussion, so I let it drop for now. Vincent took my hand and gave me a small smile. At his touch, I relaxed.

There was a lightening in the air, as if the pressure had changed in the room. We frowned and returned to the central office, letting go of each other on the way. Everything was quiet.

"What the—?" the technician said. The large central screen in the room started to light up. Vincent and I hurried over. A soft, but persistent alarm began going off. The other staff in the room looked up at the screens and started to make their way over to us.

The tech hit a few buttons and the large central screen winked out. It was soon replaced with a large satellite view of the surrounding area. Thick red lines started to overlap each other. Something in the air popped. The lightness was replaced by a feeling that the Path was being flattened. Pressure built up around us. I grabbed my head and staggered as the air popped again, pressure building faster.

Red lines began crisscrossing the computer screen. Over and over again, the lines appeared, and then they started to get closer together.

Vincent steadied me with concern filling his features. Apparently, I was the only one affected by the force being applied to the Path.

"What's going on?" Logan asked. He had his eyes on me, and I waved his attention back to the screen. The angry red lines were coming closer and closer together until there were seven distinct areas marked on the map. Vincent took a few steps away and sank into a chair, keeping an eye on me.

SHATTERED SOUL

The technician drew a deep breath. "Portals," he said softly. "Portals. I've never seen anything like this." His voice grew louder as he frantically started hitting keys on his keyboard. The smaller screens began displaying closer satellite views of areas around us. "Seven portals opening across the sector." A few more clicks of the keyboard and the alarm stopped.

Everyone in the room started groping in their pockets as cell phones rang. I sat down hard in a chair and fumbled my phone out of my jacket pocket. I pressed the screen and a text message popped up.

The screen read "911" in red letters. It was the office's automatic response system. I was sitting in the middle of the emergency so I ignored the text. Agents ran to their desks and started pounding on their keyboards. Phones started ringing as staff called in. All of the daytime agents seemed to be calling at once.

The technician never flinched away from the screens and continued to click the keys on his keyboard.

"You knew," he accused, without looking away. "What is this, Logan? Cassie?"

"It was Margaret," Logan said softly. "Margaret said to go to work, so we came."

"Sharp lady," Hank said admiringly as he strode into the room. "So, what are we in for? Why didn't you call anyone? That woman should be on the payroll." Hank sat down next to the tech and started pushing buttons. He looked in my direction and stopped his tapping on the keys. He glanced at Logan, then starting clicking away again.

Maybe I wasn't the only one affected, I thought, looking at Vincent's face. His face was deathly white. He leaned forward with his elbows on his knees, his hands were clenched tightly together and he shook. He was looking in our direction, but his eyes weren't focused.

The pressure suddenly lifted. Everything felt light, almost too light. It was like a spring that had been pressed tightly together, and then stretched too far apart. It left me light headed. The screens were showing red-orange glows in seven locations. All were away from populated areas except one, which appeared in the nearest town. The portal had opened on a street in the middle of town.

"These are not natural portals," Hank said, as screens started to scroll through data that seemed meaningless to me. "These are portals, ripped open."

"Are they dropping off or picking up?" asked Logan in a hurry.

"No way to tell," Hank replied. "Portals usually go both ways."

"They're dropping off," I said, as the spring of energy returned to its normal state. I had no idea how I knew it, but I knew it was true.

"Dropping off downtown?" an agent asked from behind us.

"Barry's on line four," someone called out.

Hank pressed line four on the nearby phone putting Barry on speaker. He wasted no time filling the boss in on the details.

Barry's orders were concise. "Send in the local cops to quarantine a four block radius downtown. Use code 593. Send whoever is closest downtown. Send another team north and another team east to the portals that had opened in those directions. We'll start there. Constant radio communication. Let's see what we are dealing with."

Barry paused as Hank gave the local police Code 593 quarantine activation instructions. Hank pointed to Logan and mouthed "downtown," then started talking to the police over the phone. We were out the door before the conversation ended.

CHAPTER 21

HAVING A FULL SCALE ANOMALY was a rare occasion, but our training had prepared us for many contingencies. Fairies and butterflies were fighting in my stomach as we neared downtown. We drove up to a cop car that blocked the entry to Broadway. An officer used a flashlight to direct the light amount of traffic away from the area. I flashed my badge in his direction and he waved us through. Logan angled past the police cruiser and headed downtown.

After putting in my coms earpiece and turning on the receiver, I heard other teams fanning out across five counties. Another team was headed in our direction, but there was no time to wait for them. Everyone was being pulled in. Part-time agents like Morgan were being pulled into the field, and new agents like Rider, were being pulled into the office to assist. Even Barry was leading a team.

Logan parked the truck and we all switched our coms over to a private channel. We didn't have time to think of other teams. We had a job to do.

"Cassie, you move straight down this side of the street. Vincent, stick with her. Assume there are civilians in the area."

We nodded and split apart. When we came to an intersection, we looked around the corners, Logan looking down my side of the street, Vincent and I checking his side. We watched for a while, and then moved on when nothing was spotted. On the other side of the street, we watched again in case we missed anything in our blind spots. Once again, it was still, so we crept forward. For two blocks, we continued like this. Then we heard scuffling and a squelching sound.

Up ahead sat a split-level building, with part of the building being below street level. We motioned to Logan, who quietly moved across the street to join us. He was stealthier than I would ever be as he skidded across the street. He ended up ahead of us, on the other side of the opening to a lower level of the building.

The noise left me unsettled. Almost like a rustling, but more fluid like a mixture of dead leaves and gentle running water. This area was lit by the store displays. It wasn't until we moved forward to check the blind spots under the stairs that we located the source of the noise.

Logan flashed a light at the hidden creature. My stomach instantly clenched and I fought to avoid retching. Under the stairs stood a pale gray creature, with no hair and large pointed ears. It was humanoid. When it turned toward me, I saw that the mouth extended beyond the face. The mouth was full of sharp teeth. The eyes were almost luminescent red. Blood and strips of meat clung to the creature. Some things my mind refused to make sense of. The strips of cloth and the stain of red on the ground were background noise compared the terrible being that lay below us.

We surprised the creature, but it was quickly on guard. Logan was radioing back to Hank what we were seeing.

"Vampire," Logan said quietly, "proceed with extreme caution."

I fixed my gaze on the beast below. I had never seen a vampire, but I had read enough office material to know they are not creatures soulfully lost, living forever amongst us mortals. In reality, they were horrible, savage beasts that rarely entered our world. Some are intelligent, and others are so blood crazed that, if they were smart once, it was long lost in their lust for blood. This creature was no different. It was a predator with a one-track mind.

The creature made eye contact with me and let out a screeching cry. Pulling my gun out, I saw that Logan and Vincent already had guns in their hands. Vincent was the first to pull the

SHATTERED SOUL

trigger. The vampire staggered back as the force of the bullet bit into his flesh. Then the vampire jumped. From a full floor below, it sprang up, landing close to Vincent and me. Logan called out, but didn't fire. Vincent landed another round, but the creature braced for it this time. It let out a shrill scream, and then lunged forward, reaching its long white arms out to try to snag me away. Vincent shoved me out of the way and I landed hard on the ground. My gun went flying.

Too fast. It happened too fast. Logan ran, the creature moved forward again. It moved within reaching distance of Vincent. It braced itself to receive another round while stretching its abnormally long clawed fingers. He was ready to attack Vincent. Ready to attack my partner that had already saved me from its grasp once.

I called on the Path to put in motion the same thing I performed yesterday on the bomb. Calling to that thought, I gripped the air around the creature and made a solid wall between it and Vincent. The creature's deadly strike bounced against the wall. Unfortunately, so did Vincent's bullet, which ricocheted away into a glass window. Concentrating as hard as I could, I ignored the breaking glass and moved the wall to wrap it around the beast, turning it into a cage. By the time the cage was around the vampire, I started to tremble. It took too much energy. It was far too draining to hold anything this way.

Logan and Vincent tried to maneuver around the creature.

"Whatever you're doing, you'd better think fast," I whispered, not sure if they were aware that I was holding the vampire.

With one hand out, I gripped the cage as the creature bashed around inside. It slammed itself repeatedly against the barrier. The energy it exerted only fed the cage, which was good, because my grip was already starting to fail. Barely noticing, I fell to my knees. This wasn't like yesterday. The Path fought my control over the vampire.

"Hold it a little longer," Logan yelled.

There was no way for me to answer, tied as I was to the

creature in front of me. There was only the vampire, the noise of the outside world, and me.

Logan yelled, "Now, Cassie." It startled me so completely that I gasped. The cage gripped tight around the vampire before disappearing completely. Looking weakly up at the creature, I knew we were screwed. It staggered a bit from the pressure of the cage, but not for long. Vincent slammed into the vampire, and both were gone.

CHAPTER 22

PAIN SEARED THROUGH MY CHEST. In a flash, the agony was gone.

"Vincent?" No answer. I pressed my hand against the remembered pain. "Vincent!" I yelled, trying to struggle to my feet. It was no use. I was too weak to walk.

"Cassie, Cassie, sit still!" I didn't listen. I couldn't stand so I crawled over to where Vincent disappeared.

"Vincent!" I cried out again. I turned and sat back on the ground facing Logan. "What happened? Where is he? Where is...it?" I asked.

"You did good, Cassie, but we weren't prepared for this." Logan looked at the spot where Vincent had disappeared and lowered his voice. "Vincent took care of it. He took the thing between the worlds."

"What?" I cried. "Is he coming back? Is he with that thing alone?"

"I'm sorry, Cassie, I didn't get the details." Logan flinched when I glared at him. "From what I understand about the area between the worlds, Vincent will be fine. He knows how to navigate the place. That vampire won't last long there." I mulled this over thinking Logan wouldn't lie to me. Keep things from me, yes, but I didn't think he was lying.

After scooting over to the rail surrounding the stairs, I leaned back into it.

"I need to do a sweep of the area," Logan said. "Make sure that was the only thing that came over. Wait here."

"Like hell," I said, already using the railing to pull myself up.

"Cassie--"

"Stay in sight, Logan. I'll watch you from out front." Logan fetched my gun and did a quick survey of the downstairs area. There wasn't much left of the man below. Logan hit the street.

I dragged myself outside and leaned against the building. Logan searched the street and stores, staying in sight the whole time.

Vincent was gone. He left this world with a monster. A monster we couldn't contain here with three of us. How was Vincent going to face that alone? I scrubbed my face, trying to push back tears before they fell. We could have killed it. Working together, we could have taken it down. Couldn't we? If the vampire wouldn't last long in the between world, how was Vincent going to survive there with a vampire full of blood lust?

I listened through my earpiece as the first reports came in from another team. Gremlins. East of town gets stinking gremlins while we were stuck in the middle of town with a bloodsucker. Gremlins would wreak havoc, especially close to the interstate, but they could bring them in.

Reluctantly, I left the spot where Vincent disappeared. I managed to walk back to the truck under my own steam, but I constantly scanned the area. Vincent was gone, giving no hint on when, or if, he would come back. Maybe he would be back right away? He'd only been around for a short time, but I had come to expect him to be there. I wanted him there. I wanted to sense him at home, down the hall from me. I wanted to feel his warm hand wrap itself around my own.

"We're a man down." Logan said. "We need to head back to the office."

Hank had already radioed ahead, so the police cruiser moved aside as we drove out. Logan waved and we were on our way. We passed another AIR truck as we headed toward the highway. The cleanup crew didn't waste any time.

I sat in numb silence. At the office, Logan jumped out of the truck as soon as he parked. Had he hesitated, it would have made it harder for me to go in.

SHATTERED SOUL

"We're going to need to fill out reports right away," Logan said. "Make sure you get all the details you remember down on paper."

"Yeah, sure," I said.

Logan lowered his voice. "Except for your part in holding the creature. Make it sound as though the creature paused, confused as to who to go after."

I nodded, not trusting myself to talk any further.

We made our way to the main control room where there was chaos everywhere with Kyrian was in charge. Barry, having been a field agent in the past, worked with a makeshift team thrown together at the last minute to check out a portal. They even called Morgan in to be muscle for the group. Their team had met a new centaur.

Hank looked up and nodded somberly to us the moment we walked in, but he went straight back to work. We received a few other glances, but with so many teams in the field, everyone's hands were full.

I told myself that it was better this way and that it was easier on me, not to face the stares, but Vincent was gone, and no one was mourning his passing.

Logan handed me some paperwork. I sat and stared at it while listening to the other teams making contact.

The gremlins were captured and on their way back to the office. Logan paused and started talking into his headset, giving language to use with the centaur. Since when did my partner become the linguist?

He relayed a few instructions and a few phrases. Markus, from the office, came over the line and started supplying other phrases.

"Where did Markus learn to speak centaur?" I asked with only a wisp of interest.

"Markus dated a mermaid for a while when he worked in the south." My confusion must have been evident because Logan continued. "Mermish is an offshoot of the centaur language. Or vice-versa, depending on who you're talking to. They live in the same world."

"I didn't know that," I confessed.

"I spent a few years there with the centaurs. They're interesting."

I nodded and stared at the paperwork once more. Logan made his way over to Hank. When I couldn't stand staring at the paper anymore, I got up and walked out.

A team rolled up as I walked into the parking lot. They backed their truck to the loading dock, and then went inside.

Once I was alone, I took a few deep breaths. Things were not supposed to turn out like this. Gremlins and centaurs were manageable, but a vampire? The scene downtown replayed itself in my head. Was there something else I could have done?

My vision got blurry and tears ran down my face.

A noise came from behind me and I whirled around to see Rider standing close behind me. He was worriedly looking at his cell phone.

I turned away and wiped my eyes. "Everything okay with your phone?" I asked without facing him.

"It is-" he stopped. "I do not-"

Once I was sure my face was dry, I turned to him again. "What's up?"

Rider hung his head. "The office gave me this, but I do not have your home number."

"Why do you need my home number?"

"I wanted to call your grandmother."

"I can give you her number." I held out my hand and Rider passed me the phone. His head was still down and he wouldn't look me in the eyes. "She may not be home right now. Do you need something?" I punched in the generic security code that all office phones started with and pulled up the contacts list.

"I wanted to know the social convention."

I punched in Gran's name and her cell number along with the home phone, and then I went ahead and entered Logan's and

SHATTERED SOUL

mine. I started to type in Vincent's name and stopped. I stared at the phone trying not to let fresh anguish carry me away, and after a few moments, I was able to force myself to back out of the contacts.

I made myself concentrate on the conversation. "Um, which social convention?"

"You. And the tears. And with Vincent." He couldn't finish a whole sentence. The pain in his face pulled at my heart.

"It's-" My voice cracked, forcing me to clear my throat. I moved closer to him briefly and held his arm. "It's not an easy one."

We stood in silence. I was unsure of what to say or even if I should say anything.

Scraping metal caught my attention. The truck at the loading dock rocked side to side.

I raised an eyebrow and looked at Rider.

"Should we see what is causing the rocking?" He asked.

"If the truck is rocking..."

"It is rocking."

"Right," I said and pulled my comms back up to my ear. "Hey, Hank."

"Logan's on his way out."

"Yeah. You might want to radio the team that trundled the gremlins up. Make sure they used the zip strips and not the handcuffs."

"Son of a bitch," Hank replied.

"Yeah, you may want to send someone out to gas the truck before we have to catch them all again." I pictured the gremlins turning the truck inside out. Hank hollered directions to someone and I broke our connection.

"I've never seen a gremlin," Rider said. "Are they tough?"

"Tough?" A loud screech of scraping metal on metal filled the air. "Not really. They are about four times the size of a fairy, but almost as fast. The thing about gremlins is that they can work wonders with metal, just not the wonders that you may want them to work. If they used metal cuffs on them, they'd have them off as soon as they woke up. Plastic stumps them, though." I kept an eye on the truck. The loading dock opened up and someone hooked something to the door of the truck. Soon the rocking stopped and the noise died away.

"How do you think they caught the gremlins if they are so fast?" Rider asked as the person on the loading dock left.

"Everything has its weakness. Gremlins can't resist metal. Throw a few metal strips out and wait for them to come. It wouldn't be that hard once they knew what they were dealing with. They probably got in a hurry and accidentally cuffed a few."

"The vampire, what is their weakness?"

I rung my hands together unsure if I wanted to continue the conversation. In the end, I decided he needed to know. "Vampires have a weakness for blood. If we needed to lure the one from this morning, we could have pricked a finger or something. They are extremely vicious and tough, though. You have to have a good plan before trying to lure one out." I looked around, hoping Vincent might appear out of nowhere. Could we have made a plan?

"I am sorry about Vincent," Rider said. Something in the way he said it made it sound so final.

"He's not dead," I said with emphasis. "He'll be back."

Rider nodded but didn't say anything.

"What about fairies? What are their weaknesses?" Rider asked.

Fairies were a safer topic. I could handle fairies. "Trying to butter up Cici or Essy?" Rider blushed a little but didn't respond. "Fairies are a little more complex, but they love new things, especially exotic things to eat. They don't travel far from home so you can share something that's hard for them to get. The bad side is that they may think you're trying to poison them. Better to bring more than one so they can see you eat it first."

"What do fairies eat?"

I stretched a little in an attempt to ward off some of the tiredness that remained. "Cici is already spoiled," I responded as I opened the truck door to sit inside. "Normally, they eat grubs, worms, or whatever fruits and nuts are in the area. They really love fireflies. Cici likes kiwi, which normally doesn't grow around here. To win her over, I would suggest an almond or maybe a star fruit. It's probably the same for Essy."

I looked over at the front door wondering if I should go back inside.

"What about you?" Rider asked. "What is your weakness?"

That was a surprise. I kept my eyes on the door for a moment longer before looking at Rider. "My weakness?" Vincent was the first thing that came to mind, but I shook the thought away. "That's insider information."

Rider looked confused, "What do I have to be inside of to get that information?"

That forced a half grin from me. I really needed to remember that Rider was not from around here.

Rider glanced up. Logan walked toward us across the parking lot.

"May I pick this conversation up later?" Rider asked.

"Sure," I replied.

The radio sprang back to life as Logan neared us. Another team neared their target.

Hank's voice came through the earpiece. "You all are going to want to come back to the office. Your prisoner is awake."

We sat stunned. Seth. The man who attempted to kidnap the sphinx and the fairy.

He's awake.

We can finally get some answers.

CHAPTER 23

READING THE PATH WASN'T NECESSARY to feel this man's anger. When I stepped into the room, his fury stirred the air.

"Let's get down to it. I want a deal." His eyes bored into Logan's.

Logan, looking good-natured, sat down in a chair across from him and brought up his cowboy drawl. "Now what makes you think we're in the habit of cutting deals?"

The man was cuffed to the table, but that provided me no comfort when I slid into my chair.

"You're going to deal or you get nothing from me."

"We don't even know you have anything." Logan leaned back in his chair, looking at ease. "In fact, I think you're just a little pawn in a bigger man's game. Pretty sure my friend rattled your brains around. You even have anything left upstairs?"

The man remained still. His eyes narrowed at Logan.

"Probably don't even remember your own name," Logan said.

"You're not getting my name until I get a deal." The man leered. "Stupid elf." The man spat out the words like a curse.

I raised my eyes in interest. He remembered Logan from the night we picked him up. He knew Logan was an elf without being told.

Logan remained unaffected. He pushed back his chair from the table. "What makes you think we don't already have your name?" Logan stood and tipped an imaginary hat before leaving the room. I followed behind quickly. We went behind

SHATTERED SOUL

the interrogation glass and watched the man. Logan no longer bore any trace of a smile.

"We don't have his name," I said. "Not his full name anyway."

"Yeah, but we got something from him."

I swallowed hard. "He knew you were an elf."

"He did, which means he has to have an elf, or at least have been familiar with them."

"No missing elves have come across the desk." I frowned and watched as Seth glared at the glass.

"Let's double check. Leave him to stew a bit." Logan left the room without another look back.

I watched the man for a minute before heading back to the control room. He had the answers and there had to be a way to get them out of him.

Back in the control room, things were chaotic. Barry was back. He looked worn from his short foray into the field. He stood at the monitors with Kyrian, watching for more portals. The tech had a display of where the portals had arrived. Nothing new was showing.

Hank, too, looked like he had run a marathon. His tie was undone and he slumped in a chair shuffling paper work.

"We need a list of the missing Lost," Logan said as we walked up.

"It's in the file," Hank said without looking up.

"We think someone might be missing from the file," Logan said.

I sat down at the desk next to us, logged into the system, and started looking up the information.

"There's no one missing from the file," Hank said.

"The man knows an elf when he sees one. Gotta be something there that we missed."

Hank looked up at Logan. "No offense, but you have giant ass ears. If I had never seen an elf, I'd still guess you were one."

"He knows we exist," Logan looked intense, "and he hasn't seen my ears. It's not like I go around wearing them in public."

201

Without thinking, I drew up the Path. My head pounded and blood rushed in my ears. They must have had the portals up and running in the basement levels. Even from the main floor, two stories above, I could see the Path curve down. Individual Paths were dragging low to the ground as if gravity affecting the Path had increased tenfold.

I closed my eyes and took a deep breath. The pounding stopped and I opened my eyes to look at my partner. Logan's anger was muted by worry. Outwardly, he kept himself in check, but I could see his anguish over the thought of a missing kinsman.

"Logan," I said, "I'll work with Hank. Will you call Jonathan and ask him to look in on Gran?" Hopefully hearing his family would calm his nerves.

Logan nodded and walked away. Hank and I watched him leave. Looking back at Hank, I saw his concern reflected in the Path.

"We haven't seen anything about missing elves," Hank said quietly.

"I see that most of the Lost in the area have been contacted."

Hank nodded. "MyTH helped us out there."

Something else stirred in Hank's Path as he opened a file on his computer. I watched as gray streaks stretched around him. Looking around the room, I saw that others had similar traces in their Path. Barry had dark gray wrapped around him as he talked to Kyrian. As Kyrian left the room, I saw that she had thin tendrils of gray so dark that they appeared black.

Two men from another team approached Hank. They too bore the marks. Guilt? Anxiety? Over the day's work, no doubt. Not for the first time did I wish I could read my own Path. How much guilt was I wearing from the day? We lost Vincent today. I told myself repeatedly that he'd be back, but he was still gone. Nothing could change his sacrifice.

Hank cleared his throat. "It's, ah--- well, I'm sorry about today."

I took another deep breath and dropped the Path. The only

SHATTERED SOUL

response I could muster was a nod. I turned my attention back to the computer and started poring over the notes from MyTH.

"We should call and check to see if MyTH has found anything new."

Hank cleared his throat again. "Yeah, I'll follow up. Make sure they've heard from any elves in the city."

Logan walked up with Rider while Hank was on the phone.

"Everything okay at home?" I asked.

"Yeah. Jonathan, Susan, and Gerald are over at your place. They're going to sit tight for the day." Logan was visibly relieved. Now that he knew his family was safe, he'd be better off.

"Everyone else is accounted for," Hank said as he got off the phone. "Listen, I probably shouldn't say anything, but we have to consider this."

"Consider what?" I asked.

Hank looked uncomfortable. "The timing of the guy downstairs waking up."

We stood staring blankly at Hank, waiting for him to fill in the blanks.

Hank sighed. "I told Barry about the prisoner. He remarked on the timing of Vincent disappearing."

"No." I shook my head. I wasn't even going to entertain that thought. "Vincent said it would be days before he woke up. It's been two days."

"I thought you all would want to know," Hank said watching Logan.

"Thanks for the heads up," Logan said. He watched as Barry headed our way. "Time to head back down to interrogation, then."

"I'll go with you," Barry said. "Did he give anything up when you went down there?"

"He knew Logan was an elf," I said. "That's the only thing we got from him."

Barry nodded. "I'll go down there with you. Rider, you help Hank out."

203

The three of us ran into Kyrian as we headed to interrogation.

Barry frowned and pulled Kyrian aside. "I thought I asked you to oversee portal transfers."

"I'm on my way down to sub level two now."

Barry nodded and watched her leave before heading once more to the interrogation room.

"Cassie, let us know if you see anything in there," Barry said. "Maybe it will throw him off guard."

That was not what I wanted to hear. Reading the Path would drive me to collapse, but I nodded. I took a few deep breaths and opened myself up. Barry didn't know of the changes to my power, and I wasn't about to offer anything. I did want to make sure that I held back the roaring tide of the Path before we faced Seth.

Logan didn't bother with the fake smile when the three of us entered the room.

There was no preamble. "I want to walk," Seth said.

Logan laughed, leaning forward in his chair. "That doesn't happen here. We can make sure you see the light of day every now and again, though."

"And if I get to prison and tell the world what they've chosen to ignore for so long?" Seth said.

"You'll look like the cell block crazy," Logan said.

"And if I tell you where the freaks are? Where they all are?" the man asked. "I'd say that's a fair deal for a walk."

"And you want us just to let you go. Let you at them again?" Logan's voice rose.

"Cell block crazy it is, then," Seth said.

Logan's laugh became condescending. "You getting to see the light of day was the deal. You tell us nothing and we're sticking you in a deep hole."

This was getting us nowhere. The Path only showed that the man was pissed off, but we could tell that by looking at him. I brought up a feeling of safety and trust and I struggled with the emotion. It didn't pour out of me so much as seep out. The

SHATTERED SOUL

emotion pushed at Seth's anger. The new emotion wrapped around the man and clung to him. Logan looked at me. I nodded.

"Let's start with your name," Logan said.

"Henry Smith."

Muddy sparks popped into the man's Path. I took a guess at their meaning.

"He's lying," I said.

Logan raised his eyebrows at Seth.

"Great. Another freak. It's Seth Grouse," Seth said.

I didn't comment when Logan looked my way, unsure if he was telling the truth or not this time.

"This is what happens when freaks and demons get involved in business," Seth said.

"Let's talk about that involvement," Logan said.

Seth leaned back as far as his cuffed hands would allow. "You're not getting anything else out of me."

Logan kept talking, but got nowhere. I worked myself into exhaustion trying to make the guy trust us. Nothing worked.

Dragging myself out of the chair was difficult. I uncuffed Seth from the table, ready to take him back into a holding cell. Barry opened the door.

"Excuse me, Director." Kyrian was walking up the hallway. She looked us over. "Did things go well here?" She glared sharply at our prisoner.

What was she doing here? My brain was foggy from lack of sleep. A sharp pain erupted in my lower abdomen. Seth elbowed me in the diaphragm and delivered a strong uppercut straight to my chin. I toppled over. He pulled my tranquilizer gun.

Logan reacted quicker than Seth expected. I could see Seth's face, but not Logan's. Seth's face paled and his gun wavered as he turned to shoot my partner. I'm not sure what he saw in my partner's face. The fight would be over almost as soon as it began.

A deafening shot filled the room. Seth fell to the floor. Loud whistling in my ears, caused by the gunshot, muffled out the voices.

I pushed myself upright against the wall. Kyrian held her gun. She looked too afraid to drop it. Barry calmly talked to Kyrian. He slipped in beside her and took her gun. Logan didn't bother to look at Barry or Kyrian. Instead, he came over to me. He handed me my gun and looked me over. He nodded and then checked Seth's pulse. I could tell by Logan's reaction that the man was dead.

What happened? Oh, shit. Is this my fault?

CHAPTER 24

THE BLOOD POOLING ON THE floor would never reach me, but I wanted to get away from it all the same. The ringing in my ears quietened as I pulled myself from the floor. Barry and Kyrian were talking outside the door.

"Call the cleaning crew to come down here," Barry said.

"I killed a witness." There was fear in her voice. "Did you get anything out of him before..."

"We got a name, but nothing else. We'll spin it for D.C. It will turn out."

Barry and Kyrian walked away.

My face started to swell. I sat down at the table opposite where Seth lay.

"I'll wait on the cleaners." My voice sounded foreign, dull and listless. Had I really caused all this? Our one witness was dead on the floor because I got distracted.

"Listen," I swallowed and took a deep breath, "about what happened in here. There are no excuses. I am so sorry I let this happen."

"I have a feeling this would have happened to any of us." Logan tried to look through the one-way mirror.

"Doesn't matter," I said. "He got my gun and aimed it at you."

"Even if he had shot, I would have taken him down before the drugs kicked in. He wouldn't have gotten to the other side of the table." Logan ran a hand through his hair. "Never got the chance to stop him, though."

"This doesn't look good for Kyrian," I said.

AMANDA BOOLOODIAN

"It doesn't," Logan said. "She killed our only witness."

I lowered my voice. "Lethal force seems out of character for her."

"Unless she has something to cover up."

I shifted in my seat and looked at Seth's lifeless body. "Do you think she's behind this?"

Logan shook his head. "It's suspicious, but we don't have any evidence. Let's keep our eyes on her."

We heard noises down the hall and halted our conversation. I stood as someone pushed the door fully open. The cleaning crew had arrived.

"Let's get you upstairs," Logan said.

I raised my eyebrow at him.

"Injury-induced altercation at work. We're off to see the doctor."

I had seen the doctor way too much lately.

Rider found us soon after Dr. Yelton gave the order to go home and get some rest. I wasn't going to argue with that order.

Everyone was already up when I made it downstairs the next morning. Rider and Logan were in the kitchen.

Gran patted my cheek when I entered the kitchen, and then cupped her hand over mine. "It sounds like Vincent knew what he was doin'. You've gotta trust in that. I'm sure he'll be home soon."

There was worry in her eyes. I tested the air around her as she left. Still blocked. Maybe tonight I could sit down with Gran and really explore what was going on with her. I could tell she was uncomfortable.

Rider gave me a worried look as I grabbed my coffee.

"That man hit you yesterday and you still have a bruise on your face. Should that still be there?" he asked.

SHATTERED SOUL

My hand immediately went to my face. The bruise was an ugly purple. "It'll fade in time," I said.

"But, why is it still there?" he asked.

"Humans are a bit more fragile than werewolves," Logan said.

I frowned at him. I hated the idea of being called fragile.

"I'm amazed," I said to the room at large, "that with all of the events of yesterday, there were not more people hurt, and no one seems to have seen anything."

"So, yesterday seems to have caused some confusion and kept you all busy," Rider said, "but caused very little damage over all."

"But why?" I asked.

"Maybe if we start with what could open the portals, it would help us find out why," Logan commented.

"Okay, so what opens a portal?" I started. "We know they happen naturally from time to time, when the energy builds up in an area, but that is obviously not the case here."

"Witches can open a portal," Logan added with a cowboy twang, "but there needs to be a lot of them working together to build up enough energy to open one."

"In my world," Rider said, "they are on lines of power. The lines are always strong enough to open a portal, but someone needs to guide that energy to one spot on the line to open it. It only takes about two or three people to open a line. One to open it and one or two to direct its energy, ensuring that it opens where we want it to open."

Logan nodded thoughtfully. "In my world, it took one person to open it and direct it, but that person couldn't be the one walking through. The energy is stored in certain materials. We build up the energy reserves over time, so a portal can be ready to open when we want it to. The materials we use are attuned to certain worlds, so direction can't be changed. For instance, the cloudy blue crystal I used to come here wouldn't take me to Rider's world or the centaur world, only to here."

"We've gathered information from natural portals. Our office portals use electricity to open when we need them to," I said. "A computer can use that information to direct the portal. When I first started, they mentioned something about vibration resonance. I didn't really understand it all, but Hank told me it was kind of like dialing into a radio frequency, only using vibrations."

"That's a lot of worlds that were dialed in today," said Logan.

"But they seemed random," I replied.

"Random would be easier than on purpose," Logan added.

"But there was no power source, at least not that I could see. Well, downtown had electrical lines and transformers." I mulled that over. "Most sites were away from everything though. Do we know if there was electricity near all the sites?"

"Not where the gremlins came in. We were lucky there wasn't metal around," Logan said.

"Can portals be opened remotely?" I asked.

Rider shrugged, but Logan thought the idea over. "Possibly, since there doesn't seem to have been a guide. A power source is missing. These portals were apparently random. Hank said the gremlins came from two different portals. Even the numbers seem to be random. Two in some areas, while only one in other areas."

"But when two were close together, they came from the same place," Rider added.

"Maybe something in the area is attuned to those worlds," I suggested. "We can check the historical data to see if any other natural portals have popped up in those areas over the years."

"Could explain the random locations," Logan mused. "Possibly the energy as well. Let's say that a natural portal bridged this world to the gremlins in the past, somewhere around this location. The energy would have flared in the area and died away. Much like we saw on the screens this morning. It probably would have happened in both worlds, but what about the area in the middle?"

"You mean between the worlds?" I asked.

"Had a chance to talk to Vincent some about the area between

SHATTERED SOUL

the worlds. The company doesn't know much about it, but as a Walker, Vincent's been there. The way that he described it made it sound almost like Wonderland and Hell all rolled up and thrown into space. It wraps itself around other worlds and portals bore their way through it. The thing is, once a portal bores through it, the ends close and the tunnels sometimes remain," Logan said.

"Vincent mentioned this?" I asked.

"Not in so many words. But with what he described and with what I know about portals, it might be possible. I wish he was here so we could get some more information," Logan said.

I looked around the room, once again hoping to see Vincent walking around a corner.

"If I'm right, though," Logan said, "it may only take a spark of energy to open the line."

"That was a lot of sparks at once," Rider said. "Who could do something like that?"

"Cassie here probably could, if she learned to control the Path in multiple areas at once. Vincent might be able to with his expertise. Other creatures could as well. Certain elementals, demons..." Logan's voice trailed away. I shivered at the thought of demons, but shoved the memories back down into the shadowy depths of my mind.

"Is there a way to control demons?" I asked. "Our prisoner seemed to know one."

Rider spoke up, "You said it yourself yesterday, Cassie. You have to know their weakness."

"Some demons have slipped into our world in the past," Logan said. "If someone actually brought them here, and found a way to exert some control over them? Well, it's possible they could have opened random portals."

I couldn't sit still any longer. I started washing out the coffee pot and cleaning the counters.

"Could one of those-- one of those things have blocked Gran?" I asked. My hand trembled as I scrubbed the counter down.

"Also possible, but someone local could have done that as well, maybe without even realizing it. She doesn't work for the company, but anyone inside the company would know that your Gran comes up with some pretty spectacular stuff," Logan said.

I froze. "Someone inside the company?" I asked, tossing that idea around. "I don't like the sound of it, but you're right. Kyrian has acted a bit strange."

"We don't want to rule anyone out yet." Logan snagged a cookie out of the jar. He didn't eat it, though. He turned it over and over in his hands and stared.

"Someone in the company could also have reason to get you out of the way, Cassie," Logan said.

"Me? Why would anyone want to get rid of me?" I said.

"Must have something to do with your abilities. Someone has set up a chain of events that could have easily killed you several times," Logan said.

"Gran's the actual psychic," I said.

"And now she's blocked," Logan said.

Rider let out a low growl, which I ignored.

"I've gotten to know Vincent a bit, and I don't think he started it. I think the one that sent him on your trail is the one behind this," Logan said.

"He said it was his office. The West Coast branch of the agency," I said.

"That's true, but I don't think they pulled your name out of a hat. I think someone would have had to suggest it. Maybe someone in house. Someone who knew you and knew of Margaret's abilities," Logan said.

"We go back to who gains from yesterday's events," Rider said.

"What could be gained from yesterday?" I asked.

Logan and Rider both shook their heads.

"Okay, let's try it this way. Rider, if you set up the events, why would you do it?" I asked.

Rider looked taken aback by the idea.

SHATTERED SOUL

"I'm not saying I think you did it," I added. "It's a hypothetical. Role-playing, if you will. What would make you be willing to set up the portals? What could you gain from it?"

"If we were back in my world, I would say it was a clan strategy. It is not open warfare, but it could be a way to lower another clan's status, having to deal with confusion and possible hostility." He shrugged. "Will this lower the status of the agency? Having hostiles at your doorsteps?"

"I guess it could look bad," I said. "Maybe we need to get more information on the West Coast branch of the company. What about you, Logan?" I asked. "What would you get out of yesterday?"

"Could be a way to sneak something or someone in or out of this world. So much confusion. I think we should have Hank look into a few things."

He grabbed the landline. "Hey, Hank, things calming down a bit?"

Logan asked Hank if all our boundaries were being watched and then invited Hank over after work to discuss the case.

Logan signed off and joined Rider at one of the stools at the counter.

"Hank's double checking everything. He'll keep us up to date. The dust is starting to settle."

"Good, I think we should have him do a bit of data diving for us," I said. Once again, Rider looked confused and I tried to explain how a computer gathers data, and how a person could go in and pull out data.

"Can we trust Hank?" Rider asked.

Now I was the one looking stumped. I never thought about if I should or should not trust Hank.

Logan didn't meet anyone's eye. "I think Cassie's the best judge of that."

Closing my eyes, I searched through all of my memories of Hank. Once I located all the memories, I poked into the feelings and energy of each memory. Opening my eyes, I blinked a few times. That had taken longer than I thought it would.

"Hank's safe, I think." I hated giving absolutes, but from what I knew of Hank, we could trust him. Logan nodded.

"Can you do that with all the employees?" Rider asked. "It may narrow down the list of who to trust and who not to trust."

"I don't really know everyone that well, and there is always some bias. People who don't like me or Logan would probably throw up red flags to me, even if they're good people," I said.

Logan nodded. "Best to save your energy. Concentrate on each person as we need them."

He was right. The short burst of energy I had needed to contemplate Hank was more than I wanted to use right now. Yesterday's activities had worn me down.

"Maybe we could track down the creature responsible?" suggested Rider.

"I'm not sure where we would start," I said.

"What about the creature who killed the troll and attacked you. Maybe we could track it down," Rider suggested.

"Anything that could throw you against a wall and hold you there by force of will is definitely something to consider. It could have supplied the portals with enough energy to open," Logan said.

I nodded glumly. "I copied what it did to me yesterday when we were fighting that vampire, I remembered what it did and I copied it. It didn't last as long, though."

Logan nodded. "You copied it during the explosion and you saved lives."

"Before I met that thing at the Sanctuary," I said, "I'm pretty sure I've never done anything like that before."

Gran's cat slunk into the room and hissed at me before walking out again. It only deepened my depression.

"What would we do if we caught the thing that attacked me at the sanctuary?" I asked.

"Is it different from what attacked you at the tunnel?" Logan asked lightly.

SHATTERED SOUL

Rider and I both nodded and I shivered.

"Definitely," I said.

"Well, if we catch it, maybe we could question it. If it opened the portals, it has to have some way to communicate," Logan said.

"It can talk," I said. They both looked at me and I shrugged. "Or at least mimic. Rider yelled my name and it repeated my name before flying off."

"You never mentioned that before," Logan said.

I shrugged again. "So much happened."

"Did you hear it, Rider?" Logan asked. Rider shook his head. "What did it sound like, Cassie?"

"It was sort of a hissing voice."

"You know I wouldn't ask if it weren't important," Logan said, "but think back, put yourself back there. Tell me everything you can." I looked at Logan and Rider then glanced around the rest of the room, reassuring myself that we were alone.

"Keep that cat away from me," I mumbled. Then I closed my eyes and pulled myself into the past.

CHAPTER 25

PUTTING MYSELF BACK TO THE attack in the Sanctuary was not as easy as pulling up thoughts of Hank. This memory was buried deeply in my mind. Forcing myself to talk as I went through the series of events wasn't painless either.

Ignoring the attack from Rider, I started with discovering the troll. Planting myself firmly in the past, I relived Rider running off and the feelings of fear when I realized I might be stepping on a dead troll. After that, I moved down the rock wall, escaping the dead body and the smell. The creature bloomed into my mind. This time, I recognized the recklessness of pulling my gun. It was a fleeting thought as I relived the moment. Once I slammed up against the wall, I attempted to step out of myself a bit and watch from the sidelines as the events played out. Being scared and weak was never something I liked to discuss, yet, here I was poring over every detail. It didn't work. Even though I couldn't see it, my own Path sucked me back in. I relived the fear while doling out details.

There were things I noticed which had been lost on me before. The vague shape of the creature started coming forward. The voice was a high-pitched hissing. The wall of air holding me up dissipated, but it did so because the thing took flight. I finished relaying the information with Rider showing up. When I opened my eyes, I realized I had been crying.

Rolling my eyes, I excused myself to the bathroom, cleaned off my face, and got myself under control. Exhaustion rolled in, despite all the coffee.

SHATTERED SOUL

When I came back out the guys were discussing the details. Feeling no need to rush back into it, I called Gran to check on her. She was finished at the mall. She and Dee Dee had retreated to the ceramic shop. Gran was painting a new ceramic mug for Halloween. We chatted long enough for me to remember the world outside of work existed. When I hung up, I joined Logan and Rider. They were bent over my laptop.

I looked over Logan's shoulder and checked out the screen. "That looks like a pterodactyl," I commented. "How did dinosaurs come up?"

"Not a pterodactyl, it's a sordis," Logan commented.

"Okay, I give, what's a sordis?" I said, returning to my chair.

"The sordis on the Internet is a dinosaur, but in Latin it means filth or scum. It's a word that comes from folklore and it referenced evil spirits. The dinosaur sordis is fairly small, but take a look, Cassie. Look at the wings, the body, and the tail. This ancient bird was reminiscent of the 'evil spirit' in an area of West Virginia over one hundred years ago. I've never seen one before, but I think what attacked you might look like a big one of these."

Raising one eyebrow at Logan, I looked over the small picture. A bone was on the ridge of the wing that went half way down. The wings were almost bat like, but looked furry. They were connected all the way down the length of the ancient bird, not just at joints at the top or on its back. I imagined those wings opening and closing. A chill shot through me. I closed my eyes and took a deep breath finding my center. Once I found it, I opened my eyes and handed the computer back to Logan.

"There are similarities," I admitted. "Do you think we should look it up through the company's archives?"

Logan shook his head. "I don't want to leave any tracks. I think we should ask Hank to take a look." We both glanced at the clock. "He should be over in about an hour. He's taking a long break with us, and then heading back into the office."

"He'll probably need to eat something," I commented, getting to my feet.

Hank had never been to my house before, so I put out the best welcome spread I could on short notice. I made some lemonade, some sweet tea, and coffee. I put out a tray of cookies.

Logan changed out the water in my flower arrangements. Rider looked a little glum at the flowers, so I got him busy wiping down the table and counters.

"Houses are not this clean where I am from. Not that this is a bad thing," he said hurriedly. "I've never seen anyone do it as much as you and Margaret. Cooking too, for that matter."

Logan burst out laughing. "You should have been warned, Rider. Cassie's Gran is a Southern Belle. Their houses are clean, their kids are well-mannered, and there is always something fresh to eat and drink for company."

"Southern Belle." Rider rolled the words over. "Are you a Southern Belle, Cassie?"

Logan laughed even harder. I crossed my arms and leaned against the counter waiting for his laughter to die down. Once he caught his breath, he answered Rider's question.

"Cassie was born in Missouri. She's not from the South, but she picked up some habits from her Gran and from her mother, I'm sure."

Logan had never met my mother. If he had, he'd know I learned very little from my mother.

"I've seen plenty of Southern Belle's in the movies, but none compare to Margaret," Logan said. "Not only is the house clean and ready for guests, but she's ready to kick butt and take names if it comes down to it. And she'll make you thank her for it too."

I couldn't help laughing.

The doorbell rang and I wiped my hands dry and went to answer. Once Hank settled at the table with a meal and coffee, Logan started easing him into our plan.

"We need some information tracked down," Logan said. "Someone went to trouble to make sure that Cassie here was attacked."

"We've looked into that. New protocols are in place to keep something like that from happening again," Hank said.

"That's great," I said, "but someone had to put things in motion."

Hank shook his head. "I've already dug in that hole."

"What do you mean?" I asked.

"I checked the message that sent Vincent out here. Checked the whole trail. It led to a dead end."

"A dead end?" I asked.

"I tried everything I could think of. I traced the message back and found nothing, and then I dug into our own systems, thinking I could find a trace," Hank said.

Logan clapped Hank on the back looking grateful. "You already did all that?"

Hank's downturned face turned into a grin. "Ages ago, my friend. I wish there was something else I could do to help."

"There's something else," Logan said. He filled Hank in on the sordis and our thoughts behind the issue.

"Do you think the kidnapping of the Lost is related to Cassie being on the hit list?" Hank asked.

"Well," Logan said with his twang, "it's a hell of a coincidence if it's not connected. Besides, Cassie has the best chance of connecting point A to point C with a weak trail."

"Good point," Hank said.

"We gotta make sure that our horses are reined in," Logan said. "Someone in the office isn't on the up and up."

"Maybe if we can find a motive, we could narrow down our search?" I suggested.

"What motive would anyone have for kidnapping innocents?" Rider asked.

"There could also be a power play somewhere along the way," Logan said.

"Kyrian was talking about someone retiring," I said.

Everyone seemed to mull that over.

"They're selling them." The thought left a bad taste in my

mouth as I spoke the words. "This could boil down to money."

Logan looked disgusted.

"Both possibilities, and that could help me narrow down my search," Hank said. "I'll start pulling information. I'll start with the sordis. If we have a demon running around, we need to bag it fast."

Logan's call came early the next morning.

"Did Hank find something already?" I asked, fumbling with the cell phone.

"We found them," Logan said.

My mind spun trying to catch up with Logan's words. "We found them?" Then realization struck. "All of them? The Lost are found?"

"Don't know if it's all of them, but gear up, we're about to find out."

We had our location at last. I threw on my gear and met Logan outside. We armed ourselves and met up with other teams. Rider joined Hank at the office. Everyone was under Logan's instruction as lead in the case.

"I haven't been here in years. It's still such a small town," I said, looking at the map of Eugene on the computer.

"We're putting our finger down on the whole town," Logan said. "There are three roads in and out, so we're blocking all three. Even if they weren't involved, they may have seen something. The heat signature though, it's there."

We set up a roadblock and pulled out maps at the entrance to town. Others drove through to block any other traffic that might try to enter or leave. Logan handed out directions over the earpieces and ticked off areas on the map. When he was done setting things up, I noticed something missing.

"We should check out the cave," I suggested.

220

SHATTERED SOUL

Logan was visibly tense. "What cave?"

"It's on the property that backs up to the house." Into the earpiece I added, "Hank, do our warrants cover the cave?"

"There is no cave on the map," Hank said through the coms.

"It's huge. How can there be no cave on the map?" I asked.

"Where is it located?" Hank asked.

"It's on private property behind the house," I said.

"All that land belongs to one person. It's covered in the warrants. We'll try to get more images of that area," Hank said.

Each team got into place. Once the roads were blocked, we went in. Logan and I were on the front door of the house with the heat signatures. Another team was at the back. I tensed as the door battered open and Logan announced our entry. My heart beat loudly in my chest as I went in to the room to the right and Logan went left. The stench of rotted food churned my stomach.

"I've got Lost, but no perps," Logan said through the coms.

The urge to drop my position and check on the Lost was strong, but I kept moving. My hand gripped the rifle so hard I could feel each groove in the grip. Trash littered the living room. I announced "clear," loudly. Others echoed the same in other parts of the house. I found the next room already covered, so I circled round to my partner.

"Get the doc in here," Logan said through the coms. "I want two teams going door to door. We need to know everyone that's come and gone from this town."

With my gun still in hand, I entered the room. The smell of waste overwhelmed my senses.

"Oh, hell." Logan's voice was barely audible. He had his gun away and he was looking around the room.

Lost were stuck in cages that had been stacked haphazardly on top of each other. I walked to the center of the room and stopped. Tears began to flow down my face, but I didn't care.

Logan started going cage by cage, starting with the ones by the door. "You're safe now. We're bringing in help." There was a desperate edge to his voice.

Doctor Yelton came in and started to take a quick assessment of the situation.

I wanted to rip open every cage and let each Lost run away. Most of them couldn't run. Faeries were slumped against the bottom of their cages, wings unmoving. Gnomes were usually a blurry streak. Here they lay listless in corners.

"Start opening cages," Logan said.

Numbly, I walked over to a cage. "You're safe. Wait here for the doctor." My voice trembled and threatened to break. "We're going to get you home."

Desperately, I tried to push the scene into the dark recesses of my brain. Force it down so I could focus on my job. It wasn't working.

I opened two more cages before my eyes narrowed in on a horrifying sight. I walked slowly to a cage in the corner. Its occupant wasn't moving. The closer I got, the more the stench of decay gripped the air. I turned away from the cage. We were too late. Numbness filled me like white noise. The lights were too bright, the noises too loud.

I turned my back and went to another cage. "You're safe now." It took me some time to get the words out. The doctor had already sent several Lost out the door with agents. Transporting everyone back to the Farm had already started.

"Go outside and clear your head," Logan said.

Someone stepped up to take my place and I silently left the house.

The sun mocked me with its bright rays. Taking a few deep breaths of the fresh air helped. I started to push away images of what we discovered inside the house.

Logan had a plan for me, or he wouldn't have sent me out here. I needed to move and be useful. The thought of going back inside made me cringe, but I wanted to be working.

Agents scoured the area around the house, but another set of eyes wouldn't hurt.

Other agents were already processing an empty shed. I

SHATTERED SOUL

stared at the outside of the house and made a circuit around the perimeter. My mind felt like it moved through sludge. Something was missing. All those small people inside. Where were the larger Lost?

Logan met me outside. "Let's saddle up and go see this cave."

Years ago, I came out here with friends. The cave had a wide entrance with several rooms carved out where they quarried stone. There was nothing at the entrance, but we explored the other rooms.

The minotaur was in the first room we inspected. I expected the large horned man to be raging. Instead, he was terribly wounded. There were lacerations across his body. Either whips or chains had stripped flesh from chest, back, arms, and legs. We called another team and the doctor over to the cave.

The minotaur was chained to the ground, unable to stand. I tried to talk to him, but received no response. We left some someone with him while we scouted the rest of the cave.

In another room, we found the centaur. He had fared little better. He tried to talk when we entered, but his voice was gone. His skin had a pinched look of severe dehydration. He stood, chained to a wall with a collar around his neck.

We tried without success to pull the chains from the wall. Logan sent me back to the truck to grab bolt cutters.

CHAPTER 26

GOING STRAIGHT TO THE MINOTAUR I tried to cut the chains. He watched listlessly as I struggled. Logan took the tool and used his immense strength to cut the chains while the doctor looked over his patient. He ordered a stretcher to take the man quickly back to the Farm.

The doctor looked weary. How long had we been here? How many patients had he already seen? The doctor did a cursory inspection of the centaur and ordered him back to the Farm. The doctor rushed to catch up with the minotaur.

We stayed at the cave. We inspected every inch, looking for signs of other Lost. In a small room carved out of the back of the cave, we found sets of chains drilled into a wall, but the chains were empty. Their wearers had moved on to unknown locations.

Logan called on me to read the Path. The landscape was marred with pain so strong that I couldn't read anything of use. We called in the clean-up crew and left the blighted stone behind.

One house and one cave. Most of the missing Lost were accounted for.

Back at the house, we fingerprinted everything before starting to load empty cages into the truck. We were careful to use gloved hands on everything. Clancy would be going over everything in minute detail.

Doing what I could, I read the Path in the house. Pain and despair had permanently leeched into the fabric of the Path. It bled into every fiber of the house. I followed each Path as it entered and left the house. For each of the Lost, I noted when they entered. Some left and never returned.

SHATTERED SOUL

Outside, I picked up apathy and greed. The kidnappers. Anger seethed inside me as I followed each of their Paths in and out of the house. Someone spent a good deal of time walking around outside.

It wasn't until Logan put his hand on my shoulder that I realized I had done too much. The Path tried to cling to me when I pushed it away. I gritted my teeth and tried not to waver when I stopped Reading. The world was dull and dark when I dropped the Path, but I welcomed the darkness after the intensity of emotions that surrounded us.

The sun had already sunk below the horizon. We'd been there for hours, but it felt like days.

As soon as we reached the offices, we started processing the Lost that were well enough to be returned home. It was heartening to know that some were only waiting for Logan to sign off on their discharge before they could leave. We quickly handled the ones that were ready to go home.

Checking into Clancy's progress, I found the man in tears. Similar to what I had felt in the house, he was taking in the emotions of each item of evidence. From the pain and fear of the cages down to the greed and gluttony of the trash left behind.

Leaving Clancy behind, I started helping the agents trudging through trash to find useful pieces of evidence. Grim images churned in my mind as I catalogued items.

Barry looked anxious and split his time between getting case updates and being on the phone with Washington. Hank pulled every satellite picture he could from the area. Dr. Taylor from MyTH and other medical staff were pouring into the Farm. The entire building was working toward one grueling task. Find those responsible.

Hank stopped on his way by my desk. "You might want to see to the new guy."

I scanned the room for Vincent, hope rising in my chest, and then my eyes landed on Rider.

"He looks worse off than you," Hank said.

225

He wasn't wrong. Our werewolf stood at the edge of the room looking forlorn.

"I've got him," I said.

Hank nodded and I went to Rider. I led him to a desk and we buried ourselves deeply in paperwork. We went over procedures and protocols until my mind was firmly fixed on training.

We went home for a few hours that night, but sleep was fueled by nightmares and didn't last.

The next day at the office, coffee flowed heavily. Logan pulled Rider and me into a conference room to debrief.

"There are holes in the case," I said to Logan.

Logan nodded. "Big ones."

Kyrian overheard as she walked by. As leads in the case, we consistently had Barry or Kyrian hovering around us.

"Reps from Washington will be here in two days," Kyrian said. "We can't have holes in the case."

Taking the comment personally, my cheeks turned pink and I narrowed my eyes at her. Logan, on the other hand, kept his cool.

"That's what we have," Logan said. "We don't know who's further up the line."

"Fix it." Kyrian walked off without another word.

I rubbed my temples after she left.

"What don't we know?" Logan asked.

He was getting all mentor-y again. My attention focused.

"We don't know who's above Seth in the organization," I said.

"Does there need to be anyone above Seth?" Logan asked.

"I think so," I said. "Seth was the one catching. I don't think he was the one selling. Plus, where did he find out about the different types of Lost?"

"Those that know about the Lost are pretty limited," Logan said.

"MyTH and AIR know about them," Rider said.

Logan nodded. "There are a few other non-profits. Other countries have their own agencies as well."

"Didn't you say something about secret societies before?" I asked.

"I don't expect them to be too involved," Logan said. "If they are, we'll have a hell of a time tracking them down."

I thought back over the last month of activity. "We're looking for more than someone who knows about the Lost. We're looking for someone who knows about portals too, and where specific Lost are located. They knew where to find the fairies, not exactly, but enough that they kept searching the area over and over again."

"That leads us to where we were before," Logan said. "Someone in the agency."

"Before we found the Lost, we were talking about the beast that killed the troll," Rider added. "We do not know if it plays a part in any of this."

"If it could have opened the portals, it may know who else is involved. It may even be at the top of the food chain itself," Logan said.

"I think that's where we should start. Let's go track a monster," I said.

Rider instantly looked eager.

Logan was a little more resigned. "Whatever this thing is, it's smart, Cassie. Tracking might be difficult. It could be just about anywhere."

"I don't think so," I replied. "If Rider is willing to help," he started nodding before I even got the words all the way out, "then we have the best tracker we can get. I think it's still in the area. If it opened those portals, it's probably been regaining its strength. If it's a part of this, it could also be waiting for payment. I think we have a good chance of tracking this thing down."

"What are we going to do once we track it down?" Logan asked.

"I think we need it alive," I ventured. "We need to knock it out somehow."

"I'm not sure we can use the tranquilizers with this thing without setting up some kind of ambush," Logan started. "I'm a good shot, but I need to be positioned right. We don't even know what it is, so there may not be a way to lure it out."

227

"Once we locate the thing, luring it out is going to be easy," I said with confidence. Logan looked at me thoughtfully, but Rider was still clueless.

"How do we lure it out if we do not know what it wants?" Rider asked.

"I think it'll want me," I said.

"No!" Rider said loudly. "We will not let you do that."

I crossed my arms and looked at Rider. Logan actually scooted his chair away some. "Won't let me? Look, I know you're new here and all, but this is something you need to know. You do not *let* me do anything. I wasn't asking for permission, and I certainly don't need permission. If you want to help, great. If you want to stay out of it, that's fine too. But unless anyone else has another suggestion, this is the best option we have."

Rider looked taken aback by my anger.

I turned to Logan, "I'm going to grab some gear."

He nodded but didn't say anything. Logan whispered something to Rider, but it was too low for me to hear. I glared at both of them before leaving the room.

I pulled my hair into a braid so it wouldn't get in my way and checked out the truck. The tranquilizer guns were there, so I loaded them up and made sure they were ready. I even checked the expiration date on the tranquilizers. When I first started working with Logan, expired tranqs made a job more difficult than expected. That was one mistake we'll never make again. I paused now and again in my preparation to pull myself back into my center. Once I was finished, I was calm and ready to go. When I went back into the conference room, Rider was there, but Logan was gone.

"He is contacting his family and speaking with Hank," Rider said.

I nodded and helped myself to more coffee. It was promising to be another long night. I asked Rider if there was anything in particular that he might want. He didn't apologize and didn't bring up the earlier discussion, both indicators that Logan had a talk with him.

SHATTERED SOUL

Since we last saw the creature at the Sanctuary, I called Travis on the way over. It was almost dark when we arrived and the place was clear except for the fairies. The ATVs were waiting when we arrived. Travis agreed to stand by on the short wave radios in case we needed the cavalry called in.

Logan led the way and Rider brought up the rear. We made two stops on the way out to the cliffs where the troll had been killed. Twice Rider called something out and stopped for a few moments before giving us the go ahead. By the time we reached the cliff, the night had turned cool.

We ditched the ATVs when we could take them no further and tromped through the woods that met the base of the cliffs. Well, okay, I tromped. Rider was almost as silent as Logan. We agreed to go over the area where the troll died and where I was attacked before trying to pick up any other trails. After so much time, I figured the scents of this area would have dissipated, but Rider assured me they were still strong enough to follow.

The area where the troll died didn't tell us anything new. Logan and I went back to where it attacked me, while Rider ran through the woods, following the creature's progress to where it actually met up with me. We didn't have long to wait. Rider said he made a loop through the woods ending up where I was attacked.

I closed my eyes and concentrated on that spot, trying to get a sense of where the creature went next. I closed my eyes twice, but they popped back open again. It wasn't until Logan and Rider moved closer that I felt safe enough to keep my eyes closed and concentrate. I was getting pretty good at opening only a small portion of the Path, but that trickle of power wasn't enough and I failed to see far enough back. Bracing myself, I opened the full raging power of the Path. Instantly, my breathing ratcheted up. Logan reached out to steady me. It struck me again how amazing his pattern was when viewing it this way. Equally amazing that it was hidden before now.

Pushing myself, I felt back to the time when I faced the

creature. Blacks and grays swirled in the memory of the creature's passing. The Path tried to resist the imprint the beast had made, but the energy hadn't yet been swept away. The Path of the creature went above me, over me. I looked up the face of the cliff. I told the guys where it had gone and we were off.

We walked back to the ATVs and started out. Rider was in the lead this time with Logan bringing up the rear. The trail went pretty far out of the way, but we were steadily climbing upwards. I'd never been to this part of the Sanctuary and I was all turned around from the twists and turns of the trail. Rider and Logan had a good sense of direction, however. They'd be able to lead us out if needed.

Rider dismounted the ATV and led us to the top of the cliff where the creature had disappeared. We followed it until he caught a scent. Since we had no idea where the scent led, we stuck together. Sometimes, the guys seemed to forget that I was slower. Rider and Logan were on the hunt. At one point, I found myself completely alone in the middle of nowhere and had no idea where to go. It scared me, which was good. Being scared quickly led me to being pissed off. Much easier to be in the woods alone in the middle night and be pissed off than it is to be alone and scared.

I crossed my arms and leaned against a nearby tree. "If I get stuck out here alone all night I'm going to get really ticked," I said lightly. There was no response so I raised my voice. "And if you stumble across my dead body, don't let that get in your way." It was a bit dramatic, but it worked. Rider popped into view and stayed closer to me.

We crossed back and forth through the woods, coming to the cliffs following one trail before catching a fresher trail and taking us away, over and over again.

"Rider, can you tell how old the scents are that we are following now?" We were working ourselves back away from the cliff again.

"Maybe three days old."

SHATTERED SOUL

"And the one we followed to the cliff previously?"

"Maybe four days."

I rolled my eyes and put my hands on my hips. "In other words, it's going back and forth from the cliffs each day?"

"It seems that way, but it takes a different path each time."

"Why don't you leave me back at the ATVs? You can follow the scents back and forth until you find the most recent ones. You'll get done faster that way."

"What if we run into it? Or it runs into you?" Logan asked.

"I don't think it will," I replied.

"Why not?" Rider asked.

"Because I think it killed the troll to take its cave." I tried not to look too pleased with myself.

CHAPTER 27

"THE TROLL WASN'T KILLED IN its cave." Logan said.

"Right," Rider added, getting excited. "It was killed well away from the cave. That way, no one would check the cave, and it would not smell up the place if no one found the troll."

"Nice work, Cassie," Logan added, "You could be right about this. Rider, find the most recent scents and follow them. I'll take Cassie back to the ATVs and we'll wait for you there. If you run into it, run away. Nothing else."

Rider nodded and disappeared. I couldn't tell how fast he moved, since there wasn't much noise, but I knew it was much faster than we had been moving together.

Logan led the way back to the ATVs and we sat together discussing tactics.

Rider joined us again. "Last trace of a scent ended at the top of the cliffs. It could still be in the cave below."

"Excellent," Logan said. "Here's our idea. Since you move fastest through the woods, circle way out and come out on the other side of the cave. You can wait there. I'll be across from you on the other side of the cave. Cassie is going to step out straight in front. If the thing's asleep, she'll get its attention. You and I will move back to be to the left and right of her. That way, we don't risk hitting her or each other. When it comes out, we shoot it."

Rider looked a little nervous. So Logan continued, "I also think that Cassie should keep a tranq dart in her hand. That way

SHATTERED SOUL

if it gets close enough, she can stab it with the dart. This will drop an elephant, so it'll drop whatever this is." Logan said something else under his breath, but I couldn't hear it.

We all hopped onto the ATVs and went back to the base of the cliffs. Hopefully, we had enough gas in the tanks, because I didn't want to think about walking out of here.

When we parked and moved toward the cave, I started to tense. Scenarios started playing themselves out in my head. When Logan guessed we were about half way to the cave, we stopped. This was where Rider jumped off. We'd give him twenty minutes to get into place before continuing on.

Before he disappeared into the night, Rider said, "Stay safe. I will be very disappointed if you two get hurt."

Twenty minutes later, Logan and I moved forward quietly. Crossing my fingers, I hoped Rider was in place. We walked for a while, but it seemed way too soon when Logan stopped and turned to face me. I moved up next to him. He didn't say anything, but pointed in the direction I needed to go. Bracing myself, I walked alone into the darkness.

The cliffs were white stone as high as a two or three story building. The moon bathed them in light until they seemed to glow. I couldn't have traveled more than thirty feet, but it seemed like a long walk to take on my own. Even among the trees, I felt exposed.

The mouth of the cave was obvious as I approached it. The black gaping maw waited for me at the base of the cliff. I stayed within the trees until I was in front of the cave opening. There was a small clearing, so I stayed among the edges of the trees.

Feeling alone, even though I knew my two friends were close by, I couldn't bring myself to yell into the cave. It felt too quiet to yell. Instead, I whistled.

Which led to nothing. Apparently, whistling was not going to do the trick.

If I spoke out loud, I knew my fear would seep through my voice. I pulled some energy into me, then formed it into a fine string and sent it forward. At first, it groped around and found nothing, but in the back of the cave, down a small side passage, I hit pay dirt. There was something in there. Bracing myself, I reached into the Path. The churning route the creature took in and out of the cave was visible. Standing out against its surroundings, the creature's Path of black flecked with red didn't ripple in the raging river of the path. It stood stark against its flowing background. Putting my finger on the newest Path was a force of will. I didn't want to touch the stuff. Immediately, I charged the line of blackness leading to the cave, forcing the creature to take notice, before dropping the line completely. Struggling, I closed off the Path and waited. If this turned out to be a groundhog or a bunny, I was going to feel really stupid, but not as stupid as I would have felt if I had yelled.

I felt the air around me change. It felt heavier and darker than before. Menace resonated. I brought up thoughts of clean crisp air and spread that around me on the path. I was able to keep most of the heavier atmosphere at bay.

Then that high-pitched reptilian voice said, "Cassie."

The voice stretched out the name in one long breath, which chilled me to my core. I tried to take deep breaths to calm myself, but it didn't work. There was no way to find my center; fear lived in its place.

Gripping the tree to my right, I forced myself not to move.

My body began to tremble. My flight or fight instinct kicked in and I gripped the dart. I wasn't sure when I had pulled it from my pocket, but I had it ready. When the thing fully emerged, I tried to get a good look at it. It's body was dark against the white stone. I expected the thing to be taken out as soon as it emerged, but for some reason, darts did not appear.

"Cassie," the thing hissed in a whisper, and then it raced with a speed I could not follow. Before I could suck in a gasp of surprise, it stood before me.

"Cassie brought friends. I'll play with them next." The slow voice drew out every syllable.

SHATTERED SOUL

Noises came from where I suspected Logan and Rider to be standing. They weren't talking, but struggling.

"Let them go!" I shouted at the thing. I could feel the Path connecting the creature and my friends. It held them tight. Would it crush them, like I almost crushed that vampire?

Taking a step toward the creature, I stabbed it with my dart. The creature lashed out against me with an invisible force throwing me back. I crashed roughly into a tree, but jumped back up. Rider and Logan were making strangled noises, which scared me much worse than the creature in front of me.

Jumping into the Path, I started lashing out at the creature. I made a small part of the Path solid and pushed it at the thing at a speed which alarmed even me. The creature slammed into the side of the cliff, but immediately recovered. I tried to imagine a cage around the creature and freeze only that part of the Path. Faster than I could follow, the fiend made a slash through the cage and moved to the side. It struck out at me again. Concentrating on the air around me, I made it solid, almost like the glassy smoothness that I felt surrounding Gran. Instead of lashing out once more, I copied its slashing move and slashed through the bonds of energy running between it and Logan, then between it and Rider.

My energy rapidly faded. There was no way I could keep this up. Once again, the beast thrashed out with its energy, hitting me like a whip. I fell to the ground. It rushed forward. With a band of energy rushing ahead of it, I was encircled and lifted into the air. The creature took flight.

We moved into the treetops. Trying everything I could, I fought against my cage, but I couldn't muster enough strength. The thing landed on a tree and sat there for a moment. It seemed to be catching its breath, or maybe it was wearing down too. I tried to sense around the beast to test its strength, but I found it was gaining strength. The Path rushed toward it from everywhere.

I put my hands out to my sides until they brushed up against my cage. The formed energy of the cage didn't ripple in the

Path, much like the Path of the monster. I closed my eyes and started pulling in the Path with all my might. The creature made a harsh hacking sound and started to fly again. I couldn't tell what it did or where it tried to drag me, but it didn't matter. I was determined it wasn't going to take me far.

My concentration was locked inside me. The energy I pulled in was dark. It didn't take long before my hands felt like they had been dipped in oil, but it didn't stop there. The oily feeling climbed up my arms and coated my torso. It slid down my legs, and then moved up to my head. Soon it felt like I floated in an oil slick. Breathing became difficult, but I kept pulling the energy in.

There was a jarring motion and I fell away from the creature, back to the ground, but that didn't stop my attempt to pull the blackness. It became almost like a hunger. Inside, the darkness was consuming me. My body went cold and rigid, and I pulled in more. Ideas and thoughts skidded through my brain.

Gruesome thoughts. Blood, bone, and carnage.

I reeled.

My concentration broke.

Drowning. I felt like I drowned in a sea of oily darkness. I screamed out and started clawing at my skin. Something grabbed me from behind and I lashed out, using my newly absorbed energy to bat it away.

When I used the energy, some of the morbid darkness slipped away. I began to feel a little lighter. Leaning forward, I put my hands on the ground and pushed. The Path that I had soaked up started to leave me, so I pushed harder. All the murkiness I had gathered, I pushed into the ground. Breathing became easier and I slowed. Concentrating hard, I skimmed the remaining obscene Path away from my mind and let it flow into the ground. As soon as I was clear from it, I pushed away from the area as fast as I could from the ground.

I only made it a few feet before my energy gave out. The air was lighter now, so after flopping over onto my back, I stayed

SHATTERED SOUL

where I was, sucking in as much oxygen as I could. My entire body felt numb, and I stared up at the treetops and onward into the stars. It would be so easy to stay here and not move.

I rolled over and looked around, looking for the creature and seeking out my friends.

"Logan," I whispered out, "Rider?" Please don't let them be dead, I thought over and over.

There was a tree next to me. I used it as leverage to push myself unsteadily to my feet. Wincing, I shifted my weight over to my left foot. My right leg didn't want to support me. Once I was standing, leaning heavily against the tree, I heard the snap of a twig.

"Rider," I breathed with relief. When I spoke his name, he walked out of the darkness. I couldn't make him out very well, and he stopped well away from me. "Rider, are you all right? Where's Logan? Where is that, that thing?"

"Logan is making sure it is drugged up. He is okay, Cassie." Rider's voice softly reached my ears.

Relief poured over me and I slid down the tree, thankful that I didn't have to force myself to stand any longer. Rider rushed over, but kept some distance between us.

"Cassie? Are you okay?" His voice remained quiet, as if he was unsure of what would happen if he spoke in a normal voice.

Up close, I could make out more details, and Rider did not look well.

"Rider," I gasped, holding my hand out to his face. He froze for a moment, but then leaned into my hand. His face was swollen and he held his arm close to his chest.

"It tried to crush us," he said simply. "We will be okay. Where are you hurt?"

"I, er, I'm not sure." My whole body was worn out, bruised and cold. "Something is wrong with my leg, but I think I'm okay." Then I felt it. The black energy that I threw into the ground was there. Like a pool of oil that led deep into the ground. Something pulled on that dark energy. Like taffy being pulled, it started stretching away into the woods.

"Rider, help me!" I said hurriedly. He pulled me upright and kept his good arm around me, supporting most of my weight. "Where's Logan? We have to get to him now."

"He is over there," Rider answered, pulling me up into his arm and carrying me through the trees. We followed the path where the darkness led.

Logan leaned over the creature, making sure it was restrained. The creature was unconscious, but feeding on the energy, soaking it into its pores. Rider sat me back on the ground, but kept his arm around me and supported me.

"Logan, it's pulling the energy back inside."

Logan stepped back. "What does that mean?"

I did a quick look over of Logan. He seemed bruised, but he moved around easily.

"I don't know. It's drugged, right?"

Logan nodded.

"I'm not sure then. How is it pulling in the energy?"

"Is there any way we can stop it?" Logan asked. "We need the thing alive, but maybe that's not an option."

Logan looked at me. He would never ask me to do anything more at this point. He understood that I was exhausted and injured. He would never hold it against me if I decided to do nothing else.

The understanding went both ways though. We don't kill things unless the circumstances are dire. Things get relocated or sent back, unless they are an immediate threat and there are no other options. He would do it if I asked him, but it also meant that we lost one piece of the puzzle. This creature was not working alone. Someone on this side was helping it, and we needed to know who.

Taking a deep breath, I closed my eyes and steeled myself. Opening them again, I looked down at the creature and the Path visible before me.

"I think there is something I can do." Rider made ready to say

SHATTERED SOUL

something but I overran him. "It needs to be done right away, so listen closely, because I am not sure how this is going to work.

"This thing is going to have to stay in my line of sight. I'm too tired to try anything from more than a few feet away. It's also going to take all of my concentration, so whatever you do, don't break that concentration."

"Cassie—" Rider started to say.

"Rider, it's okay," I said. "I'm going to trap the energy away from it."

"If this thing wakes up, know that I will kill it before I let it hurt anyone," Rider said.

"Agreed," I said. "Okay, let's do this. I'll let you know when it's okay to move out."

It took more effort than I thought it would. Pulling on my happiest memories, I began to bring brightness to the Path. This creature tried to live on darkness, so I was going to breathe light into its world. Before I moved the lighter Path close to the thing, I altered it. I made it reflect and repel the rest of the Path. The idea came from what surrounded Gran. Like a thin layer of glass, my creation surrounded the beast and cut all ties from it to the pool of dark energy swimming toward him. At some point, I know my feet left the ground, but I trusted that Rider would keep his word. The creature never left my sight.

Logan carried the creature out, while Rider brought me along. They took us to the ATVs, but I barely registered being placed in front of Rider or the ride out of the sanctuary. My eyes were locked on the creature the entire time, concentrating on keeping the energy away.

Once we were back at the truck, my concentration wavered.

CHAPTER 28

THE MOMENT MY FOCUS FELL, I could feel the creature pull sluggishly on the energy around us. The clean crisp energy of the Sanctuary didn't flow for the creature like the inky darkness that I had pulled from him.

Once I snapped the cage of energy back into place, I experimented. It took three tries to lower the amount of energy I used to keep the monster bound, but left enough for me to stay awake.

The trip back to the office seemed endless. I was bound to the creature but I took some comfort from knowing Rider was nearby. The truck stopped and voices sprang up around us, but no one strayed into my line of sight. When I moved out of the truck, the pain in my leg ran straight up my spine.

The only thing my mind could comprehend was pain. The enclosure around the creature dissipated. I tried to put it back up, but it was no use. The beast was unconscious, but how long would that last if it continued to leech energy from its surroundings?

"Move back," Dr. Yelton shouted.

I didn't realize we'd gathered a crowd on the loading docks.

"This should work." The doctor gave the beast a shot. "Chemical coma. It should keep him unconscious until we are ready."

Through gritted teeth, I watched. "It's- I think it's working."

"Excellent," Dr. Yelton said. "Your turn. Something for the pain." To Logan he said, "Take her upstairs." He eyed Rider. "You too, upstairs."

It didn't take long to diagnose my broken leg. Rider's arm

SHATTERED SOUL

was on the mend, but he was sent home under doctor's orders. There was work for a Reader at the office, so I was stuck.

Once the doctor reluctantly released me, I headed to the control room where Barry, Logan, and I had a short meeting.

"We have three men from Washington arriving in fourteen hours," Barry said. "I want this taken care of before that time. I'll be in on the interview. Cassie, do you need to be in the room to see what that thing is doing?"

I shook my head. "As long as I can see into the room, I can watch him."

"Do we know if it can talk?" Barry asked.

"It can at least mimic," I said.

"The chances of this thing speaking a language we know are slim," Logan said.

Barry put on a dark grin. "We'll find a way to get something out of it. Be ready in forty. Cassie, oversee the transfer from the doctor to the interrogation cell."

I sighed and made my way back to the holding area where the creature was being kept.

The doctor frowned as I entered. "Are you able to watch over this thing?"

"We've gotta see if he has any answers," I said.

"Maybe we can push the interrogation back?"

"The guys from DC are coming in tomorrow. We need this settled tonight if we can."

The doctor reached for his pocket. "I have something that may help. I really hate to suggest it..." There was hesitation from the doctor. "I think it will help."

My eyebrows leapt up when he pulled out a needle. It was odd he had the needle at the ready if he didn't feel good suggesting it. I wasn't in any condition to argue though.

"What is it?" I asked, rolling up my sleeve.

"It's experimental. You can say no to the suggestion, but I think it will help you through this."

"What's it do?"

241

"It will react in your system much like adrenaline, but not as strong. The effect should spread through you gradually and sustain your system for several hours. It's kind of a pick-me-up."

"I could use a pick-me-up," I said.

Within minutes of taking the shot, I started feeling great. The pain lessoned and I was more awake than I thought possible under the circumstances.

Before long, I found myself sitting and watching the creature through glass as it was chained down to the floor. Under the bright light of the interrogation room, I could see it clearly. It was much like the sordis that Logan had found online. Dull black hide with erratic patches of fur covering its body. It had leathery wings, which were now clipped behind it. It looked like bones were jutting out along the edges of the wings. It had stunted legs and feet with three talons. All the details were vivid, but somehow less real.

Over the next hour, the sordis slowly regained consciousness. It didn't take much from me to keep it from pulling in energy. Whatever the doctor gave me must have helped.

Logan and Barry were in place when the creature roused. Kyrian leaned forward and watched from beside me. A buzz of excitement filled the viewing room.

The sordis pushed against its bonds, both physical and those that I had wrapped around its Path. It wasn't able to flex out of the restraints. It hissed and watched the men closely. Barry let Logan take the lead.

"How long have you been here?" Logan asked.

There was no answer. Barry grinned cynically.

"Do you have a name?" Logan asked.

No answer. Logan tried questions in languages I didn't know and received no response.

Logan twisted in his chair. "Do you know Cassie?"

"Cassie," the creature hissed.

"Yes, Cassie," Logan said.

The creature tried to bat his clipped wings and hissed again.

SHATTERED SOUL

"Tell me about Cassie," Logan said.

"Cassie," the monster repeated. "In the way."

"In the way of what?" Logan asked.

"I have a deal," the sordis hissed. "Deals were made." He swung his head between Logan and Barry.

This isn't some monster, I thought as the creature formed his responses. *He's one of the Lost.* He wasn't some animal that escaped into this world.

"What kind of a deal?" Logan asked.

The sordis thrashed against his physical bonds.

"Deals will get you nowhere here," Barry said.

"Stupid human," the demon hissed. "Deals are forged. Fire awaits."

Logan's forehead crinkled. It was like trying to piece together a riddle with most of the words missing.

"Tell me about the portals," Logan asked.

"Arrangement. Portals opened and I go free," The sordis seethed.

Barry leaned forward at the table. "Arrangements and deals mean nothing here."

I pulled open the Path. The raging current pulled me in and I got a good look at Barry. Anger and fear swirled around him.

There was something else hidden in the Path. The creature gained strength that went unnoticed without reading the Path directly. It wasn't trying to thrash against its prison. It pulled strength from its cage and the air around itself.

"No," I whispered. "No, no, no."

Kyrian looked at me. Her excitement didn't wane, though it was hidden from her face. "What's wrong, Cassie?"

I didn't answer. Inside the interrogation room, Logan started eying Barry. The monster's gaze was also fixed on Barry.

From the Path, I could see the guilt that surrounded Barry was palpable as he faced the creature.

Panic welled up. I grabbed my crutches and hobbled out of the room as quickly as I could. I shoved the door to the interrogation room open and entered the roaring strength of the Path.

243

The air around us popped. Nausea welled up but I pushed myself into the room. The beast pulled together a monumental force. Chains snapped and it jumped on top of the table.

The sordis stretched up to full height. "You will pay for your broken deals."

Wind sped through the room and the beast lunged at Barry.

Logan tried to block the attack, but he was thrown back. The Path showed the force, solid as a wall, as it struck out against Logan. The demon sunk claws into Barry's arms. It pulled Barry forward so they were face to face. Fear coursed onto Barry's Path.

"What did you do?" Logan yelled, getting to his feet.

"Get this thing off me!" Barry screamed.

Deep in the Path, the ebb and flow washed over me. Grabbing the energy strung tightly around the beast, I turned it into an unseen rope and tried to pull the creature away.

It was no use. I wasn't strong enough.

I wedged air made solid between Barry and the Lost. The monster was forced away, but took a chunk of Barry with him. The beast's teeth dripped with blood. Barry leaned against a wall for support.

Logan had his gun in his hand. A shot fired. Screeches from the beast filled the small room. Logan's gun was smashed out of his hand by a force created by the creature. I reached for my own gun. Rough wings slammed into my chest, throwing me out the open door.

I bounced off the wall, crashing into the ground. My crutch clattered down the hall.

Roping themselves together, tendrils of energy sprung from the room and flung themselves down the halls in each direction. I tried to break the bonds between it and his feelers, but it was too quick.

A wailing alarm rang through the building. Kyrian must have triggered the lockdown. The creature's head whipped back and forth before it darted toward the control room.

SHATTERED SOUL

Logan rushed out of the room with Barry following. Blood dripped down Barry's arm and he slunk against the wall. Logan took two steps down the hall before turning on Barry. He pulled Barry out from the wall enough to slam him back into it again.

"What did you do?" Logan's fierce voice was backed by his alien appearance. His face began morphing into angles and his ears were at their points.

Logan had Barry by the throat.

"It's not what you think." Barry's voice was strained. "We were losing money."

Logan balled up his hands in Barry's shirt and lifted him off the ground. "So you sold out the Lost?"

Barry's face turned red. "No, I was helping. Washington wouldn't listen. Now they're listening!"

Logan dropped Barry and pressed an arm against his throat, pinning him to the wall. "And Cassie? What about trying to kill Cassie?"

My concentration broke. The Path fell away.

Barry's face turned blue. He tried to pry Logan's hand away. "I just wanted her out of the way. Not dead."

My face felt flush. On the other side of the hall, I used the wall and one crutch to get back on my feet.

"Why?" Logan yelled.

"I thought..." Barry struggled to talk through Logan's chokehold. "I thought she would see what was happening."

"And my grandmother?" I asked through gritted teeth.

Barry shook his head and didn't answer.

Logan made a sharp hissing sound that made my skin crawl.

Barry sputtered, "She would see the portals coming. I needed more time."

Logan drew back and let Barry fall to the ground.

"You ran this?" I asked, sneering at the man on the floor. "This whole thing. For money?"

"We needed the money," Barry said raising his voice. "We have to keep the secret and that costs money. A big case gains attention."

"Hurt a few to save the rest," Logan said, shaking his head.

"My intention wasn't to have you killed," Barry said.

My lip curled back and I felt compelled to back away.

"Not killed, no," Logan spat, "but out of action."

"I knew she would tie me to the case," Barry said.

A scream rang through the hall, closely followed by a man running at full speed. He tripped over my crutch and fell. He didn't even seem to notice us as he jumped back to his feet and started running again.

"He can't get out that way," I said, watching the man's retreating back.

Logan moved away from Barry and put his back to me. "There's no way out right now. The doors will be bolted and anything glass will be shuttered. Full containment."

Gunfire came from the control room.

I pulled out my gun and started to hobble forward.

"Not so fast," Logan said.

"We've got to get in there," I said.

Logan turned to me and looked me over. "Are you good for this fight?"

One leg broken and leaning on a crutch. I could feel bruises and pains from the long night.

It didn't matter though. We had a job to do and we knew what we were up against.

"I'm ready," I said.

Logan nodded and turned toward Barry who flinched. "We'll be right behind the boss man."

Barry stood a moment looking toward the control room. Then he pulled out his gun, checked his clip, and started down the hall.

"Let's get 'em, partner," Logan said to me.

We headed straight towards the gunfire.

CHAPTER 29

THE DOOR TO THE CONTROL room had been ripped off its hinges. As we approached, the alarm died away. Barry peered around one side of the doorframe and Logan and I looked in from the other.

The room had normal lights on, but blaring safety lights also lit the room like a stadium. The large computer screen on the wall was black with a green command line flashing, waiting for instructions. Muffled sounds came from behind desks. In the middle of the room, stalking in a circle, the sordis clawed at the floor.

Under the harsh glare of the lights, it looked unreal. The leathery skin looked like dull black latex pulled across a grotesque frame. The movements were jerky as the thing widened its circular movements. It barely paused when a desk blocked its way. A skeletal wing pushed into the metal frame. For the amount of effort the beast displayed, he might have been pushing a feather. Power surged and the desk flew up, crashing into another desk.

"How much power are we dealing with here?" Barry asked.

With the power flowing around, finding the Path wasn't difficult.

"He's gathering everything he can around him, but it's coming out of him as fast as he's taking it in," I said.

Shots erupted from somewhere out of sight. One bullet struck home, ripping through the thin skin of the creature's wing. Without looking, the creature made the air around him solidify. When the noise stopped, the wall of air dissipated. Tendrils of pure energy rippled out, latching onto a chair, which was hurled across the room toward where the shots came from. Guided by the creature, the chair moved in arcs until it crashed down into someone. They cried out as the chair ground down into them, and then there was silence. The sordis lost interest and started circling.

Barry let out a shaky breath. "Where's the energy going?"

"Down," I said. "He's pouring everything down, probing..." My voice died away as I watched the creature claw at the floor again. "He's reaching for the portals."

"They're two stories below," Barry said. "He can't do much with them from here."

I shook my head. "I think he can reach them from here. If he taps into it? I'm not sure what will happen, but I don't think it'll be good."

"Time to put a stop to him," Barry said. "I'm going to run in and grab his attention. I'll head to that desk," he gestured toward a random desk.

Logan picked it up from there. "There's an office a few yards from this door. I'll go there, and Cassie, you stay here. Wait for my signal and we'll attack from both directions."

Barry didn't reply. He slipped into the room.

"Hunker down here and stay safe," Logan said.

After that, I was alone. There is something unsettling about being alone with a brightly lit monster.

I concentrated on the flow of the Path. Wisps of smoky gray shimmered and whipped around the room while a large flowing trunk drove itself into the floor to grasp around in the unseeable floors below.

Stop the flow, stop the flow, I thought. Maybe when the distraction started? I readied my gun and aimed, waiting for someone to make a move.

Barry. It was hard to believe that he had sunk this low. Dealing with monsters to try to make Washington sit up and pay attention. In a twisted sort of way, it had worked, but how could

SHATTERED SOUL

he not see the price? How many did he hurt? If this got out, how would the Lost react to agents?

Stopping this thing was the only thing that mattered now. I knew it would raise its defenses as soon as the shots started, but maybe I could weaken them.

Barry's voice rose from somewhere out of sight. "This world isn't for you."

The beast didn't look up, but it started to raise the protective wall of air. Seeing the flow, I reached through the Path and cut through the wall. Before I could tell if my tactic worked, I started to fire.

The creature shrieked when other gunshots erupted. The wall was gone and the shots were well aimed. It folded its wings in, trying to make itself smaller. The trunk of dark energy surged downward and struck home. The power of the portals cracked open and started to pour into the creature. The lights went out, but the Path was fiery white.

The sordis turned to me. I pulled the trigger and nothing happened. The clip was spent.

It couldn't smile with a beak, but through its fury and pain, I also felt triumph.

"Broken pacts will be paid," it said.

Shots fired from Logan's direction. I tried to block the creature's defenses but it was like throwing a pebble to stop a waterfall. The beast turned and crouched. It sprang forward. Barry's scream pierced the air. I left the relative safety of the hall and entered the room while trying to form an assault on the creature's Path.

The air pressure was intense.

The sordis screeched and clawed Barry up from the floor. A swirling mass started to form beside them.

"I know my way back," it said.

Barry screamed. I tried to pull the Path, to alter it in some way, but it felt carved in stone. With no plan, I moved forward as fast as my broken leg could manage. Barry was dragged into the portal. I stopped and stared. Screams continued to tear through the hole between dimensions after Barry disappeared. Moments later, the portal closed. The pressure in the room subsided.

"He's gone." My voice came out far too loud in the still room. All traces of Path connected to Barry and the sordis had been broken. The remnants left behind swirled, as if uncertain, before morphing into the slow-paced flow of a nearly empty room.

Logan came up beside me. We stared at the place they disappeared.

Kyrian walked into the room and broke the silence. "It's gone?"

We turned. In the dim light from the hall, she looked pale and unsteady on her feet.

"They're gone," Logan said.

The thought of asking her where she had been entered my mind, but fell away just as fast. She had never been an agent. What could she have done?

Instead, I asked, "Where's Hank?"

Logan paled. "Hank?" He called out. His voice had the broken edge of panic.

Despair from Logan engulfed me before I broke away from the Path. It felt like heartbreak.

I hobbled around trying to navigate through the mangled desks and debris. "Hank?"

Kyrian joined us. "We need a head count." Her voice carried through the room. "Call out if you can hear us."

Groaning came from under a bulky computer monitor. Dropping my crutch, I pulled aside a monitor and found an agent. Blood had soaked through his shirt and trickled from his ear. Logan was staring at me apprehensively from across the room. After a quick shake of my head, I called out to two employees that had gathered, but were only staring blankly at the wreckage. They mutely took over putting pressure on the gash across the man's chest.

The crunch of metal pulling away from metal came from Logan.

SHATTERED SOUL

"Hank!"

I used my crutch for leverage and left the bleeding agent. When I made it over to Logan, he held our unconscious handler.

Logan talked to Hank in a calm but firm voice, telling him to wake up.

"Get the doctor!" I yelled across the room to Kyrian.

She had been issuing orders to people as they entered the room. "He's on his way."

Tears streaked Logan's face. I had no idea that Logan's relationship with Hank ran this deep. I started clearing away wrecked keyboards and chairs in an effort to free up more space around the two. When the doctor rushed in, bag in hand, I waved him over.

Dr. Yelton relayed orders for a brace and stretcher. He gripped Logan's arm, forcing the elf to look him in the eyes. "He's been knocked out. It doesn't look bad, but he needs a CT scan. Move him carefully upstairs and I'll meet you there."

Logan nodded and waited for the stretcher. Dr. Yelton went to examine the next person injured.

When the stretcher arrived, I started to follow my partner upstairs.

"Stay here." Logan's face was fierce. "Help where you can."

I would have protested, but a pleading look was in Logan's eyes that I had never seen before.

He wanted to be alone. It hurt, but I understood.

I fell back and examined the room. Three more men were injured. Two people were clearing walking room through the wreckage. Kyrian was in the center issuing orders.

After limping over to Kyrian, I stared mutely around. It seemed like hours had gone by. Days even. If it weren't for the shot Dr. Yelton gave me, I'd be weary and bleary eyed. Instead, I was numb.

"Barry wanted you out of the way," Kyrian said.

I couldn't bring emotion to my voice. "He did."

"He thought you could have tied him to his crimes."

251

"I should have tied him to the crime." I sighed and leaned heavily on a crutch.

"Go see the doctor," Kyrian said.

"I should help out here," I said without moving.

"Washington will be here later today," Kyrian said. "I want you checked out by the doctor and back home."

Kyrian strode off without another word.

Progress was being made around the room, but it was slow. Over the loudspeakers came three long, low tones. Lockdown was being lifted. Metal shutters on windows and doors would be rolling back. More agents would be arriving.

The place where the portal had opened and closed stood empty. I shook my head. Enough agents would be around. Someone else can keep an eye on this. As agents started arriving, I headed toward the clinic upstairs.

I was expecting similar chaos and noise around the patients' rooms, but things weren't bad. Keeping quiet, I sat in one of the hallway chairs. The MyTH doctor and extra medical staff on hand provided quick care. Rooms were in short supply. The Lost and seriously injured took the rooms, injured agents, like myself, sat out of the way.

"He's awake."

Logan was standing beside me. I hadn't noticed him walk up, but that shouldn't surprise me. He didn't look tense, which was a good sign.

"He'll be okay then?" I asked.

Logan nodded. "A knock on the noggin and a few bruises, but he'll be good as new. How about you?"

I had to think about the question before answering. "I'm good. Kyrian wanted me to see the doctor before heading home."

"Home? She doesn't want you to stick around? Be debriefed or something?"

"No, she's more worried about the guys from Washington arriving."

Logan nodded and sat down. We watched people come and

SHATTERED SOUL

go. We watched the doctor become more and more worn down.

"Listen," Logan said keeping his eyes on an agent standing down the hall. He seemed uncomfortable. "About downstairs. With Hank—"

"It's good that you found him so fast."

"Yeah," Logan said. He didn't look away from the man down the hall.

"He's going to be okay."

Logan stayed silent.

"We're all going to be okay," I said.

A corner of Logan's mouth curled up in a half grin. "Good to hear," he said.

CHAPTER 30

I 'LL BE OUT FOR A few hours," Gran said. "Logan will be here to pick you up for work soon, so we'll catch up tonight."

"I'm off work for the week," I reminded Gran.

"I know, hun, but Logan's going to need you today."

The thought of going into work made my stomach turn into knots. "Sure thing, Gran."

After Gran left, I flipped on the TV and mindlessly flipped through channels. I was under doctor's orders to take it easy for a week, and for once, I wanted to listen to those orders.

Twenty minutes later, Logan came in through the kitchen and I went to greet him.

"How are things at the office?" I asked, as I pushed a plate of cookies in his direction.

"The boys from Washington have moseyed out of town."

"They left fast." I sat down and propped my foot up.

Logan shrugged. "They got what they needed."

"Have they tracked down all the Lost yet?"

"There's one or two we're still working on, but we'll find them." Logan pulled at the collar of his shirt.

"What aren't you telling me?" I asked.

"This is the hard part. We've been placed under a gag order. No one inside the agency, outside of those already in the know, can find out about Barry."

I sneered. "What's that supposed to mean?"

"The rest of the agency is being told he died while trying to protect people from the sordis attack. Barry is being touted as a hero. Idea is that it helps with moral."

I gritted my teeth. "Someone who tried to kill me is being praised for saving our lives?"

"Seems like the real information has already been destroyed. Redacted down to nonsense."

Logan let me fume for a minute before pressing on. "Kyrian is in charge for now. That little lady is determined to drag us into the twenty first century. When you get back to the office, there's plenty of scanning and shredding to do. We're going digital."

"Gran says I'm going to work today."

"Well, I wasn't sure you should go, but Travis seemed to think he needs you. If you're up for it, we need to head over to the Sanctuary today."

"That's better than going into the office."

I grabbed my crutches and Logan drove me to the Sanctuary.

Travis and James met us in the parking lot and we rode out together in the ATVs. We took the trail slowly to accommodate my leg. It was aching fiercely when I got off the machine.

We went past the cave entrance and stepped into the woods.

I frowned and looked around. "Looks a lot different from when we dropped the troll off."

"Everything's dying," Logan said.

The leaves should have been a riot of color. Instead, they had already stripped themselves from the trees.

"The trees are starting to rot. What's worse, it's spreading." Travis pointed out toward trees at the edge of the dead ones. "The grass and bramble are dying out and the trees are starting to look sickly."

I shifted uncomfortably on my crutches. "I fed that creature's energy into the ground here."

"I invited James along. He has some ideas on how to fix the area," Travis said.

James walked slowly around the area, making sure not to step in the area where plants were dying. "They are only theories at this point. I think we need to know exactly what we're dealing with before we start."

Logan tapped his head. "See anything useful?"

I looked around at the bleak landscape once more before closing my eyes and opening the Path. It was getting easier to push back the raging flow, but it threatened to overwhelm me if I dropped my guard.

The Path in the dead ground seemed to boil up and come in my direction. "Oh, crap." I pushed the energy back using the Path.

"What is it?" Logan shifted his stance as though ready to attack.

"It startled me. The energy jumped out and wanted to join with my own Path." Pushing more firmly. "It's actually settling back into the ground with surprising ease."

Logan relaxed.

"It's energy then?" James asked. "Nothing sentient?"

I watched the nameless mass as it sunk tendrils around another tree and dragged on its Path. "It's dark and volatile, but in the end, it's energy without direction."

James smiled. "That, we can deal with."

Travis, James, and I discussed cleansing methods and came up with a plan. James lit a smudge stick and walked the outside of the area, chanting as he went. He couldn't see where the darkness started and stopped, but he must sense its edge. He never went beyond and never strayed into the muck. When he was finished, the area around the oily pool flexed. The ritual would keep the dark energy from spreading further into the woods. Before letting go of the Path, I probed the area gently. It was locked down.

We made the trek back out of the woods. We made a plan for follow up treatments, said our goodbyes, and went home.

The trip wore me out, but Halloween was around the corner and I needed a costume. With that in mind, I went out with Gran and Susan the next day and picked out a costume. Super Girl was out. Super Girl could not have a broken leg and I felt very un-Super Girlish. Instead, I chose a generic witch costume. It

SHATTERED SOUL

was long enough to work with a broken leg without showing anything I didn't want to show.

Morgan and Gran presented themselves on Halloween. They looked fantastic as the Frankenstein and his bride. They headed out to a party with Logan, dressed in his cowboy gear.

I stayed back at the house and Rider joined me to pass out candy.

We sat in the living room and I introduced Rider to the world of scary movies.

"You are looking for him, are you not?" Rider asked.

"What do you mean?"

"You have looked up at the stairs several times now."

I blinked at Rider. "I didn't even notice that I was doing it."

"He will be back. I did not know Vincent well, but I saw the two of you together several times. He will be back."

I shrugged and reflected back on Vincent. A piece of me was missing; the piece of my soul that Vincent had tucked away inside. Would I know if that piece of me had died?

Work was evolving. Under Kyrian's reign, improvements were being made. I was even thinking of taking some classes in forensics in the spring. Forging forward was the key.

Hidden World Newsletter Sign-up

ACKNOWLEDGEMENTS

While working on AIR: Shattered Soul, I've had amazing support from family and friends. Special thanks to Adria Waters. She sat next to me when I typed the first words in this novel, gave me feedback on multiple drafts, and has walked through the entire process next to me. She is a constant well of encouragement and lends a sympathetic ear when needed. I'd also like to thank Hadena James, who gave valuable feedback and consistently encouraged me to move forward and Christina Benedict, who made sure I didn't stay discouraged when I fell.

Finding a home with multiple writers' groups allowed me to receive constructive feedback from a wide variety of viewpoints. The Columbia Missouri Novelists group and the Writers In Robs Living Room have given me valuable insight. Members of Bacon provided me with support and information along the way. Leigh Michaels provided detailed comments that assisted me seeing the novel in a new light. Thank you to Frankie Sutton, my editor, for all of her assistance. Deranged Doctor Design provided me with a wonderful cover design and formatting.

I also want to thank my parents for reading everything that I put under their noses throughout my life. My sister Tamera was supportive and very understanding when I couldn't talk because I was typing away. Other thanks need to be extended to Kathie Booloodian for reading an early draft and providing feedback while encouraging me to get moving on AIR II. Also to Sharon Booloodian for providing feedback and encouragement. Also to my beta readers, Oliver and Erica Jones, and Angel Whitaker, I appreciated your help. Many, many other family, friends, and acquaintances have been incredibly supportive. Thank you all.

Most of all I must thank my husband for his continued reassurance, inspiration, and assistance in all my writing endeavors.

ABOUT THE AUTHOR

Amanda Booloodian lives in Missouri with her loving, and often times peculiar, husband. In 2006, she took part in Great Beginnings and was awarded first place in the Mystery/Thriller category. Amanda has been passionate about the written word throughout her life. Now, much of her spare time is spent at the computer, delving into worlds accessible only through vivid imagination. In warm weather, when she isn't pounding on the keyboard, she can often be found wandering through the wilderness. Occasionally she gets it into her head to SCUBA dive or to sit back at home and make wine, which can have interesting results and inspire her writing.

You can find out more about Amanda and her writing, including upcoming releases, on www.Booloodian.com. You can also find her on Facebook: Amanda Booloodian - Author, Twitter: @ajbooloodian, and Amazon: Amanda Booloodian.